The
ACCIDENTAL
ASSASSIN

a novel

NICHOLE CHASE

Copyright © 2014 by Nichole Chase
Published by Nichole Chase
Cover design by Sarah Hansen of Okay Creations
Interior design and formatting by JT Formatting

First Edition: December 2014
Library of Congress Cataloging-in-Publication Data
Chase, Nichole
The Accidental Assassin – 1st ed
ISBN-13: 978-1505275261
ISBN-10: 1505275261

www.NicholeChase.com

To KP Simmon and Rebecca Friedman.

Thanks for being on my team.

Cassie,
Thanks for
being so
awesome !
Bang Bang.
N. Chase

PROLOGUE

"THIS PROJECT NEEDS to be completed within the next two weeks." The woman leaned back casually. Nothing. No twitching, no tightening of her fingers on the arm rest, no tell-tale signs around her eyes. She might as well have been carved from marble. Her finely sculpted eyebrows raised pointedly. "And we want it to make an impression. Nothing small or mistakable."

The folder was thick with photographic evidence, but as I flipped through it, something in the woman's expression made me wary. The man she wanted killed deserved to die; he was in the slave business and killed his women when they were of no more use. But for all the expression she showed, we could be discussing cutting down a tree, or removing a stone from her front yard. Glacial coolness radiated from under a perfectly polished veneer. The lack of fear in her brown eyes, the ease with which she faced me, those were things that always put me on guard. Meeting a hitman wasn't something most people did, and she had decided to do it with no backup. Without trying to stroke my own ego, most people wouldn't even send their assistant to meet me without backup. There was a good chance that this was the actual client, not an assistant as she had introduced herself, but it would be dangerous to meet me on her own. Unless she needed to keep it from even her bodyguards. Or it could be that this was an actress hired by the real client—it wouldn't be the first time I'd run into that particular issue.

Maybe she thought she didn't need them. Maybe she felt equipped to handle me on her own.

If I let my ego run rampant like that, I wouldn't have a job. I'd just be dead.

"Well?" she asked, as I neatly restacked the evidence. "Is this a workable timeframe for you?"

"It'll be done before then." I slipped the contents back into the folder and set it on the desk. "Have you contacted anyone else about this job?"

"No." Something in her eyes shifted. If I hadn't been looking for something, I would have missed it.

"If there is someone else on this case, I need to know it." I let my fingers slide off the folder. "Professional courtesy and all."

"Mr. Walker, you came highly recommended. We have no doubts regarding your efficiency, so we have no need to hire anyone else." She leaned forward and her mouth curved into a small, seductive smile but I could see through the distraction. It was too late anyway: I'd already gotten my answer. There was something just under the surface of this job that set my teeth on edge.

"I take fifty percent upfront." I took the folder from the desk. "And the remaining fifty percent when I'm finished." Whatever was going on, I was in too far not to find out now. And I had to make sure that I wasn't in someone's eye-sights. No matter what, it didn't pay to be on the uninformed side.

"Of course." She stood up and held out her hand. Her fingers were as cool as her attitude. She knew she was in the presence of a murderer and honestly had no qualms. Or distaste. Intriguing.

"How should I address you?" It was common for hitmen to not know the name of their contractor, but I wasn't the normal hitman. I only took cases where the mark deserved to die and I was so good at my job I set the rules.

"Maria." Her smile unfolded, turning into something much more dangerous.

"I'll be in touch, Maria." I left the room with my information and the decision to get to the bottom of everything.

CHAPTER ONE

Ava

WHEN I AGREED to house sit for Tess in London, I'd decided I was going to try all things British. This included drinking tea instead of coffee, taking public transportation, and using different curse words. Regrettably, after more than a week, I still felt like an imposter and probably always would. My southern accent and love for iced sweet tea screamed American, and I'd already gotten hopelessly lost on the Tube twice. I leaned back in my chair at the tiny table and looked at the house plant I'd taken to chatting with. A week in London was hardly enough time to make new friends. Especially without anyone to introduce me.

"Have you seen the classifieds?"

The plant didn't respond. Apparently I'd asked a stupid question.

"I'm serious. If I want to extend my visa, I need to find a job." I was desperate for employment doing something other than answering phones for an aircraft engineering company like back home. Leaning forward, I opened

1

the paper to a different page. Unfortunately, I managed to hit my tea saucer with my knuckles.

"Shit." The hot tea spread across the table while I scrambled for a towel. "Bugger."

I grimaced. No, it still sounded weird when I said it. I snatched the dish rag from the sink and tried to sop up the brown liquid. Well, creamy brown liquid. I'd added more than my share of milk and sugar to the cup. I picked up the now-soaked newspaper and threw it in the sink. I'd have to look up the story about the visiting prince and duchess online now. Once I had everything clean, I took a shower and put on real clothing.

Tess swore that the internet was easy to use, but I could never get my laptop to connect at her new flat. If I wanted to look for a job, I'd have to buy a new paper, or better yet, head to the local café for some free wi-fi. I grabbed my keys and threw the strap of my computer case over my shoulder.

"Don't wait up for me, Mr. Green. I might go sightseeing." As usual the plant didn't respond.

I passed Mr. Song in the hallway and nodded my head. He jerked his chin in a short acknowledgement, but never said anything. I knew he spoke English, I'd heard him complaining to the woman in the apartment across from Tess's about her cats. Flat—not apartment, I corrected mentally. So I felt it safe to assume that he was just a grump, not that he hated me. Not that I would have really cared, but I couldn't stand the thought of alienating one of Tess's neighbors. She had been so excited about moving to London with her new husband, I think she'd been a bit disappointed that she was leaving on her honeymoon almost immediately. Danny had gone all out with a month-long trip in Italy, though, so she couldn't be too upset. Besides, she'd be able to do the tourist thing here when she got back. It would feel like an extension of their honeymoon.

I shuddered as I passed the hallway that led to the building's parking garage. I had tried to drive Danny's car my second day here and had hated every second of it. Everything was backward. The steering column was on the wrong side. I had to drive on the wrong side of the road. Combine that with all of the roundabouts and new-city-confusion, and it spelled disaster. I'd made it to the airport to pick up the luggage that had been delayed, but when I got back, I drank half a bottle of wine to calm my nerves. I'd never thought I'd have such a hard time doing something different. Then again, I did prefer to stick to my routine.

Which is exactly why I was here in London, trying to shake things up. After my college graduation, I'd found myself in a rut. My degree seemed useless and I still hadn't left the aircraft builder's office where I'd been working during school. I still drove the same car, used the same shampoo, and did everything the exact same as I had when I first left for college. And then Danny proposed to Tess. And Tess, one of my rocks, said yes. Before I knew it, I was helping her pick out dresses and look at flats—ha! I got it right that time—online. As I watched her move forward, I realized that I was going nowhere. The more I delved into my life, the more static it started to seem. I even realized that the men I had dated over the years had all been the same. Boring, predictable, and even more lackluster in bed. In my mind I had thought that meant stable, but it really just meant…mind-numbing.

3

Coffee smells wafted from the little café at the corner of the street and I smiled. So far, I'd tried eight new drinks. Rachel, the barista, always brightened when I came in. She said that most people ordered the same thing every time, but that I was always a surprise.

"There she is! How are you, Ava?" Rachel leaned a hip against the counter. Her bright dreadlocks swayed around her head and her nose piercing shined brightly.

"Good, you?" I stepped around a mother wiping up her daughter's spilt juice.

"Excellent. What are you going to try today?"

"I'm not sure." I looked up at the board above her head. "Why don't you surprise me?"

"Really?" She stood up straight. "Anything you don't want?"

I almost said tea, but bit my tongue. "Nope. You make it, I'll try it."

"Have I mentioned how much I love it when you come in here?" she asked. "And not just because of your cute American accent." She rubbed her hands together. "I get to experiment on you."

"I prefer to think of it as expressing your creativity."

"Same thing, isn't it?" She moved over to her machines and started mixing things in a cup. I watched and tried to pick out the ingredients. When she brought it over to me, she watched expectantly, so I took a test sip.

"Caramel." I took another sip. "Pumpkin?"

"Got it. Better than the raspberry?"

"Definitely." The raspberry coffee had made me want to gag. Fruit and coffee was apparently not my thing. I handed her some money and waved for her to keep the change. Rachel was one of the few people that I had met

4

the past week who had become familiar. Mostly because she was a sucker for my accent. Which was funny, because I was a sucker for hers.

The first couple of days I'd sat at the same table when I came in, but when I realized I was falling into yet another safe routine, I'd started picking random spots. The chair closest to one of the open windows called my name, so I decided it would do for the day. My eyes drifted over to the seat I'd used yesterday and froze. A man in a suit sat in the corner, his arm draped over the back of the chair, a paper in his hand. Sharp cheek bones, combined with a light sprinkling of stubble and piercing green eyes, combined for a heavy shot of lust.

As if sensing my scrutiny, he looked up and met my gaze. There was a quick zing that zipped through my body as our regard held. I jerked my eyes away guiltily before chastising myself. It was an instant reaction to being caught ogling, but I should have just smiled and looked down. I couldn't bring myself to look back over at him, so I focused on pulling my laptop out and connecting to the internet. I didn't realize he had left the café until I saw him walk past my window. He smiled at me when I looked up, but didn't say anything. I watched his back with interest as he headed down the street. It was a rather nice backside and it had been a while since I'd enjoyed a good romp in bed. I was a bit surprised by the immediate attraction though. All of the men I'd dated in the past had been a bit callous, rough around the edges, but this one had been very nicely put together.

"Looks like you've got an admirer." Rachel sat a new cup down on the table.

"What?" I looked up at her, confused.

"The hottie got this for you. Said to get you another cup of whatever had made you smile." She grinned broadly at me.

"Hottie?"I looked at the cup and felt my cheeks grow hot. He had definitely noticed me staring.

"I saw you checking him out. Not that I blame you. Those eyes were to die for." She cocked her head to the side. "Had a dangerous feel to him, too. Rugged, but not in a mountain man sort of way."

"Caught." I held up my hands in defeat. "Sexy. He was sexy."

"And he knew it."

"They usually do." I shook my head and looked at the cup.

"Don't worry. I made it, so it's not drugged or anything." Rachel laughed.

"Good to know." I looked back out the window but didn't see him anymore. "That was nice of him. Who is he?"

"Dunna know." She shrugged. "Never been in before, but I hope he comes back." She raised an eyebrow and I laughed.

"He certainly doesn't hurt the décor."

"You can say that again." She went back to her counter in a swish of bright skirts, leaving me to think about the mystery man.

After an hour and several emails about job openings, I decided to head out and see more of the city. I was used to being by myself. Tess was the closest thing I had to family, so it wasn't unusual for me to visit places without anyone. I'd learned at an early age that doing things alone could be liberating. I didn't have to worry about what other people wanted to eat, or bathroom breaks, but there were times I wished I could share something with someone —have that connection. There was an American family with a daughter in line to see Buckingham Palace that made me laugh. She kept asking if there were any princesses at the castle and I knew that her parents would always remember her excitement.

"I heard that America's Duchess was going to be here." I smiled down at the girl. "Maybe we'll get lucky and see her and her prince charming too!"

The little girl squealed loudly before slapping both hands over her mouth. She danced in spot for a moment, trying to contain her excitement.

"That's right." The mother smiled down at her daughter. "They're in town for the christening of the baby prince!"

"Oh my gosh. Oh my gosh!" The girl bounced up and down on her toes. "I can't believe it! A real princess and prince!"

Her parents laughed, soaking up her excitement as it spilled out. I did too. There was something contagious about watching a child faced with a dream come true.

I wonder what moments my parents had shared with me that I could no longer remember. They had died when I was twelve, and at twenty-three, some of my memories were becoming fuzzy. Maybe that was because I had no one to remind me of them, or maybe it was simply a side effect of growing older. I'd lived with my grandmother until I went to college. She passed away a year later, leaving me completely alone. Maybe all of that upheaval was the reason I'd stuck so closely to a routine in the past—a need for normality.

The palace was huge, breathtaking, and everything I had hoped. The queen wasn't in residence, but would be back soon for the christening of her new grandbaby. I could imagine her dressed in one of her elegant gowns and talking with dignitaries. In fact, the christening is why there was a story about the Lilarian royalty in the paper. In between sending my resume to different employers, I had finished the article about the visiting prince and soon-to-be princess. Like most of America, I had been enthralled by America's Duchess, but I also felt a bit bad for her. Not too bad, considering her hunky fiancé, but bad for all of the upheaval in her life. This was ironic, when you considered that I was working hard to cause disruption in my own life. At least I didn't have cameras following me through mine, though.

I spent a good while in the palace, looking at the art work and peeking down hallways. I was amazed by the artifacts—by the history itself. Many important historical figures had graced these halls. Outside I snapped pictures of the guards in their red suits and big black hats. I strolled aimlessly for a while, taking pictures and soaking up the culture. We might speak the same language, but there were a lot of differences between Americans and the British. There were a lot of similarities of course, more than the differences, but it was tiny things that reminded me I was somewhere new. I walked through a shop and perused a shelf of tea. I'd tried two other brands so far, but would keep working to see if I found one I liked. I picked up a box with a smiling, grey haired woman on the front, and took it to the counter.

Just like everywhere, the clerk wasn't exactly excited about her job, but I didn't care. I took my tea and made my way back to Tess and Danny's apartment. Flat. Not apartment.

I smiled at the doorman as he opened the door for me. "How are you?"

"Very well, madam. Thank you. I hope you've had a nice day as well." He offered a disinterested smile.

"I have. Thank you." I tried to not sigh.

I took the elevator, thinking I'd walked enough for the day. Leaning against the rail inside, I thought about maybe hitting up a pub the next day. I was trying to do different things, but going to a pub by myself was intimidating. I knew they weren't like the bars back home, but it was hard to push that image out of my head. When the elevator dinged, I stepped forward without looking and ran smack into the chest of someone tall.

"Bugger!" I bounced backward, but congratulated myself for using the right word. "I'm so sorry." I looked up into bright green eyes and froze. Even though I'd only seen him briefly, I wasn't likely to forget his face. There was something so arresting about his presence that I was sure I'd have remembered him a year later. He was attractive, refined without being pretty, and the hint of steel in his jaw implied danger. His nose had a slight hump in the middle that made it seem off center. Full, firm lips pulled to one side in a small smile and of course, there were the gorgeous eyes bound to make most women weak in knees.

"Never a problem when bumping into a lovely woman." He smiled down at me and I froze. Was he? Yes. He was flirting with me. Did he remember that I was the lady at the coffee shop or did he give out so many drinks that I was just a blurry face? I wasn't bad to look at it, but I was a far cry from the type of woman that would be on his arm.

9

"Um. Thank you?"

"You're welcome." He reached out with a hand to motion for me to step by him. "Is this your floor?"

"What floor is it?" I sounded like a dumbass. A complete dumbass.

"Fifth." His mouth twitched.

"Ah, yes. It is." He didn't say anything, just watched me. "My floor, I mean. It's my floor."

"Here, let me get out of your way." He stepped aside and I realized that he was being polite while I had been staring again.

"Thank you." Taking a breath, I stepped out of the elevator and was going to head to the flat, but found myself turning around to ask if he lived in the building.

"I hope you enjoyed your drink at the café." He held the door open with his hand while his eyes traveled over me in a lazy perusal. I fought the urge to look down and check what I was wearing. I was pretty sure it wasn't anything that should garner that much attention.

"I-I did." I cleared my throat and smiled at him. "Thank you."

"Ah, there it is." He stepped back, letting go of the door, and pressed a button. "You have a lovely smile."

"Thank you." I felt my lips curve upward even more just as the doors closed. I walked back to the flat, a little pep to my step. Even if I never saw him again, the compliment was a nice one.

CHAPTER TWO

Owen

I LEANED AGAINST the wall of the elevator and fiddled with the lock picks in my pocket. Running into the girl with the bright eyes and killer smile had been a nice surprise. I'd barely been able to take my eyes off her when she came into the little café. Her chipper American accent and friendliness with the staff had been charming. When leaving, I'd decided to send her a drink—a small way to thank her for brightening up a dreary day. In a city this large, I hadn't expected to see her again. Certainly not in the building where my target lived.

Turning back to business, I ran over what I had found. Song's apartment had been spotless, but I'd expected as much. The man had been in the trade for entirely too long to not make sure his hands were clean. The tell-tale sign was that he was *too* clean. There wasn't a porno or single inappropriate email on his hard drive, but there had been a key tracker I'd had to disable. I had enough in the portfolio I'd received to be convinced of his involvement, but I kept hanging back.

The elevator dinged to signal I'd reached the ground floor and I stepped out. Something about this hit felt off and I was uneasy. I'd learned over the last few years to trust my gut even if my brain couldn't figure out why.

Pushing through the doors, I nodded to the doorman and made my way around the corner to my hotel. I'd decided to stay close so that I could do a little more snooping before completing the assignment. It wasn't a fancy place, but more than met my needs. Hell of a lot better than the last place I stayed. Bangkok had been a dirty nightmare.

I pulled at my tie as I shut my door and opened my laptop. Using the passwords one of my contacts had sent me, I downloaded videos from the local traffic cameras.

Song left every morning and took one of three routes to a small office in Canary Wharf. He wasn't varied in which path he took each day. The man had fallen into a pattern that would be his ultimate downfall if I couldn't get to him in his apartment. Flipping through the images, I paused on the car he drove. Other than a bullet, a bomb would be the simplest way to get rid of the pig. Even if it was much messier—which would probably make my client happy.

I snorted and got up to pour myself a drink. Any pimp that had been in the trade for as long as he had didn't have an easy death coming to him. Considering the harsh life my mother had lived, I never turned down the chance to kill a pimp. I looked down at the amber liquid in my cup and frowned. He certainly didn't deserve an easy death. Then again, most of the people I came in contact with didn't; myself included.

I glanced back at the images of the dead prostitutes. High class women that brought in large amounts of money. These weren't the women you would find on the corner or in a dark alley. No, you'd find them on the arm of a parliament member or a rich businessman. He had used them and then got rid of them for some reason. And in ways that had been particularly painful for the victims. The last one stared up at me with glossed over blue eyes. They would have been pretty before she died, would have shined with seduction and the promise of long nights, and behind that would have been the bored gaze of a person doing their job. I'd seen the type before.

My thoughts drifted back to the blue eyed girl in the elevator and I tried to push her out of my mind. Her eyes were so open, so unguarded. I'd seen the surprise in her face when I ran into her at the apartment, her self-consciousness when I'd looked her over, her embarrassment at being caught staring at me. It had all been there like an open book, beautifully written in the delicate lines of her face.

Monsters didn't belong with the innocent. I was looking at pictures of dead call girls. I murdered people for a living. *And I was fucking good at it,* I reminded myself. It takes all kinds of people to make the world go around, and I was like the vultures that cleaned up the carrion on the side of the road. I got rid of the diseased pests that made the world a darker place. I was far from an avenging angel; I liked what I did. The satisfaction of taking out the garbage. But I knew better than to think I deserved a happily ever after. There would be no picket fence in my future.

Shoving the bright smile from my mind, I went through the rest of the information I had on Song, his contacts, and the people that worked in his office, before deciding what type of bomb to use on his car. I had several options, but I wanted one that would make a statement. Opening a small case I'd brought with me, I pulled out some of the pieces I needed and set to work. Tiny wires, a burner cell phone, and explosives. It didn't have to be complicated, just effective.

Once it was ready I leaned back in my chair and drained the last of my scotch before setting the empty glass next to my creation. It was an ugly thing that would make an even uglier scene. Every time I'd been in the garage this week no one had been near Song's car, which meant the risk of bystanders was low. I'd be close enough to monitor the situation and make sure no one innocent came anywhere near the blast zone, but far enough away that I wouldn't have to risk exposure.

The next morning I nodded at the owner as I left the hotel to head for Song's building. The owner was squinting at her computer, but looked up and smiled at me.

"You're up early, Mr. Martin. It's not even in six in the morning! Will you be returning for breakfast?"

"No, I'm meeting a friend today." I smiled back, easy with the lie and fake name. I wanted to get to Song's apartment with enough time to do everything I needed.

"Ah, well. Have a good morning." The crinkles at the corners of her eyes deepened.

"Thank you. You too." I pushed through the door and walked the short few blocks to the building that housed Song's flat. It had rained already this morning and more was forecasted. I hoped it would hold out until after the job was complete. I stopped and bought a paper from the man at the stand on the corner of Song's block. I flipped through the pages, organizing the paper as I looked for the business section and scanned the street.

The doorman wasn't at the entrance, which raised a red flag. He had been at his post every morning for the last week—so what was different today? I hung back for a while, watching the entrances to see if anyone came or went. Eventually the doorman exited the building with a blonde woman wearing a business suit. They spoke for a few minutes before he pointed to the garage. She laughed and turned toward the ramp that led to the cars. From what I could hear, she was there to pick up an employer's vehicle. She tripped a bit on her way inside and giggled, her briefcase swinging wildly.

I narrowed my eyes as I watched her enter the building. My gut told me to not trust her cheerful façade. I looked down at the paper in my hand and debated leaving for the day. If Song kept to his schedule, he wouldn't be using his car again until next week, which meant this was my last chance for a bomb. Otherwise I'd be stuck with something more personal and that wouldn't create the same type of message. My contact had assured me that no one else was on the same case, but I couldn't shake the feeling that something was off.

For the first time I cursed not having a partner. Some assassins worked with teams, but I'd always thought that was the best way to get themselves killed. The first thing you learned in this business was to trust no one. If you trust someone, they can betray you. If they betray you, you're dead. But I had to admit it would be helpful to have someone else monitoring the building while I climbed under a car. Shooting Song on his drive to work would have been much easier, but would likely kill bystanders.

The garage was quiet, except for the woman chatting on her cell phone. I could hear some of her inane gossip as she fiddled with her car keys before climbing into the driver side. I made my way to Song's car and watched the woman pull out of the garage from the corner of my eye.

I sidled up to the trunk and crouched down to look at the underside of the vehicle. It was a foreign model; one of the more expensive sedans. I worked quickly, careful to keep track of time while making sure everything was set up correctly. I wanted to be able to detonate the bomb once he was in the street, not in the building. It would make the largest splash that way and I was nothing if not thorough.

Once I had it ready, I slid it out from under the car and checked the burner phone one more time. Everything was ready to go; I just needed to wait for Song. Making sure that no one was watching, I headed for the exit.

CHAPTER
THREE

Ava

THE RAIN WAS thick this morning and I had to fight my urge to stay in bed and sleep away the day. I was trying to go to the gym every morning, but perhaps it would be good to break that routine, too. Of course, I'd started working out every day so I would take better care of myself, which wasn't really a habit that I should break. Or should I? I could try.

I rolled over and squished my pillow into a comfortable shape but couldn't go back to sleep. I tried to remind my body that it was still early back home and that sleeping in would be understandable, but it wasn't working. My internal clock was all over the place.

Sighing, I gave up and headed for the shower. The shower was nice, large, with a special nozzle that was supposed to simulate rain. In fact, everything in Danny's place was nice. Fancy stove, expensive American style refrigerator, and art work that made me drool. Not to mention the apartment—flat—itself was in one of the most expensive buildings in the neighborhood. I hadn't thought a contractor would be able to afford something like this, but maybe his job explained his expensive taste. Or, more likely, he got all of his expensive fixtures at a discount.

Unimpressed with the weather, I sat down at the table and looked at Mr. Green the Plant. "So far England is amazing. Everything has this undertone of history mixed with modern technology. But the rain? Every day. Every. Day. What's up with that?"

I didn't wait for the answer that would never come and thought about my options. Not exactly a great day to go exploring. I could hit up the coffee shop and stop by the store across the street to stock up on ingredients for one of the new recipes I wanted to try. That would keep me busy, at least, and somewhat dry.

As I got dressed, I noticed my phone flashing on the night stand. Thinking it might be Tess checking in, I grabbed it and waited for the voice mail.

"Ms. McKenzie, I'm calling from The Studio on Fourth about our open position. I know it's last minute, but we had a cancellation this morning and would like you to come in for an interview. We look forward to speaking with you at eight."

"Holy shit!" I scrambled around for something to write their address on and shut the phone off. I never thought I'd get an interview with that designer. An interview. In less than an hour. This could be my chance to stop answering phones and finally start using my art degree. "Oh, shit."

I looked out the window and groaned. I'd have to drive. There was no way I'd be able to get there on public transit in time. The thought made my stomach clench and I debated not going at all. The new me, the try-everything, give-everything-a-shot-me, put her foot down. I couldn't miss out on the chance to have job and a reason to stay in exciting London. I had to try.

I searched the closet for something suitable to wear and threw on a dark dress suit before pulling my hair up into a bun. Dumping my jewelry bag out on the bed, I chose large teal earrings and a chunky necklace. Designing jewelry was my passion and I wanted to wear pieces that would show off my skills.

I glanced in the mirror briefly and hurried out the door before realizing I'd left my phone and needed to go back inside for it. I locked the door again and made it halfway down the hall before I remembered I'd left the address on the table.

"Fuck me!" I said just as one of the other tenants opened their door. I frowned at the little old man staring at me. "Excuse me."

"I'll take the first option." He cackled and I felt my face flush.

"Not really up for consideration." I hurried past him, ignoring the leer he directed at me.

"Then don't offer!" He slammed the door and I fought the urge to shoot him the bird. Grumpy old cuss. Grumpy, old, perverted cuss.

If this morning was any indication of how this interview would go, I was already screwed six ways to Sunday. By the time I made it to the garage, I was a complete mess. My stomach was in knots. The rain had started again and I could hear it pounding away outside. Driving would be a nightmare and I was already nervous about the interview.

I made my way to the car and pressed the unlock key. I was halfway into the seat before I realized I was on the wrong side.

"Oh, for fuck's sake! Will anything go right today?" I got out and stomped around to the other side. "Stupid ass car with the steering wheel on the wrong damn side." I muttered under my breath as I climbed in, situating my stuff and taking a deep breath. I clenched the steering wheel as my stomach knotted even tighter.

Something dark fluttered beside my car, like a shadow shifting feet. I leaned forward and looked around. Nothing. There was nothing there and I was stalling.

"I can do this." I could do this. I was going to drive all the way to this interview and then kick ass. It was going to be good. English driving had to be better the second time around, right? I'd have picked up some stuff. I shouldn't be so afraid.

I put the car in reverse, my eyes on the rear view mirror, and reached down to turn on the GPS. Someone shouted as I slid out of the spot and I slammed my foot down on the pedal.

Unfortunately, it was the wrong pedal. A loud sick crunch filled the car as it slammed into something solid, and I saw a dark shape fly across the parking lot.

My heart froze as my brain processed what had just happened. Thankfully the rest of my body kept moving and I threw the car into park before jumping out of my seat.

"Oh my god!" My heart stuttered in my chest and panic lit my veins like fire. Blood pooled under the man's head and his body was twisted at an unnatural angle. A long stick with a mirror attached to the end lay a few feet away. I couldn't see his face, but I recognized the severe haircut.

"Mr. Song? Mr. Song, are you okay? I'm so sorry. I never saw you." I knelt down to check the man. He didn't move and I reached out to check for a pulse. It was so weak I couldn't even find it. "Mr. Song? Oh, God. Oh no. Oh no."

I stood up to go call for help, my eyes swung wildly around the empty garage. My heart was beating so loudly I never heard the person behind me. Someone grabbed my wrist and spun me against the car.

"It was an accident!" I immediately assumed I was being arrested. It was the only thing that made sense to me, but it didn't stop me from trying to stand back up. "You have to help him!"

"I fucking knew they'd sent someone else." A hand pushed me forward so my face was pressed against the trunk. "Who sent you?" The voice sounded familiar. The man's hand slid around my waist and along my small belt.

"What are you doing? That man's dying!" I hollered and tried to wiggle away. Fear made it hard to breathe. "We need to get him help. Let me go!"

"He's not dying. He's dead." His free hand slid down the outside of my leg before sliding up the inside of my thighs, brushing along my panties. "How did he know about the bomb?"

"Hey! Fuck off, pervert!" I stepped back, my heel landing on his instep just like I'd learned in college, but he didn't budge. If this was a cop, he'd just crossed my boundaries. I tried to wiggle away from him again and he just grunted.

"Who do you work for?" He leaned close, his body pressing into mine so that he could keep me in place as his hands rummaged through my pockets before moving to trace the underwire of my bra with strong fingers. "Where's your weapon?"

"Get off me!" I managed to get one arm free and twisted in his grasp, just enough for my elbow to make contact with his jaw.

He stepped back and I spun away from the car, intent on making a run for it. Stepping to the side, he blocked the most direct route to the exit, and officially filled my view. His narrowed gaze did nothing to diminish the impact of his green eyes and I wanted to punch him for turning out to be a creep.

"You?" I frowned, disoriented. "What the hell is wrong with you? We need to get help for him! And you need to keep your hands to yourself." I shoved him and tried to get back to Mr. Song.

"You can drop the innocent act. He's dead." He stepped closer and gripped my arm. "And I don't appreciate you taking my hit. When did they hire you?"

"What are you talking about?" I tried to edge further away from him. "He's dead?" Hit? My breath hitched. I'd killed someone? I'd killed someone on my way to an interview. Oh my God, I killed him. Nausea washed over me and I sucked in air like a dying fish.

"What's your name?" Green Eyes considered my face carefully. He seemed to be studying me, processing whatever he saw in my eyes. With a jerk of his head he motioned toward Mr. Song's mangled body and I shuddered. "Two weeks and he never once checked his car. Until today. Have you been tailing me?"

"Tailing you?" I yanked myself away from him and wrapped my arms around my midsection. I was a murderer. Was it manslaughter, or vehicular homicide? Did they use those terms in the UK? My brain couldn't process the fact that I had killed a man so it resorted to being angry. It was like there were short circuits in my grey matter. It didn't compute; didn't make sense. How could I have killed a man, just like that?

"Your name." It wasn't a question.

"Go to hell! I'm not telling you my name." I looked away from Song's body and fought the bile rising in my throat.

"We're standing over a dead man that you just killed in a parking garage. I'd think telling me your name would be the least of your worries." His mouth twitched.

"Or it's a really good damn reason not to! Now get out of my way so I can go get him help." I started to step around him, but he moved to block my way.

"You really didn't mean to kill him." The realization swept over his face.

"No shit, Sherlock." My heart was beating so fast I could swear he could hear it. I stared into his eyes, wishing that I could understand what was going on. Wishing that we were talking under different circumstances.

A loud shot filled the garage and Green Eyes threw himself into me and pulled me to the ground.

"What the fuck?" I tried to scramble away from him, but he wouldn't let me up.

"Be still!" He looked down at me and I froze. There was no denying the serious look in his eyes. "Don't move."

He slid off of me and rolled onto his side, scanning under the cars. I could hear the steps of someone as they walked across the concrete, and I felt the flutters of panic grip my throat. I looked around trying to pinpoint where the sound was coming from. Warm fingers closed on my wrist and I looked to where Green Eyes jerked his chin.

About four cars away I could see red heels next to a tire. Squeezing my hand to get my attention, this man that had just felt me up now motioned for me to be quiet and follow him. He pointed for me to climb into the driver side of the car next to us and I shook my head. Hadn't he been here five minutes ago when I ran someone over? He jerked his head again and pointed at me, then back at the car.

I shook my head and pointed at the dead man whose blood was slowly creeping across the pavement toward us. I'd killed the poor man, I wasn't about to steal his car, too. And now someone was trying to kill us. Probably a bodyguard or maybe the police.

Another shot slammed into the side of Danny's car and I moved without thinking. Apparently self-preservation was an instinct. Yanking open the door of Song's car, I flew into the driver seat and searched for the keys. I was vaguely aware of Green Eyes standing up and calmly pointing a gun over the roof of the car before firing.

"Fuck, fuck, fuck!" My grandmother would be horrified at my language, but damn it, if there was ever a time to use it, it was now ! "There's no key!" I looked over at the man coolly sliding into the passenger seat.

The coldest green eyes I'd ever seen met mine and I shivered. He handed me a single silver key—obviously a copy of the original, but I didn't care. I shoved it into the ignition and threw the car in reverse. There was a sickening crunch, but I didn't have time to feel bad about running over Mr. Song again. A loud crack had me ducking as a bullet slammed into the back window. It didn't shatter though, and in some distant part of my mind I wondered why Mr. Song had bulletproof glass.

"Feel free to run over anyone else in our way." Calmly he turned in his seat and lowered his window. Humor warmed his eyes.

"Not funny." I turned the first corner of the garage just as he fired another shot. The sound made me wince and I jerked the steering wheel. The car clipped the bumper of a delivery van and threw Green Eyes against his door.

"I was joking. Please try to not do that." He looked at me, his expression serious. "There's a bomb on the bottom of this car."

I turned to look at him and felt my mouth fall open. "A bomb! There's a bomb in this car? Why is there a bomb in this car? What kind of bomb?"

"The kind that goes boom. It was meant for Mr. Song, who you managed to kill without a bomb, and technically it's on the car, not in it." He twisted in his seat so that he was facing forward again. "It should be fine. It's set to go off by remote and I have that right here." He patted his pocket.

I twisted the steering wheel sharply as I exited the garage and almost knocked over the doorman. But he was holding a large gun in one hand and to my shock he fired directly at my window. The glass shattered, but I didn't feel any pain, which I hoped meant I wasn't hit. I ducked in a belated reaction and the car swerved wildly, but the gun-toting hottie next to me steadied the wheel.

"I knew that doorman didn't like me." I gritted my teeth. "What an asshole. He's almost as bad as you are."

"I'll drive now, if you'd like." He said it like we were taking turns on a road trip, not running for our lives. Maybe he wasn't running for his life. But I was still running for mine. I didn't know what this guy wanted with me. Was I supposed to just let him drive me to some creepy kill room? An image of walls draped in plastic, knives on a table, and a bed with chains filled my mind. I didn't think so.

"Now? You want to drive now?" My voice rose with each word. "Sure, I'll pull over at the corner for a snack and let you take over. Holy shit! Are you crazy?"

"Has anyone ever told you that for such a beautiful woman you have a very dirty mouth?" He smiled at me as my mouth worked silently. "I think I like the odd combination."

"Fuck you." I glared at the road.

"So does that mean you don't want me to drive?" He nodded toward the traffic that was growing thicker. "Do you have a plan for where to go?"

"The cops." I didn't mention that I had no idea where they would be located. I'd just stop the first one I saw. "And you told me to get in the driver seat."

"You're sure you want to go to the police?" He leaned back into his seat, getting comfortable. He looked, for all the world, as if riding around in a car with a bomb attached to it was normal. "You killed a man and fled the scene in his stolen car—which has a bomb attached to it. Oh, and someone was trying to kill you. I'm sure being locked in a tiny room with nowhere to run will make their job much more difficult."

"Maybe they were trying to kill you. I can imagine why they'd want to." I growled and turned down a street that was one way only. And I was going the wrong way. I muttered under my breath as I dodged cars and people honked at me. "I should've stayed in bed today."

"Possibly. They were very sloppy." He pointed to a street. "You should turn here and take the roundabout."

"Roundabout?" My heart dropped into my stomach and I broke into a cold sweat. "That seems like a bad idea."

Roundabouts were the devil. If you've ever tried to drive through a roundabout after years of driving in America, you'd understand. Everything was completely backward to how you instinctually drove. It gave me an ulcer just thinking about it.

"We're being followed. We need to lose them." He looked at me with serious eyes. "If you want to live, we need to put distance between us and the people in the black sedan."

"Oh, Jesus." I jerked the wheel and our car shot down the road toward the evil traffic circle of death.

"Don't stop, go around them." I swerved into oncoming traffic to avoid the cars waiting at the stop sign. Horns blared, people shouted, and I gritted my teeth. If I made it out of this alive, I'd kiss the ground.

I could hear people screeching to a halt as I blew into the traffic circle and weaved between the cars.

"Here." He pointed to a road and I didn't hesitate as I turned. Belatedly, I wondered where the police were. Surely there should be screeching sirens and flashing lights in my rearview mirror at any minute. The part of me that wasn't required to pay attention prayed to have someone else to turn this mess over to, someone to make sense of the last thirty minutes.

Had it even been thirty minutes? Probably closer to five minutes. It felt like hours.

A pedestrian stepped into a crosswalk and I slammed on my brakes. Dear God, don't let me kill anyone else. The rear tires slid in a wild fishtail and my arms locked stiffly as I fought the wheel to keep control. Without thinking I took my foot off of the brake and slammed it onto the gas pedal, wrenching the vehicle around the dazed man and through the intersection.

"Nice." Green Eyes nodded his head as if I had done something impressive when I had only been trying to not pee my pants.

"If I can't go to the cops, where do you suggest I go?" I gritted my teeth as I tore through another intersection.

"Out of town would be best." His head ducked so he could look out the mirror on his side of the car. "The less people around, the better we can stay hidden."

I took a deep breath. "So I'm stuck with you?"

"It could be worse." He shrugged.

"How could it possibly be worse? I just killed a man in a fucking parking garage! I killed him! His brains are probably stuck to the cement!"

"Well, you could be trapped with the people shooting at you right now." He pointed toward a side street. "And it's not your fault. Song was creeping through the garage trying to not be seen. There was no way you could know that he was behind you. The blood splatter would prove your innocence."

Pedestrians stopped to watch as our car squealed by.

"You thought I killed him on purpose." I gripped the steering wheel.

"I thought you had very cleverly stolen my ticket, but once I calmed down I realized you hadn't meant to do it."

"Ticket?" I was innocent. I knew I was innocent, but I

still felt horrible. Guilt gnawed at my stomach and squeezed my chest.

"You need to turn. You've been on this street for too long."

Yanking the wheel, the car slid around the corner and onto an empty road. I could still see the other car in my side mirror and had no idea how I was supposed to lose them.

"What do we do?" I turned the car down a different road without being told to. I had no idea where I was going, except for away.

"We need to get on the motorway." My eyes must've widened, because he reached out and touched my arm. His gaze was steady, no signs that he was panicked or worried about lying. "We can switch. I'll keep you safe."

My gaze darted to his. "What's your name?"

There was a moment's hesitation before he answered. "Owen."

"Ava." I looked back at the road and swerved around a car that had stopped to let someone out.

"It's nice to meet you, Ava." His lips turned up and I felt something different than guilt flutter through my chest. "Will you let me drive now?"

"How?" I couldn't stop. Who knew what would happen if I stopped. Would they just start shooting at us? Would they shoot other people in their attempt to get us?

"Get on the M1 and we'll trade." His fingers squeezed my arm. "It'll be easy." There was no way switching drivers while on some sort of expressway would be easy.

"Where is the M1?" Something slammed into the back windshield and I ducked. They had shot at us. In public. So much for hoping they were trying to get us somewhere quiet.

"We're not far. Can you get us a few more blocks?" His eyes were so calm, as if nothing was happening and we were just practicing driving around the town.

"Pfft. No problem. I've gotten us this far." Where the hell this bravado was coming from, I had no idea. But I noticed the smile on his face, and knew that I'd put it there.

"That's my girl."

His girl? Hardly. Under other circumstances... well, that wasn't an option now. Following his directions, we made our way to the on ramp without any accidents. The car tailing us never disappeared, no matter how hard I mentally wished flat tires on them. I sped up, going around cars until we had a nice swatch of clear road. I looked on the dash until I found the cruise control and hit the little button.

"Okay."

He reached over and unbuckled the seat belt I hadn't realized I had put on. Sliding his arm behind my back, he shifted over the center console and moved closer to me. Carefully I used my feet to push up so he could slide underneath me. His body pushed against mine and I could feel every manly inch of him pressed behind me, down to the muscles his button up shirt concealed. As his hands slid around my waist to help steady me, his thumbs pressed against my back and rubbed soft circles, as if he was trying to comfort me—but instead it was accomplishing the exact opposite. I let the weight off of my feet, easing down on to his lap so I could move to the other seat.

"I'm ready." His voice was husky in my ear and for a second I thought about telling him I was more than ready myself. Thankfully I was able to keep my senses and re-member that there was someone intent on killing me in a car not far behind us.

With extreme caution I tried to lift my left leg so that I could step over the console, but my skirt was too tight. Understanding the problem, his hands slid moved down my hips and over my skirt so he could slip it up my thighs. Goosebumps erupted along my skin as his knuckles brushed along my legs. Once the material was high enough that I could lift my leg, I slid into the other seat and let him take control of the steering wheel.

"Buckle up." He smiled at me as he took the car off cruise control and hit the gas pedal.

CHAPTER FOUR

Owen

I HAD TO force my mind back onto the task at hand as Ava adjusted herself in her seat. She checked the side mirror before turning to look at me.

"What are you going to do?" Her voice held a throaty edge that made me smile. Apparently she had enjoyed changing seats as much as I had. It was certainly a better sound than the horror it had held earlier.

"Lose them." I wrenched the car around a tour bus and tried to put a little more distance between us and the idiots following close behind. There were only two real options. Lose them in traffic, or take them out. And I had a feeling that Ava would be upset if I used my particular skill set right now.

Knowing that there was road construction nearby, I headed there. It would be one of the easiest ways to lose our tail. And then I needed to get somewhere safe so I could work out just what was going on here.

"Ava? Why would someone want to kill you?"

"Me? I don't know! What about you? You put bombs

under people's cars. Maybe they're trying to kill you."

"They were aiming for you, Ava." I swerved around another family car and gritted my teeth when our tail almost clipped their bumper. "I was just collateral damage in that scenario."

"They're stopping!" Ava reached up and grabbed the handle above her door.

"Yes."

"Then why are you speeding up?" Her voice rose in pitch.

"To try and lose the car behind us in the construction zone." I swerved and clipped the side mirror on the railing in a shower of sparks. "Or would you rather have me stop so we can try to talk out our differences?"

The hand that wasn't bracing her jerked out and slammed into my arm.

I swerved just a little and she gasped loudly. "Sorry."

"This is going to be close." Up ahead I could see some of the equipment moving and seized my chance. As cars merged into one lane, I whipped into the narrowing emergency lane. Up ahead the extra space was being used for regular traffic and that would be our best chance at bottlenecking our chaser. We sideswiped a taxi and I could hear Ava cursing under her breath and muttering about the bomb, but we made it through.

Loud pops had Ava ducking in her seat, but we had managed to get them trapped for at least a couple of minutes, which would give us time to lose them.

"Shit. Where are the cops?" Ava peeked over her shoulder and out the window.

"Oh, I'm sure they're coming." I pulled off at an exit and turned down a quiet road. "We need to change cars."

"Great. Now you're a car thief?" Ava wrinkled her nose.

"You killed a man in a parking garage. What's a little grand theft auto now?" I watched her out of the corner of my eye as she frowned and looked out the window.

"I guess we already stole one car." Her breath sounded heavy and I wondered if she would cry. A lot of people would in her situation.

"True." I turned into a different parking garage. "And we did it to save your life."

"Our lives." Her face whitened. "I still can't believe I killed Mr. Song."

"I told you, it was his fault. And don't feel bad for him." My voice clipped out the words. "He was not a nice man."

"How would you know?" She looked at me, her eyes narrowed.

"I was there to kill him." I pulled around the garage until I found a corner with a broken light. I put the car in park and looked at her. "Mr. Song ran a prostitute ring. He sold young girls and women to men and made a very healthy living doing so."

"He sold girls? Hookers?" She shook her head. "How can you know that?"

"I'm very particular about the cases I take on. When the girls started showing up dead, one of his associates decided it was time to call his number." I looked around the garage before opening my door. "I need to defuse the bomb. I don't want it accidently going off when the police find the vehicle."

"Shit." She scrambled in her seat to undo her belt before jumping out of the car. She was looking at the stairs

34

leading outside and chewing on her lip when I climbed out of my seat.

"Ava?" I leveled my eyes at her over the car. "You're free to run, but your chances are exponentially better with me."

She looked at me, but didn't say anything. I couldn't blame her for wanting to run. I'd admitted to being a hit-man and she'd been chased by people trying to kill her, not to mention the dead man she left behind. That was a lot for most people to digest.

"Take care of the bomb." She looked away from me. "And then we need to talk."

I nodded my head, relieved she hadn't decided to run. I knew that if she went off on her own she wouldn't make it long. Even the idiots that had been following her would have an easy time taking her down. I could walk, could disappear for a while and wait for this to blow over. But I needed to know what had happened back there, if for no other reason than to make sure I hadn't been set up. And Ava was my best link to the whole mess. It was also a convenient excuse. My bleeding fucking heart was getting the better of me.

"Watch for anyone approaching." She nodded, but didn't look back at me. Still pissed and frightened, I guessed. Understandable.

I slid under the bumper and carefully undid the wires that connected the device to the explosive. I considered removing it all and taking it with me, but I didn't want to have to worry about carrying it. Besides, I knew how to get more if I needed it. Something tapped my leg and I realized Ava was kicking me softly. I crawled out and looked around carefully. There was someone walking toward a car on our side of the garage.

"Found it, honey." I held my hand up as if I'd found an earring before wrapping my arm around her shoulders. I kept my voice casual as I led her toward the nearest exit. "It looks like it's broken. You'll have to get it repaired."

"That's a shame." Her voice was steady, but I could see the tightness around her eyes as she leaned into me.

We walked down the road a ways as I scouted for a new vehicle. Preferably something older that wouldn't be easy to trace. The farther we walked, the more I found myself enjoying the fact that Ava was tucked against my side. Most of my time spent with women was very business-like. We were there to scratch an itch for each other. There was no cuddling or holding hands. I couldn't remember the last time I'd spent a moment with a woman tucked against me for anything other than sex.

I slid my arm from her shoulders down to her waist and she stiffened slightly before falling back into pace with me.

"Loosen up, Ava. If we look happy, that's all anyone will see." I leaned close so I could whisper in her ear. "Just a happy couple walking down the street—not people worried about being followed."

"I'm trying." She stopped and looked up at me, our breaths mingling, and my gaze dipped down to her lips. A lock of her hair had fallen loose and was whipping against her cheek. Slowly I raised my fingers and tucked it back behind her ear, letting my hand linger along her neck.

"You're doing great." Turning away from her I urged us onward. I had no doubt that the people following us would catch up unless we put more space between ourselves and the city.

When we happened upon a quiet row of houses with cars parked along the curb, I turned and walked until I found an older Land Rover. I stopped and bent over to tie my shoe, checking the sidewalk and nearby homes for people that might notice us. Once I was sure we were in the clear, I stood up, pulling the lock picks out of my pocket.

I made quick work of the door and slid into the driver seat before leaning over and opening the door passenger side for Ava. She climbed into her seat Ava climbed inside and discreetly kept watch out the passenger side window. I found it amusing that she had slipped into the role of look-out so quickly. I pulled away from the curb and headed out of town.

We'd stick to as many back roads as possible and keep a low profile. I had a safe house in Oxford that would give us a place to regroup. We needed to change clothes and I needed to talk to some people.

"Where are you going to go?" Ava asked as I navigated the busy roads. Her eyes didn't have the happy glow that had been in them the day before. A couple of hours with me was all it had taken. I didn't blame her.

"Oxford. I need to make some calls and figure out what's going on."

"Are you going to kill me?" she asked. Her voice was steady, but there was no mistaking the fear behind her words.

I sighed. "I don't normally announce when I'm going to kill someone, but no. I'm not going to kill you. If you haven't noticed, I've been trying to keep you alive."

We sat in silence and I focused on staying under the radar. Avoiding suspicious behavior was important while driving a stolen car. My mind ran over the events, trying to piece together an exact timeline. Had I seen that woman at any point before this morning? And the doorman had been in place for quite a while. How long had people been planning on killing Ava?

"Why not kill me?" Her voice broke my train of thought and I looked at her confused.

"What?"

"It would be easier. If there really is a bounty on my head you could just collect the money yourself." She crossed her arms over her chest. I reached out and turned up the heater. It was nearing the end of summer and there was a chill in the air today.

"You're not my contract." I shrugged. "And I only take contracts for people who deserve it." I was not going to go into my philosophy for my job. There was no making what I did okay. I was a murderer.

"How do you know I don't? I didn't know Mr. Song was such a horrible man." She leaned her head back against the seat. "I mean, he was unfriendly, but I never would have looked at him and thought he was involved in some kind of sex scandal."

"I just know." Mr. Song's death wouldn't bother her if she trafficked in the darker parts of humanity. Her eyes were too bright, too innocent—it wasn't something you could fake.

She was looking at me like I was a puzzle and for the first time in a long ages, I felt nervous. I reached up and pulled at my tie so it hung loosely and focused on the road. I'd faced down some of the most disgusting people on the planet, but her bright eyes made me feel undone. I needed to get a grip. Or get laid. How long had it been? I couldn't remember—which was a sad thing.

We lapsed into silence again and I debated our next move. Information was a must. There were too many unknowns in this situation and I didn't like being blind. What were the odds that two people living in the same building, on the same floor, would have hits out for them at the same time? Whoever was after Ava must have some connection with Mr. Song, which meant I was involved whether I wanted to be or not. And I certainly didn't want to be involved.

"Look, I can drop you anywhere you want, but you can't go back to London. It's not safe there right now. For either of us."

"I don't have anywhere else to go," she said miserably.

I shot Ava a quick glance as we wove our way through traffic. She was looking out the window, chewing on her thumbnail. Unshed tears glistened along her eyelashes and made my heart do something funny. A lot of women would be screaming or hysterical. Ava was trying to not let me see her cry.

"Stay with me," I said.

"You're dangerous," Ava pointed out.

"That's why you need me."

She wiped at her eyes, and I could sense she was wavering—but when she finally nodded, I felt relief wash over me. Because at that moment, I understood I had a new job: to protect her.

Shit.

I was definitely involved.

CHAPTER
FIVE

Ava

I WOULD NOT become a blubbering mess. I would not cry like a little girl. I would remain calm so I could retain some kind of control of the situation.

Or I would stare out the window and glare at the world that passed by while pretending like I wasn't crying. I hated to cry. I really fucking hated to cry, especially while trapped in a car with an insanely hot self-confessed murderer.

Then again, wasn't I a murderer now, too?

The memory of blood creeping across the concrete filled my mind. No, no. Can't go down that road right now. It was too much to think about. And I had to concentrate on what was happening to me right now. Had to stay calm so I could figure out what I needed to do next.

Not that I had a clue what that was. I should be looking for a cop, distancing myself from Owen, but I had agreed to let him help me and besides I had nothing with me; no money, no passport, no cell phone. Nothing. Everything was in my purse, back in the car that killed Mr.

Song. I wasn't sure I could even remember Tess's new phone number. I mean, who bothered memorizing phone numbers anymore? And surely the police had gotten to Song by now. They would go through my purse and call out to all of the officers to start looking for the American with torn stockings, blue eyes, and brown hair.

I was so screwed. Right now my entire life hinged on the guy driving this stolen car—on what he decided to do next. And I wasn't exactly comfortable with that. But my options were limited. Very limited. I sighed.

"What's in Oxford?" We passed a small sign with the city name.

"My house." He cleared his throat and sat up a little straighter. "A safe house."

His house or a safe house? And was I really okay with going to a strange house with him? Did I have a choice?

"What are we going to do there?"

"After I have my way with you I think I'll order pizza and catch a game."

My mouth fell open and for a minute my stomach did all sorts of flips. When he saw my expression his lips pulled back into a wide grin and I felt my cheeks heat.

"Very funny," I said, but he only laughed.

Though I didn't want to admit it, for a moment I'd hoped he was serious. It had been almost a year since I'd rolled around in the sheets with someone other than George, my battery operated toy.

"I told you I wasn't going to kill you." A deep chuckle filled the car.

"You're an ass."

"And you're disappointed I wasn't serious." His

smirk made me itch to hit him again.

"You wish." You wish? Was that the best I could come up with?

"We need to figure out why someone is trying to kill you and what we can do about it." He glanced at me slyly. "Then if you want…"

"You know, maybe after the pizza..." I raised one eyebrow. His eyes darted down to my mouth then slowly back up to meet my gaze. "We could discuss strategy. I'm starving."

He smiled slowly and looked back at the road. Ha. Score one for me. He wasn't the only one who could play that game.

I tried to pay attention to landmarks as we drove through town. The last thing I wanted was to be completely lost. There were lots of little storefronts, old buildings, and students meandering through the streets. If I wasn't worried about someone trying to kill me I would have had a blast poking through the old shops and bookstores.

"What is that?" I pointed at a row of houses. One of them seemed to have a giant fish sticking out of the roof like a missile that hadn't detonated.

"A shark." Owen chuckled.

"Why is there a giant shark sticking out of that roof?" I shook my head.

"An expression of outrage about nuclear issues." He shrugged and I leaned back in my seat. "The city tried to have it removed but failed."

"It adds a certain amount of charm, don't you think?" I wished I had my camera. A shark sticking out of a roof would make a fun picture. Of course, my camera was back in Tess's apartment, which was probably being combed by officers wearing latex gloves and searching for finger-prints.

"It's certainly eye catching." His shoulders seemed to relax, even though I hadn't realized that he was carrying tension in them. Part of me wondered if he ever rode around with someone, just talking.

"What else is there to see in Oxford?" I wanted to keep him talking, see him unwind even more. If nothing else, it made me feel more relaxed.

"Museums, the Carfax tower, the Bridge of Sighs." He rattled off the list as he made a turn down a narrow lane.

"The Bridge of Sighs?" I smiled. "That sounds romantic."

"It's very similar to the bridges you find in Venice, but that's as romantic as it gets." Laughter lit his eyes as he talked. "It's not far from the Turf."

"The Turf? Turf as in grass?"

"As in Turf Tavern. It's near the colleges. A lot of the students gather there. Always a good time. Or good trouble." A note in his voice caught my attention. Pride?

"You grew up here?" I offered the guess. It was definitely not just a safe house that we were going to.

"For a while." It was like a metal door dropped down and his chipper attitude dissipated in a cloud of smoke.

I didn't ask anything else as we drove through town. Curiosity raged inside me, demanding to know what would shut him down so quickly, but I knew better than to push for any answers. It didn't take a psychology degree to see he had some serious issues. Could you be an assassin without some kind of baggage? I seriously doubted it.

Eventually the buildings of town thinned out and we

turned down a small country lane that wound through bushes and trees. A small cottage sat nestled amongst the brush. The red door was a little dingy, but the cottage looked to be in good shape otherwise. We climbed out of the car and I stood there looking around the small clearing.

Owen knelt down in front of the Land Rover and used a knife to remove the license plate. I watched, not sure what else I should do.

"Come on." Owen opened the door for me, waiting for me to go inside. I squeezed past him, conscious of how close we were.

The curtains were closed, leaving the cottage draped in shadow. I moved forward slowly, not wanting to trip. The door creaked as Owen stepped inside and pushed it closed. As he moved close to me I froze, my heart rate accelerating. Leaning forward he reached past me and light flared to life. His bright green eyes bore into mine without looking around the small room.

"Ava?"

"Yes?" I licked my lips.

"You're safe here." He didn't touch me. Didn't squeeze my hand or even smile. Yet, I did feel comforted. I had a feeling that he didn't tell people that often. And if he was telling me, that meant he believed it.

"What are we going to do?" I said the words quietly. He had offered me help, I'd have been a fool to not accept it. Even if I was still wary.

"Why don't you change and I'll get some food ready? We can talk while we eat."

"I don't have anything with me." I looked down at my dirty dress and torn stockings.

He looked me up and down before walking into an

adjoining room. I watched as he opened a few drawers and pulled things out. I chewed on my nail as he walked back to me and proffered his bounty.

"The bathroom is right over there." He motioned to a door next to the bedroom.

"Thanks." I took the clothes and walked past him. The bathroom was small but functional. It was neat, with a fine coating of dust on everything that suggested it had been a while since anyone had used the cottage.

I locked the door as quietly as I could. It wasn't that I thought Owen was going to peek in, it was just more of a precaution. That man didn't have to go peeking into bathrooms to see naked women. They probably lined up on the sidewalks waving their panties for him.

When I looked into the mirror I frowned at my reflection. My makeup had not held up well to rolling around on the pavement. Of course, being shot at hadn't helped either. I looked through the shelves in the corner until I found a wash cloth and used it to clean up. I didn't know what was going to happen next, but looking like I had just pulled an all-nighter at a club probably wasn't a good idea.

Owen had given me a cable knit sweater that was a little large and a pair of jeans that were snug enough to make me consider not buttoning them. I decided that if I had to do any more rolling around on the ground I didn't want to lose my pants so sucked it in and zipped them up. My hair was a mess, hanging around my face in clumps, so I pulled it all the way down and tried to work some of the knots out. It was silly to care what I looked like, but it felt good to take a few minutes to do something so normal.

When I was finished I took my clothes and shoes out to the living room. Owen was on the phone while stirring a pot on the stove, his jacket and tie discarded on the sofa. There was a tattoo on his left forearm that curved up and around, but I couldn't see exactly what it was. I took a seat at the table, quiet so I wouldn't interrupt. I had no idea who he was talking to or what they needed to know, but I didn't want to announce my presence.

"No. Tell him there was a complication. Nothing I can't handle." He stepped away from the stove to grab two bowls from a shelf. He stone-cold voice was so at odds with his movements, I felt like I was watching two versions of him battling for reality. "He knows how to reach me."

He set the bowls down before throwing the phone on the counter. I watched as he worked, enjoying the complete contradiction of him working in the kitchen. He was definitely at home in the cottage, even if there were no photographs on the walls. There was no hesitation when he reached for something, because he must've reached for it a hundred times in the past. It made him seem normal, not a hardened hired killer.

"I was going to make tea, but it seems we're out." He flung a dish towel over his shoulder and leaned against the counter. "The clothes fit?"

As his eyes ran over me I fought the urge to fidget with the giant sweater. I felt like I might as well be naked under his scrutiny. His gaze lingered on my shoulder where the wide neck of the sweater kept slipping off. Instinctively I reached up and touched the spot he stared at, wondering what it would feel like to have his mouth there instead. The moment seemed to draw out and I realized I hadn't answered his question.

"They're fine." I cleared my throat and looked down

46

at the table. "What are you making?"

"Canned soup. I don't keep perishables here." He nodded toward the open cupboard. Cans lined the shelf.

"Not here often." It wasn't a question.

"No." He folded his arms over his chest as he regarded me. I wasn't sure what he was looking for so I sat there quietly. "How are you holding up?"

I shrugged. What could I say? I'm fine? That would be a lie. I wasn't bleeding or having a panic attack, but I also wasn't comfortable or happy.

"You seem to be handling this pretty well." He turned to stir the pot again.

"No. I'm not. Inside I'm huddled in a corner and crying." I folded my hands on the table in front of me. "I have no idea what's going on, I'm in a stranger's cabin wearing a stranger's clothes, and all of my belongings, including my passport, are back at Tess's apartment."

"Tess?" He turned around and looked back at me.

"My friend. I'm housesitting for her while she's on her honeymoon." My stomach clenched. I wasn't sure why it hadn't occurred to me until that moment, but what if those people hadn't been looking for me? "Oh my God. I need to call her. She might be in danger."

"Hold on a minute." He took the pot off the stove and ladled the soup into the bowls. "Was that your car in the garage?"

"No. That's Danny's car. Her husband." I twisted my fingers together. "I'm just housesitting and got a call for a job interview. I hate driving here, but I didn't have any other options."

"Your friend, is she American as well?" He sat a bowl down in front of me before taking the opposite chair.

NICHOLE CHASE

"Yeah. She met Danny in the States and they went straight on their honeymoon." Sitting back in my chair I shook my head. "I need to call her."

God damnit. I didn't even know her new number.

"That's not a good idea." Owen shook his head. "They could be monitoring her."

"What if it's not me that they were after? What if they really meant to kill Tess? I have to warn her!" I stood up and stepped toward the counter.

"And if she wasn't their target, you'll be putting her in their sights." Owen didn't get up, just waited for me to think it over. "Let me see what kind of information I can get before we do anything. There is something weird going on and I don't like it."

"You mean weirder than running over a man, being shot at, and stealing cars?"

"That's a normal work day for me, love." He winked at me and I thought about punching myself for the giddiness that coursed through my veins. Maybe I should just punch him. Anger was better than panic, right?

"Yeah, I'm beginning to get that." I sat back down and picked up my spoon. "Who did you call?"

"My handler." He took a few sips of his soup. "I need to check in and let him know the hit went amiss. I'm also going to ask if there are any hits out for an American woman. Try to feel out the case."

My stomach clenched. Would he decide to take the job himself once he knew how to get the money? I looked down at my bowl and tried to not show my nerves. One minute I felt completely at ease, contemplating his ass while he cooked, and the next I was shaking like there was a velociraptor watching me while I ate gelatin. I was apparently insane. Or in a really odd situation. Jesus, I wish there was a script I could follow.

He got up from his seat without a word and opened a small drawer next to the stove. When he pulled out the black gun I sat up straight, watching him. If he decided to shoot me there wasn't anything I could do about it. Casually he checked the chamber and slid the gun across the table to me. I looked from it to him.

"You need to be able to defend yourself." He sat back down in front of his soup.

"From who?" I slid the gun closer to me. I had used guns on Grandma's farm. Mostly shotguns or rifles, but it had been a long time.

"From anyone you think is a threat." He dug back into his soup.

"Would this gun stop you?" I lifted the gun, wrapping my fingers around the grip, careful to avoid the trigger. I dropped the clip and checked the chamber. A large bullet fell onto the table, spinning for a moment. I popped the clip back into the handle, cocked the gun, dropped the clip and replaced the bullet. And I managed to do it all without shaking hands.

"It could." His amused smile made an appearance. "You know your way around a gun?"

"Some." I set the pistol back down on the table and decided to eat. I had a feeling it was important to keep my stamina up. "My grandmother owned a farm. So, I know the basics. Mainly it was just shotguns or rifles. Trying to scare predators away from the chickens or occasionally dealing with a sick animal. We didn't have much to do with pistols, but I did win a couple of sharp shooting competitions in 4H. I didn't keep up with the training though."

I sighed and tried to not think about that too much. I'd had to put down one of our cattle the year Granny had passed. She'd been too weak to do it and I couldn't look at the cow suffering any longer.

"Good. Then I don't have to worry about you shooting yourself."

"I'd be more worried that I'd accidently shoot you." I laughed at his expression. "Thank you."

"You're welcome." He stood up and went back to the stove for more food. "No one should feel helpless."

His words rang through the quiet little house. Oddly, I did feel better having the gun. If he was going to kill me, he could have done it already, and certainly wouldn't have given me a way to defend myself.

I finished my soup quickly. You'd think I wouldn't be hungry with everything that was going on. I *had* killed a man today—shouldn't I feel bad? But instead of praying or offering up Hail Marys, I was scraping the bowl with my spoon like it would magically spout out more chicken.

"I can make more." Owen watched me, amusement in his expression.

"I don't know why I'm so hungry." I pushed back in my seat. "I'll do it if you don't mind."

"Help yourself." He threw an arm over the back of his chair and watched as I got up and moved through his kitchen.

I looked over the cupboard offerings and picked a can of clam chowder. With the overcast weather and soft patter of rain it seemed like the perfect fit. I took my time as I rinsed out the pot and used the handheld can opener. His eyes followed my every move and I tried to not show how it affected me. There was a tension between us that was

50

undeniable and the new me might have jumped all over that fact, except for everything that was going on.

"Where was your job interview?" His voice rumbled through the room.

"A jewelry designer." I sighed. "I really wanted it, too."

"Is that what you were doing at the café? Filling out job applications?"

My cheeks heated at the reminder that he had been watching me. "Yeah. I didn't expect to hear back from them so quickly."

"When did you hear from them?" His eyes narrowed.

"This morning. I barely had enough time to get ready." I stirred the pot on the stove. "I wonder if I would've gotten the job?"

"Had you made it, I'm betting they wouldn't have had any idea why you were there."

"What do you mean?" I turned to look at him, for a moment thinking he was implying I wasn't good enough for the position.

"It was a set up. They were drawing you out so they could make the hit."

"But—"

"Think about it, Ava. What are the odds that someone would call you before normal business hours to ask you to come in for an interview?" His head cocked to the side. "They were hoping to take you out without causing a scene. The garage was typically empty at that time of the morning."

My mouth opened and then closed. "How could they…"

"Hacking into email isn't difficult." He walked to the

51

sink and rinsed his bowl. "I should know."

"But—but." I shook my head. "So I didn't get the job interview?"

"Is that the part that upsets you the most?" His smile mocked me and I glared at him.

"I really wanted it. I wanted to get a job so I could get a work visa." I leaned my hip against the counter and crossed my arms.

"You don't plan on going back to the States?"

"I won't have a choice if I can't find a job." I turned back to the stove and stirred the pot again. I was still shocked that I had been set up, that my computer had been hacked, and I had no idea. How long had the woman in red heels been following me? The doorman had been at the building since I'd arrived during a thunderstorm with nothing but my carry-on bags.

"Don't you have a job and family back home?" He moved a little closer and I could feel his eyes on me like a caress. It was so odd to look at him and find the balance between the murderous monster that lurked behind his eyes and the gentle manner with which he looked at me.

I shrugged.

"No?"

"No family. Quit my job." I looked up at him, surprised that he was so close. "When Tess got married I realized I needed to change. Stop doing all of the same things. Try something new."

"Seems like you're accomplishing your goal." The laughter in his voice made me meet his stare.

"I guess so." I felt the corners of my mouth turning up. "Killing people in garages, a mad car chase through London…guess I can mark those off my to-do list now.

You sure know how to show a girl a good time."

"And I'm not even trying yet."

"Yet?" Did my voice sound heavy? I looked up at him.

"Yet." Hunger lit his eyes. Oh my.

"That so?" I bit my bottom lip.

"So." He reached out and brushed some of the hair away from my face.

We stood there like that for a few minutes, our gazes locked as we contemplated each other. The hiss of the soup boiling over broke the moment and I turned around to turn the stove off. Owen grabbed a rag from the sink and cleaned up the mess while I dished food into our bowls.

"Is there any reason someone would be after your friend?" Owen leaned against the corner before spooning some of the soup into his mouth.

"Tess? God, no. Everyone loves her." I pursed my lips. "I can't imagine anyone wanting to hurt her."

"What about her husband?"

"Danny?" My initial reaction was to say the same thing. Danny was funny, personable, and put everyone at ease. But the truth was, I didn't know him very well. He and Tess had only dated for a few months before deciding to elope. "I don't know."

"What does he do?" Owen set his empty bowl in the sink.

"He's a contractor. Builds things."

"What type of things?" Owen cocked his head to the side. "Maybe he's upset someone."

"Upset someone? Danny is one of the easiest guys to get along with, I can't imagine he would do something that would upset someone that badly without trying to make it right." I needed to talk to Tess. I was terrified she would wander into a terrible situation and be completely blind.

"Maybe he doesn't know that he's done something wrong."

"Then I'm not going to know what it is." I shook my head and added my empty bowl to the sink. "For that matter, maybe I've done something and I just don't know what it is."

"Have you gone anywhere unusual, met any abnormal people?" He turned the water on and started cleaning the dishes. "Other than me?" He threw me a smile that had me shaking my head.

"Not that I know of." I plucked the clean bowl from his hand and the towel from his shoulder. I thought it over as I dried and he cleaned. Where all had I been, what had I done? Nothing outlandish or uncommon came to mind. The typical tourist traps and landmarks in London, but hadn't really had much contact with anyone other than Rachel at the café.

"What about in the States?" He leveled his gaze at me. "Are you running from anything?"

"Boredom." He didn't laugh which made me sigh. "Honestly, I just wanted to shake life up a bit."

"I'm serious, Ava. An ex-lover holding a grudge? Someone you owe a debt to?"

"No and no. I parted amicably with my last boyfriend and my grandmother left me enough money that I wouldn't have to go into debt." I sat the towel down on the counter.

"Someone after your money?" He looked at me intently.

"It wasn't that much, just enough to cushion me if I

was careful." I wasn't going to explain the details of my bank account. After I paid Gran's debts off, I'd had just under twenty thousand left. It was a nice amount of padding, but we weren't talking millions. Surely not enough to make it worthwhile to hire a hitman.

"Then we're back to your friends. Is it possible people didn't know what Tess looked like?" He walked over to a wall and pulled a picture down. There was a safe behind it and he quickly entered a code before opening the door. He pulled out a stack of money in various currencies, a few passports, some folders, and a laptop.

"I guess so." I sat down on a large stuffed chair and ran my fingers over the arms. "They got married in the States and barely stopped in London before going on their honeymoon. They're going to be gone for a month, so Tess asked me to house sit—take care of their plants. I think she just wanted to give me an escape. She felt bad for leaving me."

"Escape from what?" Owen set the laptop down and flipped through his folders.

"Life." I shrugged uncomfortably when he looked up at me. "I'm twenty-three and was living like a cat woman. Minus the cat."

"Cat woman?" He smirked.

"I never did anything interesting or spontaneous. I wasn't even using my art degree because I was comfortable in the boring job I had been doing for the last three years. I was just…existing." I tucked my feet up under me and picked at the jeans. The knees were wearing thin, like they had been someone's favorite pair. "I thought London would give me the chance to break out of my routine."

"Well, I think it's fair to say you accomplished that."

He smiled before looking down at his computer.

"More like blew it to smithereens." I propped my chin on my knee and watched him as he typed. "What are you doing?"

"Checking email, trying to see if there are any rumors online. Hints as to what's going on." His voice drifted as he searched. "I knew there was something wrong with this hit from the beginning."

"So is there an assassin chat room? Online support group? A top secret forum?" I leaned forward to try and peek at the computer screen.

"Something like that." His eyebrows drew together and he frowned. A familiar blue light lit his features and I gasped.

"Oh my God. Are you on Facebook?" I laughed when he turned the computer away from my prying eyes.

"No. I am *not* on Facebook. What kind of self-respecting assassin would have a Facebook group?"

"Let me see your profile picture." I reached for the computer and he moved it further away. "Don't tell me. You're holding a gun, Bond style."

"Bond wishes he was as cool as I am." Laughter lit his eyes as he looked up at me.

"Uh huh." I shifted back in my seat. "Do you think I could send Tess an email?" That was one thing I could remember; her email had been the same since we had met.

"That is the worst thing you could do right now." He didn't look up, just continued to stare at whatever was on the screen.

"Then how do you suggest I let her know she may be in danger?" I tried to reel my temper in, because it wasn't his fault I was being targeted, but the fact was that I was in a terrible situation. "Or that I'm alive? I'm sure the cops had to have traced Danny's car by now. Tess probably thinks I'm dead or worse."

"Worse than dead?" Owen raised an eyebrow.

"Well, I could've been taken and sold as a sex slave." I shrugged. "It happened in that movie where the dad kills everyone, only I don't have a bad-ass to come save me. And fuck, I ran over a murderous pimp in his garage!"

"You really do have a foul mouth." He leveled a disapproving stare at me.

"Are you kidding me? You're an assassin. Stop throwing stones."

"Point. But I might argue that I manage to kill people while maintaining a sense of propriety."

"You kill people with a sense of propriety?" Laughter erupted from my mouth. "What? Do you leave a thank you note? Do you design your own assassin stationery? Dear Sir or Madam…" My laughter choked my words.

"I didn't say I was nice about it. Just proper."

"Proper." I shook my head.

"Yes, clean and quick." He watched stuff scroll across his screen. "Usually."

I didn't want to think about what that meant. Instead I turned back to what I felt I could control.

"So why would it be a bad idea to let her know that I'm alive? That she may be in danger?"

"They may be monitoring your email. It could lead them to you or her. Think about it. If they are after you and you let them know she is important to you, then it will send them after her to use against you. If they are after her, it could just alert them to wherever she is right now." He frowned at me. "Where is she?"

"Italy? I didn't ask for a detailed itinerary. It's their honeymoon. They're probably holed up naked in a little villa somewhere." Standing up, I went to look out the windows. "I think they were driving, so they could be anywhere."

We were silent for a while, the only noise the sound of his fingers dancing across the keyboard. I was starting to feel drained, the insanity of the day catching up with me now that the adrenaline had calmed.

"I don't like this."

"Which part?"

"Any of it. All of it. This is a giant fuc—stupid mess." Using my fingers I pushed the blinds open wide enough to see through. "I don't have a passport, I don't have any money—I have nothing."

"That's not true." Owen's voice rumbled through the room.

"What?" I shot him a look over my shoulder. "I'm baggage for you. Nothing but a hassle to give you a headache."

"Not true." He sat back from the little table in front of the sofa. "And you have a gun. I've found that those are just as helpful as money or passports at times."

I smiled at him and turned back around to look at the gravel path in front of the house. I didn't want to show him just how vulnerable I felt at that moment, but I could feel him watching me out of the corner of my eye.

"Ava, I'm not going to dump you on the street." I heard him stand up, but didn't turn around. "It may not be comforting, but you're my best link to all of this and I need to know what's going on."

"Your handler can help you with that." I shrugged.

"Or your Facebook group."

"No one has heard anything. Seems like the wires are too quiet right now. My contacts are antsy." He had moved closer to me, but I still didn't turn around. "Something is happening and everyone is on guard."

"So, it is a Facebook group?" I glanced over my shoulder at where he stood. He was watching out the window with me.

"I'll send you a friend request." His chuckle did a lot to make me feel better.

"What will your likes be? Shooting? Maiming? Do you take James Bond quizzes and post your results? Which Bond are you?" I shifted so I was facing him.

"I guess you'll find out." He reached out and tugged a lock of my hair.

"I'm not ready to die, Owen." I looked at him with steady eyes. "I just decided to start living."

"I'll never lie to you, Ava." He lowered his voice like we weren't already alone. "I don't know what's going to happen, but I'll do my best to make sure you get to live your life the way you want to."

"Why?" I was always good at asking questions when I probably shouldn't.

"I don't know. Maybe I like the challenge of doing something different." He paused. "Or maybe I just want to see you happy. I miss that smile from the café."

I had no idea how to respond. Instead of saying anything, I leaned forward and kissed his cheek. His stubble brushed against my skin and I fought the urge to turn into him and nuzzle along his neck. I knew I should be ashamed for being attracted to a man who killed people for a living. Knew I should be trying to get away from him and running to the police. And yet…

And yet, I was still there, putting my trust in a man that I met while he was trying to kill another man. There was something seriously wrong with my decision making abilities right then, but there was nothing I could do to change how I felt.

CHAPTER
SIX

Ava

BY THE TIME it was dark outside I was going stir crazy. There was a television, but nothing could hold my attention. Owen still hadn't heard from his contacts and wasn't saying much. I had a feeling that he was lost in his head. Maybe plotting to take down a government or steal someone's ice cream cone. Okay, I didn't really think he would steal someone's ice cream, but I honestly wasn't sure what was going on in that head of his.

I also wasn't sure what was going on in my head. I went back and forth between trying to figure out what I would tell the police and how I could contact Tess without attracting unwanted attention. The pistol Owen had given me was sitting on the arm of the chair I was using.

My imagination got the best of me at one point and I wondered how many people that gun had been used to kill. But then the sensible part of me kicked in and I refused to worry about it. Those people were dead and I needed to protect myself. Callous? Maybe. Didn't make it less true. And feeling bad about it did nothing but cloud my need to keep myself safe.

Besides, I'm sure they didn't care.

Owen stood up from his spot on the couch and stretched. I watched him, my eyes traveling over his body as he twisted and turned. He wasn't very bulky, built more like a swimmer. Tall and lanky with muscles that made my mouth water. I shouldn't stare at him, but my modesty had run out the door when I decided the gun was my friend.

"Get some sleep." He looked over at me. "You should try to grab some while you can."

"I don't think I can sleep." I shook my head.

"Why don't you go try? There's a bed in the other room. I'll stay out here and sleep on the sofa."

"What if someone shows up?" A shiver raced down my spine.

"There are alarms and security cameras." He turned his computer to face me. The screen was broken up into four different images. One of the front of the house, one of the back, another showing the narrow driveway that led down the side of the house and the last one was pointed at a barn of some sort just in front of a tree line.

"Are all of your safe houses this well guarded?"

"No." His eyes stared at the computer and I had the impression that he was avoiding looking at me.

"This one must be special."

"It's vulnerable. The security system makes it less so." He gave a lazy shrug.

"Uh huh." Not the whole story, but that was okay. It was his story to keep.

"We'll be safe, Ava. Go get some sleep. We don't know when we'll have another chance."

I chewed on my lip and thought about it. Sleep didn't

sound that bad, but how could I trust that nothing would happen to me while I slept? What if he decided to ditch me? What if someone came looking for us while we were unconscious?

"How do you do it?"

"Do what?" He raised one eyebrow.

"Sleep, knowing that you have enemies." I played with the hem of my sweater.

"I trust my equipment." He stood up and held his hand out to me.

"It must be pretty good equipment, then." I felt my cheeks flush at the unintentional flirtation. But that smile was playing across his lips again, and I liked seeing it.

"Yes it is."

I let him pull me to my feet. I grabbed the pistol from the chair arm and let it hang loosely in my fingers. Tugging gently, he pulled me toward the bedroom where he had gotten my clothes earlier. The room was dark, but he flipped on a light on the small table next to the bed. I watched as he pulled back the blanket and fluffed the pillows. He turned to look at me once he was finished and stuck his hands in his pockets. That simple gesture made him seem somewhat vulnerable.

"It's not fancy, but it's comfortable."

"It's great. Thank you." I looked at the bed and forced myself to smile. If he wasn't an assassin I would think he was trying to be sweet.

"Get some rest." He turned and paused by the door. "I'll be on the couch. Nothing will get past me."

"Will you be able to sleep?"

"Don't worry about me, Ava. This is a normal day for me."

He closed the door without looking back. I sat down on the bed and took a deep breath. The bed was comfortable and if I wasn't running for my life I might even have appreciated the charm of the little cottage I was stuck in, but right then I was too busy trying to make sense out of the craziness that had completely taken over my day.

Eventually I lay down and tried to get comfortable. Owen was right; I needed to sleep. Exhaustion weighed heavily on my shoulders and I felt like there was a beach's worth of sand under my eyelids. While my mind was racing, my body was waving a white flag. There would be time to worry about everything in the morning. If Owen decided to bail on me, I'd figure out something. If he decided to kill me…well, there probably wasn't much I could do to stop him.

I shivered and pulled the quilt up higher on my shoulders. Deep down, I didn't feel threatened by Owen. He'd had his opportunity to ditch me and hadn't done it, but I still wasn't sure about his motives. Did assassins have scruples? He might be British, but he wasn't exactly James Bond. He did his job for money, not out of duty to Crown and Country. He wasn't Tom Cruise in Mission: Impossible, either. Though I had a feeling he lived in a world that was cold and lonely much like those two characters.

My eyes drifted shut as I contemplated my murderous knight in shining armor. Even in my dreams I couldn't escape my reality. Rachel at the coffee shop made a gun with the foam on my café mocha before chasing me down the block with a knife, but the worst were the ones about Mr. Song. He was walking through the building where I used to answer phones and the lights were flickering. I chased him past airplanes that were half-built, begging him for forgiveness, but he never stopped, never looked back. Instead he stopped at the door to the engineering wing, his shoes drenched in blood, and knocked.

"Please forgive me!" My fists clenched. There was blood on my hands, caked under my nails.

"Ava."

"I didn't mean to kill you."

"Ava."

"Please!" I reached out to touch Song.

A hand closed on my shoulder and I woke screaming. Owen looked down at me with sad eyes.

"Shh. You're okay. It was just a dream."

I took in a lungful of cool air and choked. Bile rose in my throat and I covered my mouth. Pushing past Owen I ran to the bathroom and got rid of last night's soup. I clung to the cool porcelain and wept as quietly as I could. I tried to choke back my sobs but there was no stopping them. My eyes burned and every muscle in my body felt as if I had just completed a marathon by the time I was finished. Pushing away from the toilet I leaned back against the bathtub and rubbed the back of my hand across my nose.

Owen knelt down next to me and held out a wet wash cloth. "Finished?"

"Think so." I took the wet rag from him and pressed it to my face. "Sorry 'bout that."

"No need to apologize." He sat down on the floor and leaned against the tub next to me. "I thought it would happen yesterday."

"You thought I would break down and toss my guts yesterday?" I leaned my head back and looked at him from the corner of my eye.

"Killing isn't easy. The first time is always the

worst."

"Did you throw up after your first... kill?" Hit? Mark? Murder? I didn't know the lingo.

He let his head fall back and closed his eyes. I watched as he swallowed and wondered if he was reliving it in his head.

"Two days later." For all the emotion he expressed he could have been an android. Which meant it was probably more important in some way than he would let on.

"A real tough guy, huh? Two days." I shrugged. "I guess I shouldn't be ashamed that I lasted a whole day. That's almost as good as you." Which was probably only because I had been too busy running for my life to stop and really think about it all. Or maybe my moral compass was off. I'd been too worried about my life to think of the one I had accidentally taken.

His lips curved upward just a hair.

"Was he really a bad guy?" I turned my face to watch him carefully.

"Yes." His deep voice was firm. I didn't have to say who I meant.

"He killed women and girls?"

"Most prostitutes don't retire, Ava. They live a life where they trade part of themselves for money; sex and companionship are commodities. It's a high stakes world and Song was brutal."

"How do you know for sure it was him?" I tried to brush some of my tear dampened hair out of my face.

"A local madam lost some of her girls to Song. They ended up dead not long after."

"And what, she cared about the turncoats?" I frowned. "If it's such a brutal world, you'd think she'd

66

have chalked it up to what they deserved. Not spend money to avenge their deaths."

"Too right." His chin jerked decisively. "From what I found, she was more angry that some of her high rollers followed the girls to Song's business and never came back, even after their favorite girls were gone. That's bad for profits so she decided to make a spectacle and remove him from the scene. He encroached on her territory and then spat in her face."

I thought it over. "Why not just lure his girls away from him?"

"Money. If those girls come to her looking for a job she has the upper hand and can pay less. She'd have to dangle a large carrot to get them to come to her otherwise."

"It's a prostitute turf war." I shook my head. "Like in a movie."

"Fiction is usually grounded in some sort of reality." He stood up and offered me his hand. "Would you like to get some breakfast?"

"I'd really like to brush my teeth." I let him pull me to my feet.

"Extra toothbrushes in the medicine cabinet. Then we eat." He closed the door behind him and I stared at my reflection. I had hopped on the carousel of death and had no idea which way it was going to take me.

CHAPTER SEVEN

Owen

DECIDING WHICH VEHICLE to take to town gave me pause. We could use the stolen car because I'd changed the tag while Ava was sleeping. Or we could take the old farm truck from the garage. Then again, people might recognize the truck and it would be better to keep a low profile here. Most of the people I ran with long ago were gone or locked up, but it paid to be safe.

Ava might object to using the stolen car, though. Watching her cry in my mother's bathroom had been like a knife to the gut. How was I supposed to comfort her over killing someone? Patting her on the back would have been patronizing. Any sort of comment I made would sound empty. I would have made tea, but we were out. So I'd gotten her a rag and sat on the floor instead.

The gentlemanly thing would be to take the truck so I didn't upset her any more, but my pragmatic side pointed out that it would be better to keep her alive than to soothe her feelings. She was just going to have to suck it up.

The bathroom door knob turned and I stopped pacing.

I'd felt heat before, but having someone else by my side as I dealt with dangerous people was a new experience. It made me uneasy to feel responsible for another person's safety, and it was wearing on my nerves. With slow, deliberate moves I picked up my laptop and placed it back in the safe. No reason to telegraph my unease.

I closed the safe and froze when I saw Ava. All traces of the makeup she had worn the day before were gone, letting a vulnerability shine through her eyes that was at odds with the defiant way she held her chin. When her gaze met mine it was like being kicked in the gut. I'd just watched her get rid of everything I'd fed her the night before. There were circles under her eyes and she was pale, her hands twisting the hem of the over-sized sweater she was wearing, leaving the material disfigured. But something in her eyes remained fierce.

I'd never seen anyone so beautiful in my life.

I couldn't tell you what it was that drew me. She would never be a model and she wasn't sultry or glamorous, but just a look at her made me want to bundle her up somewhere safe so that I could enjoy her smiles forever.

"Ready?" I cleared my throat.

"Where are we going?" Her voice was low, hoarse from her earlier sickness.

"Breakfast." I slid my guns into my shoulder harness and slipped my blazer over them. I hadn't taken the time to change since we'd gotten to Oxford.

"And then where?" She looked around the room and then shook her head. She had nothing to bring with us.

"We need more supplies." I opened the front door and waited for her to go through.

"Duct tape, tarps?" Her lips quirked into a smile.

69

"Har, har. Look who woke up with a funny bone." I rolled my eyes. "I meant more food, maybe some soap."

She didn't respond, just shook her head.

"Besides, I have plenty of the other stuff in my super-secret kill room."

She stumbled a bit and shot a glare in my direction. "Not funny."

"You started joke hour." I quickened my pace so I could get to the car and open the door.

"I'm officially shutting it down." She tried to look annoyed but couldn't hide the amusement in her eyes.

"Kill joy." I closed her door and moved around to the driver's side.

"Nope, that's your job."

Ouch. That one stung.

"Way to beat a dead horse, Ava." I set the car in drive and headed for town.

She snickered loudly. "What, that doesn't fall under your job description, too?"

"I leave the animal slaughtering to my apprentice."

"You have an apprentice?" Her tone lost some of its laughter.

"No, Ava. I don't have an apprentice. There is no as-sassins' guild. No journeymen trying to work their way up the ranks. No apprentices mucking bloody rooms." I sighed. "And I don't beat animals."

"Sorry." I could see her suck her bottom lip into her mouth. "I'm in unfamiliar territory."

"No problem." I kept my voice calm. "You're going to have to trust me and if that means answering random questions then I will do my best to supply the correct re-sponse."

"Look, I'm not used to depending on other people. I take care of myself." She frowned out the window. "So this is new for me."

"And you don't like it." If the roles were reversed I wouldn't like it either.

"Of course I don't like it. And it's not exactly like you're upstanding citizen material." She waved her hands in front of her. "I mean you're not a police officer or secretly a knight in the Queen's Royal Guard."

"Why are you so sure I'm not a secret knight in the Queen's Guard?" I raised an eyebrow but kept my eyes on the road.

Silence filled the car.

When I finally looked over at my companion her mouth was ajar. I couldn't help the smile that split my face.

"You asshole. I knew you weren't some secret agent." She crossed her arms.

"You thought about it."

Her eyebrows narrowed and she squinted at me. "You're awfully chipper today. Aren't you breaking some kind of assassin rule?"

"Nowhere in the indoctrination did it say I had to frown while killing people."

"I bet you had classes on how to annoy people, too." She looked out the window but I could see a small smile in her reflection. "For your exam you would just stare at the instructor with that smug grin plastered across your face."

"Top of the class."

"I can imagine." She shook her head. "Did you wear bullet proof vests to class? Or were you expected to protect yourself with bare hands from ninjas that jumped out

71

from nowhere?"

"You have a very active imagination." I turned onto the road that would take us to town.

"Maybe, but I never imagined I would kill someone in a parking garage or run away with an assassin." She cracked the window and lifted her head as if trying to get a good breath. "Or that I would be riding along a back road in a stolen car."

"Well, killing Song was an accident. An accident that he caused." I shrugged and turned on the windshield wipers. The misty rain was making it difficult to see the road. "No one imagines they're going to run over a pimp in a car garage."

A soft chuckle escaped her soft lips that blossomed into a throaty laugh. "Oh God. I killed a pimp in a London car garage. A pimp. A well dressed, non-fur wearing pimp."

"Yes, you did." Worry crept up my throat. "Are you about to lose it again?"

"No." She laughed again. "Maybe. Actually, I think I've already lost it."

I swerved for the edge of the road.

"Not lose it as in my lunch. I mean my mind. I'm pretty sure I've lost my mind." Her laugh took on a shrill note. "Look at me. I'm wearing a stranger's clothes, riding in a stolen car, a murderer, and running around with a hot hitman. I wanted to shake up my life a little, but this is a bit much."

"You think I'm hot?" I slowed the car to turn into a parking lot.

"Is that all you heard? Yes. You're hot. Okay? It's not like you don't know that. Your targets probably throw themselves at your feet with a smile. That's not my point." She waved her hands in the air and her cheeks turned a pretty red. It amused me to no end. "My damn point is that my life is a fucking mess right now! I'm a freaking mess right now. And we're...shopping? Where are we? Is this a meat market?"

She turned her large blue eyes in my direction while flinging a hand in the direction of a sign that was shaped like chicken riding a pig.

"Yes, this is a meat market. No, me being hot was not the only thing I heard you say." Though it had been a bright point in her rambling. I opened the door and walked around to her side of the car. She was still pointing at the sign.

"That pig doesn't look very happy." Her eyes met mine as I opened her door.

"Sure he is. They're romping...through a field having a great time." I looked at the sign. "It's like pig and chicken heaven. They're running through the Elysian Fields. Avoiding meat cleavers."

"So, you're saying that the pig and chicken were gladiators and now ride each other around the Greek version of heaven for fun." She took my hand and let me pull her out of the car.

"Yes. That's exactly what I'm saying." I raised my eyebrows and gave her my best innocent expression.

"Right." Her nose furrowed. "Are you going to tell me why we're at a meat market? If we're here to get dinner, I don't think it'll keep well in the car while we shop for other stuff."

"We're not here for steak, I just need to see an old friend."

She stopped walking.

"Is this old friend really someone that you have an iffy business arrangement with, who might kill you rather than talk to you?"

"There goes that imagination again." I shook my head and kept walking. "No, Mrs. Abernathy inherited the butcher shop from her dead husband and has been running it with her sons for as long as I've been alive. As far as I know she has no kind of under the table dealings." And I would know. I'd researched everyone from my past.

"Uh huh." She wasn't convinced, but she followed me inside.

"Just stick with the same routine we used yesterday."

"You mean where I'm a love sick girl hanging onto you like I can't use my own legs?" She cocked an eyebrow at me.

"I know, sticking close to the truth is safer." I winked at her. "If you feel the need to swoon to sell it, go right ahead."

She opened her mouth but stopped when the bell above the door rang softly to announce our presence.

"Just a moment!" Mrs. Abernathy's voice floated from the back of the shop.

Ava gave me an aggravated look before stalking past me into the store.

The building had the same dank, raw meat smell that most butcher shops contained. The white tile floor and counters seemed to enjoy showing the leftover blood droplets in deep contrast. Everything was mostly clean, but it would be impossible to catch everything. A shelf sat against the far wall, advertising marinades and special sauces.

Ava walked around the small room inspecting the shelves and baskets of vegetables. She clasped her hands in front of her like a child scared to touch anything. Maybe she was worried about getting her fingerprints on anything.

There was a small refrigerator next to the register that housed different cool drinks. The quiet hum filled the shop as we waited. Mrs. Abernathy appeared from a back room wiping her hands on a rag.

"Owen Walker, it's been too long!" She came around the counter and kissed my cheeks.

"Indeed." I kissed her cheek and then pointed to Ava. "This is my friend, Ava. Ava, this is Mrs. Abernathy."

"Nice to meet you." Ava held her hand out and smiled at the older woman.

"And you, dear." Mrs. Abernathy took in Ava's appearance with a critical eye. To her credit, Ava didn't blush, but instead stood there with her hand still in Mrs. Abernathy's.

The shop owner looked back over at me and frowned. "You're in trouble?"

"I'm not sure I would call it trouble, more of an interesting situation." I shrugged.

"Come to the back and I'll make tea." She headed for the door through which she had just entered. "Then you can tell me all about this situation."

While Ava didn't say a word, her expression spoke volumes. Intrigue, suspicion, and amusement battled for dominance.

I waved my hand ahead of me and followed her through the doorway. The back room was mostly used for meat preparation, but there was a small office off to the side with comfortable chairs, a table, and an old desktop

75

computer. Mrs. Abernathy set a kettle on the portable stove top and turned the dials.

"I hope you don't mind powdered creamer. Johnny used the last of the milk yesterday."

"Powdered would be fine." Ava offered a smile, but it was a little thin around the edges.

At first look, Mrs. Abernathy seemed like a helpless old woman, bent with age. But here, in the back, you could see the intelligence that shined through her eyes. She was confident and radiated power. When I was younger I'd been convinced that she was a Russian spy or at least someone important hiding from bad guys.

Now here I was, the bad guy, sitting across from her, knowing that the strength in her voice, the steel in her eyes, all came from living a hard life. Despite any troubles she had encountered, she had managed to carve out a slice of something good for herself and her family. That wasn't something most people managed to do.

Mrs. Abernathy was a survivor.

That was probably why I felt such a deep kinship with the woman. I'd been dealt difficult cards in life as well, but unlike her, I couldn't see how to carve out my own piece of happiness, so I settled for a life where I could simply feel satisfaction over a job well done.

"It's been a while since we had tea, you and I." Mrs. Abernathy smiled. "I remember when you would come in here with your mum before you moved to the city. Big eyes, big ears, but always so quiet. You're still too quiet."

I could feel Ava's eyes on me, but I paid her no attention.

"My mother thought a great deal of you." I picked up my tea and sipped. "She also told me that when children

76

misbehaved in your shop you made them clean the floors in the back with their toothbrushes."

"Once. I did that once and it will follow me to my grave." She laughed. "And yet, you always came back to see me."

"You'd sneak me crisps when mum wasn't looking."

I was hyperaware of Ava's presence. It was difficult to open up about my life in front of anyone, much less someone I'd only known for a little over a day. But she didn't speak, didn't judge.

"You needed to be fattened up." She leaned forward and cupped her tea in both hands. "But I don't think you're here for crisps this time."

"No, I'm not." I leaned back in my chair and sat the tea back on the table. "I need to know if you've noticed anything odd in town. If any of my old friends are still running around. If anyone has been talking about me."

"Aye. Johnny said Edgar Herndon was in here asking for you yesterday. I was out for an appointment." She frowned. "Never cared for Edgar. Even as a boy, you could tell there was something missing in his eyes. Some part of his humanity was gone."

"Did Johnny say anything else?" I fought my urge to lean forward. I didn't want to telegraph my unease.

Edgar Herndon was a name from my past I'd rather forget. His mother had 'worked' with my mother and we'd moved to the city at the same time. When I'd run with the local crowd he'd hated me. I was his biggest rival in his eyes, but he knew that in a fight I would win. That meant I'd spent years looking over my shoulder, waiting for him to stab me in the back. If he was back in town asking for me, it meant bad things; I just wasn't sure what those bad things were yet. The last I'd heard of him, he was locked up for assault and petty theft.

"He asked if you'd been in recently." She looked past my shoulder as she thought. "He had some excuse about wanting to see old friends, but Johnny said he was acting shifty. If he's looking for you then you don't want to find him."

I wasn't worried about Edgar Herndon himself. I was much more concerned about the fact that he was tangled up in this confusing web. And if he came to this shop looking for answers, it meant that I wouldn't be visiting again for a while. I couldn't jeopardize the Abernathy family. They'd been a shining example of normalcy during my childhood and for that I'd do whatever it took to keep them safe.

"Anyone else back in town?" I ran my fingers along the chipped handle of the cup in front of me.

"Marilynn Jones is back in town. Well, I suppose it's Marilynn White now. She's married with a little one on the way." She narrowed her eyes. "But I'm sure that's not the kind of gossip you're looking for."

I wasn't thinking about Marilynn. Marilynn had ceased to exist years ago for me. It was likely I would pass her in the street and not realize it. "If I asked you for a favor, Mrs. Abernathy, would you help me?"

"Of course, Owen." She reached across the table and touched my hand. "I've always thought of you as one of my own. I won't speak ill of your mother, but there were many times I wished I could just keep you with me."

I swallowed to get rid of the lump in my throat before speaking. "Close the shop for the rest of the week. Get out of town and take a break. Holiday somewhere pretty and just relax for a while. I can help you pay for it."

"Why would you want me to do that? People need their meat. Besides, I just took a long weekend last month."

"I don't like that Edgar Herndon came here—to see you—about me. You're right about him. He's dangerous and you can't trust anything that he says."

"And what about you? Are you leaving town as well?" Her eyes narrowed.

"Don't worry about me." I shook my head.

"Then what about your lady?" She looked at Ava who had remained so quiet through the entire conversation I'd almost forgotten she was there. "I'd hate to think of Edgar running into her in town."

"That won't happen." The crisp words exited my mouth in a harsh whisper. If he tried to harm one hair on Ava's head I would beat him until he couldn't get up.

"If Edgar is as dangerous as you say—"

"I'm not worried about Herndon." I let my disguise slip and the beast—the murderer—I kept chained tightly in the back of my mind peered out of my eyes.

"I see." Her eyes turned sad and she leaned back in my chair. "I wanted so much more for you. After that nasty business with your mother, I'd hoped you would stay on the straight path. Find something that would make you happy. Avenging angels are forever lonely, walking the world with no chance of heaven."

"I'll be happy if I know you are safe." She opened her mouth to say something, but Ava broke her silence.

"Mrs. Abernathy, if Owen is telling you to go I'm sure he has a very good reason for doing so. If he knows you're safe, then he'll be able to concentrate on the problem at hand."

Huh. I looked at Ava and then back to Mrs. Abernathy. Was I really that transparent? No. Just to Ava. She seemed to see so much more than I wanted to show.

"If it means that much to you, I'll go stay at the family cottage by the coast. I'll take walks along the beach every morning and tell people the doctor suggested it."

"That sounds like a great idea." Ava smiled.

"Are you going to give me any more information? Or do I just tell my boys to take the week off?" She stood up and I followed suit.

"If I had more information I would gladly offer it, but that's the problem." I held my palms up to show my hands were empty. "I have nothing that makes sense."

"It's settled then. I'll close the shop for the week and take my grandchildren to the coast. Johnny just had a new one, you know. A little girl. This will give him a chance to spend some quiet time with his wife and wee one."

"Congratulations." Ava smiled at Mrs. Abernathy.

"Thank you, dear. There's nothing quite as wonderful as grandchildren." She laughed. "I'd love to see Owen's children someday. I wonder if they would have his big ears."

"I think I've grown into my ears." I lifted an eyebrow. Children. That was something I would never live to see.

"Turned into a handsome devil, that's for sure." She led us back to the front of the store. "You need someone to keep you in check."

"You aren't lying, lady," Ava muttered.

"I'm accepting applications," I whispered back. Her cheeks flushed but she rolled her eyes.

Mrs. Abernathy chuckled. "He's trouble, Ava, but I

think you could handle him."

Her blush deepened and she looked around the store front for a distraction.

"Would you mind if I buy a soda before we leave?" She walked over to the small refrigerator and picked out a bottle. "I could use the caffeine."

"It's on the house, dear." Mrs. Abernathy patted her shoulder.

"I'll take care of it." I stepped forward and set an envelope down on the counter. "That should cover the drink."

"That's more than change for a drink. By the looks of it, that would fund our shop for a year." Mrs. Abernathy picked up the envelope and weighed it in her hand before giving it back to me. "I make my own money. I don't need any handouts."

"You are leaving because of me. That means I have a responsibility for you." I stared down at the small woman that was like family. "If you don't take it, I'll find another way to make sure you get it."

"Stubborn man." Mrs. Abernathy stood on her toes and kissed my cheek. "Get out of here and get this woman some clothes that fit."

Ava looked down at her clothes and shrugged. I hadn't noticed but she was wearing the high heels from the day before. With the tight jeans, my old sweater, and her bare face she looked like something out of a lingerie magazine. Or a pornographic movie.

I liked it.

"I'll add that to the list." Without thinking I held my hand out to Ava and to my surprise she accepted it. "We're leaving. You turn the closed sign on as soon as we're out the door."

"Bossy git." Mrs. Abernathy waved her hands at us. "Get out of here, Owen Walker. Or I'll find a toothbrush for you to use on my floors."

CHAPTER EIGHT

Ava

OXFORD WAS GORGEOUS. Each building screamed with history. Spires reached from the top of the buildings in an effort to bring the long dead architects closer to heaven. Owen eventually found a parking lot he was happy with and we left the car. People walked everywhere or rode bicycles. Bikes lined the streets in an orderly fashion and I couldn't help but think they were so close together I'd knock them all over trying to extract one.

Owen took us to a little place for breakfast. It sat between a pub and a small bookstore, and even from down the street the smell of food had my stomach growling loudly. The shop owner took our order and suggested the fresh squeezed orange juice, which was divine. We ate in companionable silence. He picked the olives out of his omelet and I scooped them onto my plate. When I pushed my grilled tomato away, he helped himself. There was nothing strained or awkward, which was amusing when you considered our situation. I should have been looking over my shoulder and flinching whenever I saw someone with a badge, but instead, my nerves seemed to have disappeared in a state of exhaustion.

We walked down the sidewalks, stopping in shops so Owen could get things or speak to someone quietly while I peeked through the different stalls. It was odd to watch him with people. Some he charmed, others he gave what I decided was his 'assassin stare.' Either way, he seemed to know exactly which he would need for each person.

Eventually we ended up at a little store that sold clothing and essentials. The racks were full of basic shirts and jeans, but even a clean pair of underwear sounded like a luxury at this point.

"Get what you need." Owen nodded at the store. "I'll be back to pay for it."

"Where are you going?" I pushed my hair out of my face and fought to calm my heart.

"Next door. I'll only be gone for a moment."

"And you're not going to tell me what you're doing." I kept my face blank. I felt exposed without him by my side. Would I ever feel safe in public again?

He smiled and squeezed my hand. "I'll be back soon."

We had held hands for most of the day. At first I'd told myself that it was part of our cover—looking like a happy couple. But eventually I realized I found comfort in his touch, in the way his warm fingers wrapped around mine. My wildest revelation was when I realized that he seemed to be just as content with the contact.

"I don't like secrets." I stepped closer and lowered my voice.

"I promised I wouldn't lie to you, Ava, and now isn't the time to talk about it." His lips brushed along my hairline and I forced some of the tension out of my shoulders. It was his way of reminding me that we were supposed to be happy, but it mainly served to make my heart race.

"Hurry back." I smiled sweetly up at him and his eyes locked on my lips. Temptation swept through his features and I was sure he was going to kiss me. My stomach coiled tight with anticipation and desire. I'd been with my share of men, but none of them had made me feel like that with just a look. But then, just as quickly, distance slammed down in his eyes and the moment was broken.

"Back before you know it." He pulled away from me and left.

"Whoa," a voice echoed from behind me.

I turned and looked at the girl behind the register, who still stared after Owen.

"Yeah." I sighed. That pretty much summed up Owen.

"Your boyfriend?" The girl leaned forward over the counter. "He's a killer."

"Um, yeah." I had to look away so I wouldn't laugh at her word choice. I picked through the racks and grabbed a couple of shirts I thought would fit.

"American, huh?" She pursed her lips.

"Yep." I smiled, but didn't elaborate.

"Southern state, right?" She walked around the counter and rifled through some of the shirts before holding one out for me. "This will look nice with your eyes."

"Thanks." I added it to the pile in my arms. "Arkansas."

Bad. I was a very bad liar. Even when I just said one word.

"I have a friend that moved to Florida. She works at a

theme park." She turned to look through a different rack. "She likes all the sun."

"Florida is nice." Florida is nice? That's all I've got? "The beaches are beautiful."

"Maybe I'll get to visit her one day." The girl held her hands out for the clothes in my arms. I took a quick glance at her name tag. Heather with curly-cues on each side of her name. "Here, I'll go start you a dressing room."

I almost objected but decided it might look weird. There was no way I was going to be caught with my pants down in a dressing room. I'd just have to stand in there and pretend.

As I expected the jeans weren't in American sizes, so I had to do my best to eyeball the right size. After narrowing it down, I took two shirts and a pair of jeans to the front counter before going to look at the shoes. There were sandals, a few small slip-ons, and some athletic shoes. I opted for the athletic shoes even though they weren't very attractive. I'd rather be able to run than look cute.

I added socks and underwear to my growing pile, but Owen still wasn't back. Trying to not look worried was hard, so I ended up trying on sunglasses, picking out a shampoo, and eventually ended up by the paperback books. There wasn't a large selection, but I read the back cover of one that actually caught my interest. It was a Christmas romance with a puppy on the front cover.

"Oooh. I read that one last year. You should definitely get it." The accommodating cashier peeked over my shoulder. "I love happy endings."

The door chimed and I looked up to see a petite blond woman enter the shop. She was breathtaking. Small delicate features, big brown eyes, and a shape that would leave men drooling in her wake. It was like looking at one of Shakespeare's fairies brought to life.

"Can I help you?" Helpful Heather pounced on the new customer.

"Mm. Do you have the local paper? No one else on this block has one." Her voice was low and sultry. She had a very upper crust London accent.

"Let me go check in the back." The rapt clerk disappeared behind a curtain leaving me with the well-dressed woman.

I tried to not stare, but something about her made me uneasy. She caught me looking at her and smiled.

"Can you believe no one has the paper? I'm new and looking for a place to stay." Her voice was friendly, it hit every note that it should, and every hair on my body stood on end anyway.

"I guess you could try looking online."

"Oh, American!" She held out her hand. "I'm Jilly."

Well, shit. Now I had to shake her hand. I guess if she tried to put me in a headlock I could just step on her.

"Taylor." I held out my hand. Hopefully if someone was looking for me, they wouldn't recognize my middle name.

"Pleasure to meet you." Her eyes were so genuinely friendly, I was sure she was acting. She pointed at the book I had forgotten I was still holding. "I love that author. I buy everything of hers. She writes the best happy endings."

"I've got one left, if you don't mind a few bent corners." Helpful Heather reappeared.

"Oh, that would be perfect. I just need the real estate section." Jilly turned her bright smile on Heather. She paid for her paper and turned back to us at the door. "Nice to meet you, Taylor! Maybe I'll see you around."

"Good luck with your house hunt." I smiled, but I knew it didn't reach my eyes. Maybe I was being paranoid. Okay, I *was* being paranoid, but that didn't mean I was wrong to be suspicious.

She could be guilty of something that had nothing to do with me and I was just picking up on it. I looked back at the book in my hand and shrugged.

Well, I figured I could really use a happy ending at that point. I sat the book on my stack and looked back around the shop.

"Feel like you're forgetting something?" Heather tilted her head in sympathy.

"I just can't remember what I'm missing." I shrugged my shoulders. If Owen didn't show up soon to pay, I was going to look like a giant ass. It had been almost an hour since he'd left and I was starting to wonder. "Makeup! That's what I'm missing."

I could kill some time staring at the cosmetics. I tried not to grimace when I found the small section of makeup.

"Airline lose your luggage?" Helpful Heather asked.

"Can you believe it? And I had some really cute things to wear for...well, you know." I tried to chuckle but it sounded demented. I really couldn't lie.

"From what I saw, I don't think he cares." She laughed.

The door chimed and Owen walked back into the shop. I almost melted in relief. He was carrying a small black bag slung over his shoulder and his hair was a little windblown.

"Sorry, love." He wrapped his arm around my shoulder and nodded his head at my personal shopper. "Ran into an old friend who wanted to catch up. Couldn't get away."

"That's okay. I've had fun shopping." God, that made me sound like an airhead. And was he speaking in code? Should I be ducking behind something heavy and covering my head? "Did you invite them to dinner?"

"They had plans." He nuzzled my cheek and I tried to not whimper as his stubble rubbed across my skin. "Looks like it will just be the two of us."

"Good." My voice came out in a husky whisper as I stared up at him and I watched his pupils dilate.

"Well, let's get your things and head back." He barely noticed the giant pile of things I had collected while I waited, but he did smile at the Christmas book.

"In case I have time to read." I shrugged.

"Hm. We'll see about that." His voice all but purred and I was tempted to check and see if my panties had spontaneously combusted.

Helpful Heather was staring at him with her mouth slightly ajar and I felt a flash of jealousy and the need to reassert my fictional claim on him. I leaned against his chest and stroked my hand across his midsection.

Whoa. Those were some nice abs. Owen the Assassin was ripped.

Mentally I took inventory to make sure that I wasn't drooling on his button up shirt and that I was still completely dressed. I had this wild desire to rip all of my clothes off when I was this close to him. Helpful Heather's expression turned a little less helpful as she watched my hand.

I looked up at Owen and male pride smiled down at me. I really couldn't fault him. My hand was still stroking along those hard lines and I had to force it to be still. His smile widened but he didn't say anything. Which was good. I was embarrassed as it was, and I wasn't sure I could keep up the charade if he called me out for groping him so shamelessly.

Charade? Who was I kidding? On some level I was eating the attention up.

Jealous Heather told us the total and quickly bagged up my new clothes. Her eyes were glued to Owen's backside as we left the store. I turned around and waved bye.

"Thanks for all the help!"

Her head jerked up in embarrassment. I should have felt bad, but I didn't.

"Any more errands?" I was developing a blister on my left foot from walking all day in the heels, and I mentally congratulated myself for the sensible new shoes I'd just picked out.

"I dropped off some food at the car before I came back to the shop." He put his arm around me, but I could tell his mind was elsewhere. His eyes swept back and forth across the street, waiting.

"Are we looking for something in particular or just letting paranoia reign?"

"I really did run into someone. Or rather, saw them and followed them." A frown pulled at the corners of his mouth. "We need to get back to the house."

"Followed them where?" I shivered.

"A store." He looked down at me and I could see the hesitation in his eyes as he wrestled with saying something.

"What is it?" He had promised to not lie. Of course, that didn't mean he wouldn't just refuse to answer.

"They had your picture."

I stumbled and looked around in fear. I spun in a circle like a puppy chasing its tail. The bad guys could be anywhere. I thought I might actually pass out.

"Ava." Owen said my name softly, but I started forward, intent on getting to our car, to temporary safety. He gently pushed me back against a nearby vehicle and put a hand on either side of my face. "Breathe, Ava. I need you to keep it together. You can do this."

"My picture. There are people here trying to kill me and I still don't know why." My breath was ragged. I felt like there was a flashing target over my head. How was I going to survive with all of these people out to collect some bounty?

"It's okay, Ava. They didn't know your name, just that you were American. There are a ton of ex-pats in Oxford." He lifted my chin, forcing me to meet his gaze. "Breathe, Ava, you have to breathe."

The only problem was that it was just as hard to breathe when he looked at me. All of that intense scrutiny made me want to wiggle against him.

"Take that shit somewhere else," a drunken man called from a group of guys meandering down the sidewalk. I froze, my heart speeding into a panic. Were these people here to kill us?

"Get a room!" another man called.

"Nah, I wanna watch." He stopped and leered in our direction.

"Mind your business." Owen turned to look at the men and they sped up, pulling their drunken brother with them. I couldn't see his face as he looked at them, but it must've been menacing. When he turned to look back at me, he had already managed to school his features back to normal.

"I'm scared." I whispered the words. I'd never felt so alone and frightened. "For just a little while I'd let myself forget. Forget that everyone wanted me dead for some reason. I picked out a book to read."

"I'm not going to let them hurt you." He leaned closer, his eyes intense. "Do you trust me?"

I thought about it. Really thought about it. Did I trust Owen? I did. I didn't know why, but I trusted him. And I was probably a giant idiot for it. But...he had come back for me. He hadn't led the witch hunters to the little shop. He'd been by my side every step of the way.

"Yes." I let the word out on an exhale.

"Good. That's good." He pulled away from me and opened the car door. I hadn't realized we'd gotten back to our stolen ride. "We need to get going."

I didn't talk on the way back to his safe house. I was too shaken up to hold an intelligent conversation. Every muscle in my body felt like jelly and my head throbbed.

At the safe house, Owen insisted on carrying all of the bags himself. I busied myself in the kitchen, putting up the new groceries and heating more soup. It was almost dark and we hadn't eaten since our late breakfast.

Owen made a fire and we sat on the floor eating our soup and watching the flames. It would've been peaceful if I didn't jump at every noise that seemed out of the ordinary.

"I'm sorry for freaking out," I sighed.

"Don't worry about it."

My mind rolled over things and I tried to make sense of it all. One thing was certain: I needed to make some decisions. If I was going to trust Owen, I needed to trust him. If he was going to give me up, then I wouldn't be able to stop him. I didn't know much self-defense and wasn't sure I could hit anything with a pistol. It had been years since I'd fired a gun.

But despite the unusual way that we had met, I liked Owen. Not because of the way he looked with firelight twinkling in his eyes. Well, not just because of that. But because of the way he had looked at Mrs. Abernathy, the way he puttered around this old house, and had gone out of his way to fluff my pillows. There were more sides to him than even he realized.

I also needed to get in touch with Tess. I wasn't sure how I was going to do it, but it needed to happen soon. No one else would be worried about me, but I knew that Tess would search until she figured out where I was. Or until something happened to her in the process. But I couldn't afford to think that way.

I leaned back against the couch and set my bowl on the table. The soup had been good, and I felt warmed from the inside and out. I closed my eyes and tried to figure out how I was going to get out of all this mess.

CHAPTER NINE

Ava

I WOKE ON the couch, a blanket tucked around me, and tried to figure out how I'd gotten up there. Tapping drew my attention to floor at the foot of the couch. Owen was leaned back against the sofa, the keyboard in his lap. His eyebrows were drawn together and I watched as he frowned at the screen.

Worry was etched across his tight jaw and I wondered what had him so upset. Even when we were running from the people shooting at us, he had seemed so calm and in control. He bent over the keyboard and his hair fell across his forehead, obscuring his eyes. His fingers tapped furiously across the keys and he blew out a deep breath before leaning back and dragging a hand through his hair. I could just barely make out the screen, but I saw my picture with a news station logo plastered in the corner.

Instead of freaking out the way I had the night before, I felt oddly resigned. I should have been worried, scared, and confused; instead I just wanted everything to be over.

"If you tell me how to get there, I'll turn myself in to

the police."

His head jerked in my direction and I noted the growth of stubble along his jaw line and the way his eyes flared.

"You are not turning yourself in, not to anyone." His words were soft. "Besides, they're just saying that you're a person of interest."

"I'm weighing you down, Owen." I sat up and noticed that my shoes were on the floor. Had I taken those off or had Owen, when he put me on the couch?

"Stop it, Ava." He closed the computer and sat it on the floor next to him. "Does it look like you're weighing me down?"

"Well, yeah, a little. When was the last time you slept?" I adjusted my sweater so it wasn't twisted around my waist.

"I've slept some each night that we've been here." It was still dark in the room, and the sun wasn't fully up yet. I watched him in the early grey light of dawn thinking about all that he had done for me.

"If I turn myself in to the police, they can give me an extra guard and you can slip away. I'll tell everyone that I managed to evade the other people by myself." I shrugged. "I'm American. I grew up on action movies. They'll buy it."

"No."

"Owen—"

"No. They can't protect you the way I can. I realize I'm not exactly the knight in shining armor most women imagine, but I've got the skill set you need right now." He frowned. "Something serious is going on. Big players in the business are disappearing. Some of my contacts are gone. Vanished. No one has heard anything from them for weeks. This is bigger than just you. You're going to need me to help you get through it. And you're my best link to everything that's going on. You're not the only one on the news. They are reporting about Song and say he was the head of a sex slave ring, but they believe someone else is pulling the strings from behind the scenes. Somehow you're connected to all of this."

"So, I'm a means to an end?" I scrubbed at my face. Made sense.

"Yes. No. I don't like it, but we need each other. You won't last long without me, and I'm not going to get any information without you. If I could, I'd ship you off somewhere remote and make sure you never had to deal with any of this again." His voice took on an earnest tone and I caught a glimpse of vulnerability in his eyes.

"It's not your job to protect me." I kept my voice soft. He looked on edge.

"I've made it my job." The words sounded like a gruff promise.

"I can't pay you much, but I've got some money." I played with the blanket, afraid to meet his gaze. If he was looking for money, then I could keep him at arms-length. If he was doing it for something else…I was in a whole different type of trouble.

"I don't need your money, Ava." He stood up and looked at me. "I have a hundred thousand quid in that safe and this place is only one of my safe homes."

"Why?" My voice cracked. "Why are you helping me?"

"Because you need it." His eyes ran over my face. "Because I want to."

I wanted to say something, anything, but I didn't know what. Instead I stood up and folded the blanket and placed it back on the couch and smoothed it out. I turned back to Owen and met his stare.

"Thank you."

"No need to thank me." He stepped back and bent over to pick up his laptop.

I watched as he moved over to the small dining table and opened the computer again. Without another word I went to the kitchen and opened the fridge. He'd bought eggs and milk the night before and I was ready for something other than soup.

We spent the day quietly, each of us lost in our thoughts. He was busy on the internet, shaking his head and muttering under his breath. It wasn't until I heard him mention bodies that I asked him to clarify.

"Are you talking about dead bodies?" I tried to not shiver.

"Someone discovered eleven dead women in a warehouse in Singapore. Normally that wouldn't make our news, but most of them were from England." His eyes narrowed. "They'd been raped and drugged. Most of them were malnourished."

"You think that's linked to Mr. Song." I let out a sharp breath.

He nodded his head. "And to us."

I had nothing to say for that and we lapsed back into silence. At one point he hopped up from the table and took three steps before turning around and walking back to his seat. He found a phone book and looked at the pages as if he were reading a map.

For my part, television wasn't an option. My face was

on every channel and the panic it inspired wasn't helping anything. I sat on the couch and read my new book. Helpful Heather had been right. The book was good.

"I thought you might be hungry."

I looked up from my book to see Owen and a plate of sliced fruit and cheese. The pen he had been using earlier was tucked behind his ear.

"Thanks." I set the book on the table and made room for him to sit down beside me

"Well, you made breakfast. Figured it was my turn." He bit into a slice of apple.

"Did you find anything interesting on Facebook?"

His face darkened. "Nothing good."

I layered a slice of apple with a piece of cheese. "More people disappearing?"

He nodded. "There could be a number of reasons for it, but I think it best that we assume those that aren't active are looking for us."

"Huh." The apple in my mouth suddenly didn't taste as good. "And how many is that?"

"Seven."

"I guess it could be worse." I swallowed. "Seven highly trained assassins out looking for us is better than twenty highly trained assassins out looking for us."

"I'm more concerned with the disappearance of my sources." He leaned back on the sofa and put his feet on the table. For some reason I found it fascinating that he wasn't wearing shoes or socks. You'd think that assassins were always fully dressed, ready for a fight.

I forced myself to focus on what he was talking about. "That would mean someone you trust is removing your resources."

"Yes." He ran a hand over his face. "I trust very few people and none of them have access to all of my contacts."

"So, at least two people are working together." I picked up another slice of apple and looked at it. "Or someone has been keeping tabs on you."

"That would be nearly impossible." He shook his head. "I'm thorough, but one thing is certain. They aren't just after you, love. We're in this together."

"Have you heard back from your handler?" I knew it was a common expression, but I always felt a thrill when he called me 'love.'

"No." He didn't elaborate and I didn't push for an explanation. I could sense that careful boundary of his just behind the scenes.

The rest of the night followed the same pattern. He checked email, watched the news, surfed the nets, and I read my book. When I realized I was nearing the end, I slowed down, trying to savor the ending. I put the book down and stocked the fireplace so we could stay warm through the chilly night.

I curled up in my spot on the sofa and watched the flames dance along the bark. The couch seemed to mold to my body.

"Who knows about this house?" I leaned my head against the arm rest.

"My handler might, but it's more likely that he wouldn't even think I used it." He looked away from me. "He doesn't know I own it."

I wanted to ask him why. I wanted to know why this particular place was a little more important than the others. The answer danced just out of reach, but I couldn't figure it out. My eyes were too heavy to keep open, my mind too tired to search the maze of Owen's mind. I fell asleep in my same spot, content to bask in the warm glow of the fire.

The next day was much of the same thing. If the bad guys didn't find me and kill me, the waiting would. It was hard to keep my mind occupied. I'd finished my book, cleaned the living room, and rearranged all of the food in the kitchen. Owen didn't want me to go outside, so I was left pacing the house.

I caught Owen staring at his phone. No one had called him back the entire time we'd been here. Instead he spent his time on the internet, checking the news and who knew what.

I suppose I should be glad that he was staying busy. With all of this time on our hands there was no knowing what would happen. And the more time I spent around the man, the more I wanted to know about him. There was something sexy in the way he offered to do things for me, as if he wasn't used to spending time with someone and he was rusty at being companionable—that he was only trying for me.

Down that road was trouble, though, and I needed to get my mind on something else.

Tessa. I sat down in a chair facing the front windows.

I was worried about my friend. What if they had found her and planned to hurt her if I didn't go to them first? Were the police making her stay somewhere else? Did she and Danny have to go get his bloody car out of impound?

I needed to talk to her. Reach out and make sure she was okay in some way. She was the only family I had left.

"I'm going to take a shower." Owen stood up and stretched. With quick movements he undid the buttons of his shirt and I couldn't tear my eyes away from his fingers as they worked. When he finished he threw it on the back of the couch with his discarded tie. I could feel his gaze on me the entire time, but couldn't find it in myself to be embarrassed. The man was delicious and he knew it. I looked up into his darkened eyes and contemplated offering to scrub his back.

"Okay." The word exited my mouth softly. Apparently I wasn't brave enough to follow through with my little fantasy.

"Do you want one?" He raised an eyebrow and my pulse quickened.

"Want a shower?" Damn it. Did I sound too excited?

"You could go before me. The hot water heater isn't very large." He smiled, his teeth gleaming in the low light.

"Oh. No, go ahead." Yep. That was definitely disappointment in my voice.

"I'll be quick." As he walked away, he pulled his undershirt off over his head and tossed it on the couch. The muscles of his back rippled and I fought the urge to jump up and shout *I VOLUNTEER*! The thought of watching soap run over his skin made me want to…

I shot out of my chair and paced back and forth. I needed a distraction. I needed to get a grip. My eyes fell on his laptop and I stopped in my tracks.

I needed to contact Tess.

I heard the water in the bathroom come on and I tiptoed across the room to listen at the door. Once I was sure I could I could hear him splashing I ran across the room and lifted the lid to his laptop. It was password locked.

Damn it. I tried a few words and then gave up. Closing the lid, I made sure it was in the same spot he had left it and looked around the room. His phone was still on the table so I picked it up and smiled. He had been streaming the internet with it and it hadn't shut down all the way. Quickly I flipped through his apps and signed into an old email address of mine.

How could I let her know she was in trouble in a way that wouldn't let others know it was me? In the subject line I kept it simple. An old nickname she had when we were in school—Grumpy. She was anything but grumpy, but it drove her crazy when people called her that. In the end our friends had all ended up with a nickname from Snow White and the Seven Dwarves—including me.

Congrats. Heard you got married and ran away to Italy. If I was you I'd stay there for a really long time. Leave the trouble of the city behind and enjoy the peace and quiet.

Speaking of peace and quiet I've gone to visit the country. Met a friend and he's helping me find a place to stay.

All my love,
Sleepy

I hit the send button and signed out quickly, then went back and made sure my login didn't pop up when you reopened the app. I set the phone back on the table trying to make sure it was just like it had been. Feeling as though I had finally accomplished something, I decided to reward myself with some food.

The soup from earlier hadn't really cut it and I was

craving something more substantial. In fact, I was starting to hate the thought of soup. I'd probably never eat the stuff again. There were canned beans, vegetables, and some kind of tinned meat that scared me. I did find some crackers and a can of beef stew. It would probably taste like dog food, but at this point I wasn't going to be too picky. I picked up the can opener from the counter and started working on the beef stew.

Something moved out back by a shed and I froze. It was dark out, but I could have sworn I saw a person. I ducked out of sight of the window and tried to catch my breath. A moment later I peeked back around the cabinets but couldn't see anything. Taking a deep breath I walked into the living room with my can and can opener still clutched in my hands. I tiptoed across the carpet and lifted one of the blinds with a finger. The crunch of gravel drew my attention to the road and I saw a dark car with no lights making its way toward the house.

I jerked back around and dove for the chair where my gun was still lying. I threw the beef stew on the couch and wrapped my fingers around the pistol's grip. My body was moving without thought, some kind of survival instinct kicking in. Every cell practically screamed, "Don't die! Don't die!" I sort of floated to the bathroom door. It didn't feel like my feet ever touched the ground. One minute I was scrambling for my gun and the next I was pressed against the wooden door. Not sure if anyone was listening to what was going on in the house, I rapped gently with my knuckles.

"Owen! There's someone here!" I hissed the words and increased my rapping when he didn't answer right away. "Owen! Damn it! Answer the door!"

The bathroom door opened and I practically fell into his wet arms. My body slid against his in a delicious tangle of damp skin that I shouldn't have even noticed. The shower was still running, but he'd taken the time to wrap a towel around his waist. I looked up at him, water dripping from his hair onto my face.

"There's someone here!" I whispered as I stood up and pointed to the front door. "And in the back!" I swung my arm behind me.

Without a word he turned around and dropped the towel. My mouth fell open at the view and I felt my head tilt to the side as he bent over to grab his underwear. The man had a lot to work with. He pulled the tight shorts up and I wondered why all men didn't wear those.

Probably because they wouldn't all look like Owen in them.

His hand grabbed mine as he slid past me and into the bedroom, pulling me along with him. He opened the closet and punched a hole into the plaster in the back. He reemerged holding a gun, a duffle bag, and a long rifle. I leaned against the wall and tried to listen for anything happening outside.

"Grab me some pants." He nodded to the dresser and I opened the middle drawer and shoved the clothes around. I found a pair of slacks and a shirt and threw them on the bed. Looking around the room, I spotted my new running shoes. No way was I going to run around in the stupid heels I had worn earlier. Owen checked the rifle before tossing it to me.

"Heads up. You said you were better with a rifle."

"I said I had shot them, not that I was good with them." I caught it and checked the slide before slipping the sling over my shoulder. I wasn't bad, but I wasn't a marksman either. I'd also never shot at a living person or while running for my life. Too bad I hadn't thought to practice that type of stuff instead of just shooting at empty cans.

"Let's hope you're better than you think." He smiled at me as he pulled his pants up and slid the shirt over his head. Light danced across his eyes and a wild excitement lit his face.

"What are we going to do? Is it the same people from earlier?" I whispered.

He moved along the wall to peer out the side of the blinds. "Can't tell. Different car." He slid his feet into some shoes by the bedroom door and stepped close to me. "Are you ready?"

"For what?" I could feel my eyes go wide. I was growing more and more nervous while he seemed to be slipping into his stride.

"To make our getaway." He used a finger to tilt my chin up. I opened my mouth to respond but he didn't wait for my words. His head dipped down, his lips capturing mine in a kiss. The heat from his body next to mine made my head spin and the soft touch of his mouth enticed me more than any other man ever had. I could've melted into him right there, the danger to our lives forgotten. His touch was like electricity that ran over my body from head to toe. When his tongue slipped across my lips, I gasped in shocked pleasure. When he pulled back he smiled at my dazed expression. "For luck."

I swallowed and tried to catch my breath as he pulled his bag over his shoulder and laced his fingers mine. Tugging gently he pulled me through the living room toward the back door.

I crept along behind him and tried to keep my head down. The silence in the house rang in my ears as I strained to hear something from the people outside. Owen held up his hand and I froze mid-step. Pointing to the kitchen counter, he motioned for me to move. I scuttle-walked to the side of the back door.

I could hear the soft scratching of metal on metal as the door knob twisted slowly. One man entered, followed quickly and quietly by another as they slipped into the kitchen. They were wearing normal street clothes and carrying small machine guns. I flattened against the cabinet I was leaning against, but one of them saw me. As he swung in my direction a shot rang out and the man toppled forward, landing against me. I shoved him off just as the lights in the house went out. There was a grunt and the sound of flesh hitting flesh, but I couldn't tell who was beating who.

When fingers closed around my wrist I jerked backward and almost fell over the dead man.

"It's me." Owen pulled me to the door and hit a switch on the way out. The front yard was suddenly bathed in bright strobe lights that blinked in and out every couple of seconds. Shouts came from the front, followed by gunshots, but Owen didn't stop. We reached the shed in the back and ducked in through a small door on the side.

"Drive or shoot?"

I looked at him like he was crazy. Both were bad options for me.

"Okay. You drive. Do exactly what I say." He pushed me toward the door of an old farm truck. "We have to go out the front way."

"Okay." I unslung the rifle and climbed into the truck. The key was in the ignition and I prayed it would start. Owen undid the latch on the barn style doors before the truck and ran back to the passenger side.

As soon as he was in I turned the key and hit the gas. The truck came to life immediately and I said a silent prayer of thanks. I shifted into drive and slammed my foot down on the pedal. We blew through the doors in an angry crash and I almost ran over two men with guns pointed at us. You'd think with my record they would have made sure to not be in my way. Owen fired quickly and I saw one man go down, but was too busy trying to drive to keep up with it all.

"This is going to be loud." Reaching into his bag he came out with two small canister shaped objects. Rolling his window down, he hurled them at the two cars in front of his house. Explosions rocked the clearing, but I kept us steady as the truck tore down the gravel path.

"Right at the road."

"'Kay." I never hit the brake, just jerked the wheel. The tires squealed as we swung onto the pavement. Someone honked at us and I looked up in time to see a little old lady in a big hat giving me the finger. Well, I guessed I deserved it.

"At the stop sign make a left. The road is curvy so hopefully they won't see us as quickly."

"Blowing up their cars won't stop them?" I clutched the steering wheel tightly. "Holy fucking shit. Who was that?"

"Only one other person knows where that house is." Owen stared ahead with a grim expression.

"Who?" I looked at him out of the corner of my eye

as knowledge dawned.

"Marcus." If I hadn't been looking I wouldn't have seen him clench his hand around the gun he was holding. "My handler."

"Oh. Well." I turned at the stop sign and gunned it again. I wanted to get around a few curves before anyone had a chance to come looking for us. "That sucks."

"Yes."

"Where are we going?"

"To see Marcus."

"Well, that'll be fun." I stared at the road ahead of me, trying to anticipate the curves, but there was no telling which way the road was going to turn.

My eyes dropped down to the gas gauge. Thankfully we had a full tank of gas. I remembered my grandmother always telling me to never leave a car with only half a tank of gas. I guessed Owen had been told the same thing. Or he was just prepared for things like people showing up at your house with the intent to kill you.

It was probably the second thing.

"And what are we going to do with Marcus?"

"Ask him why he's trying to kill us."

"Hmm. And when you say ask…"

"I mean beat the shit out of him until he tells me."

"Look who's being all proper now." I reached over and pushed his shoulder.

"Well, when your brother decides to have you killed it doesn't inspire much brotherly affection." He looked at me with a twisted smile.

"Your brother?" I gasped. He'd mentioned his handler, but not once given any kind of sign that he was family. "What, did you forget his birthday? Are you serious?"

When I thought of siblings I thought of my friends and their family. They fought over leftovers and who had to take the dog for a walk. When they got older they fought over who spent Christmas with the parents, but they always loved each other.

"We have more of a business relationship. He passes the jobs on to me and I get it done. He takes a cut and I get the rest." He looked out the window for a minute.

"How did you become a hitman?" I rubbed my hands along the steering wheel. "Answer an ad in the paper?"

"The job found me." He looked back at me. "There is always some garbage that needs to be taken out, and someone willing to pay me to help with the chore."

I tried to think of how you could just end up a hitman. A favor to someone? Being in a gang or working for a bad guy? Or was it to protect himself or his brother?

"Marcus always knew someone that needed a job done." Owen moved the bag at his feet out of the way. "It didn't take long before I made a name for us. I only take certain jobs and Marcus weeds them out. He likes being the face of the organization."

"What do you mean you only take certain cases?"

"I don't help people knock off business rivals or family for insurance money. No cheating spouses. No petty revenge jobs." He pulled out a folder from his bag and flipped through documents. There were passports and other types of identification inside. "The rich pedophile that bought his way out of jail, drug lords, slave traders. There are more than enough douchebags to keep me busy."

"Like Mr. Song." I took a deep breath. "But how do you know you're not doing the dirty work for a competitor?"

"Marcus sends me the files for review. He's supposed to vet everyone that comes through, but I still do my research."

I didn't point out the obvious. That if Marcus was trying to kill Owen, he might not be so trustworthy. Instead I reached over and toggled the heat switch on. It was chilly despite the season.

"Alright. Where does dear brother Marcus live?"

CHAPTER TEN

Owen

WE STOPPED AT a run-down inn on the outskirts of London. Somewhere I could pay cash and not worry about anything. The owner barely batted an eyelash at us which was exactly what I had been looking for when we chose the place. We'd put the truck in a garage a few blocks away. It wouldn't be on the street for someone to spot and was far enough away that we'd be safe for the night.

Ava was staring at the little room in concern. Her nose was wrinkled and she hadn't touched anything. I was trying not to laugh, but it was hard when she leaned over to examine the film of dust growing on the crystals hanging from one of the lamp shades.

She had tucked her pistol in her pants and tore down the rifle so it would fit in my bag, but the old room offended her. Who would have guessed that the sweet woman at the café would know how to handle a gun? She seemed nervous with them and I guessed it had been a while since she had used one, but at least she hadn't screamed and run away.

"It doesn't look that bad." I sat the bag down on the chair.

"What room are you looking at? It smells like someone died in here."

"It's possible." I shrugged and opened the blinds to look out over the street.

"Oh my God."

"Relax. I'm sure they washed the sheets." I snapped the blinds closed and turned on the television and flipped through the channels. There was nothing on the news about the disaster at my place, so I turned it back off.

"I need to check a few things." I tossed the remote on the bed. Ava turned around, her blue eyes wide. "I'll pick up some food while I'm out."

"You're going to leave?" She said the words flatly, even though I could see the panic in her eyes.

"I'll be back soon." I went through the bag and pocketed some of the money before grabbing one of the belt holsters for my pistol. The .45 was my favorite and I wasn't going anywhere without it.

"What if you aren't?" She chewed on her bottom lip. "What if you don't come back?"

"I'm coming back, Ava."

"You think you're coming back." She took a deep breath. "What if you can't come back?"

"If I don't come back, use the money to get to your consulate. Tell them I kidnapped you but you managed to get away." She could do that while I was gone, but I had to show her trust to get trust. And I wanted her to trust me. "But I am coming back."

She stared at me and for a moment I felt lost in her eyes. There was so much emotion trapped there that I wondered how she was staying so calm.

"Okay." She nodded her head.

"Lock the door and stay away from the window. I'll be back with some food soon." I didn't smile. I wanted her to know I was serious, that I would be back—even if I had to climb out of the grave to do so.

There was a very short list of things that scared me. And I'd managed to fall head first into my number one fear—caring about someone. In less than a week, Ava had managed to turn my entire, well-compartmentalized world upside down. Turning away from her, I left the room quickly. No reason to draw this out.

I heard the deadbolt click into place after I left. Good girl. No one knew we were here and Marcus would have no reason to look for me at this place. Not only did I never share the details about my hits with him, I never stayed in the same hotel or inn. In a place like London, that wasn't a hard thing to do. Every grandmother or uncle owned an inn or a hotel in this town.

It was summer time, but there was still enough chill in the air to wear a light jacket. There had been an old jumper in the back of the truck, so I pulled the hood up around my face and headed for a nearby store. I needed a burner phone and some supplies. A change of clothes would be nice as well.

I stopped in a small store and grabbed a basket. I threw in some essentials: soap, shampoo for Ava, a knife sharpener, deodorant, toothpaste, and some duct tape. There were racks of clothing on the other side of the store. I guessed at sizes for Ava and grabbed a few things for me. There were some clearance items at the front of the store and I grabbed a shirt for Ava to sleep in.

There were very few people that I trusted; of the few people I had met over the years, Roger was one of the people I would trust the most. He lived in a small house within walking distance, which is why I had chosen this side of town. It wouldn't take me long to get there so I skipped the Tube. I bought a lot of my firearms from him and I could always count on him to get me explosives. There wasn't much Roger couldn't find.

I watched from a nearby store for a while before going in his gate. The man was trustworthy, but paranoid as all hell. He wouldn't take kindly to me just showing up at his home, but he'd have to deal. This was a special circumstance.

I rang the doorbell and waited. I kept my hands out of my pockets so he could see them and pushed my hood back far enough that he would recognize my face. The door opened a crack and Roger peered out at me.

"Well, fuck it all." The door snapped shut while he undid the chain and then back open. "Get in! Hurry the fuck up before someone sees you."

"Nice to see you too, Rog." I slid in past him and pushed the hood back the rest of the way.

"What the fuck happened to you? The fucking internet has blown up. Did you know there is a hit out on you? Mavis still hasn't checked in with our group and Thomas Delaney is apparently dead. You've got some nerve showing up at my house right now. You could have led them straight to me." He walked past me toward a small kitchen. "Sit down. I'll make tea."

"Thanks, but I'm in a hurry." His dog looked up at me from where he lay on the floor. "Who put the contract out?"

Roger didn't answer me, just putted around the kitchen for a few minutes. He rinsed his kettle out before filling it back up and setting it on the stove. He took out two cups and set them on the counter. The handle of one of them was a pistol grip. I took it and managed to not shake my head in dismay.

"Have you spoken to your brother?"

"No, but I intend to." I sat down on the stool at the counter. Roger was the only person I worked with that knew of my connection to Marcus.

"Then you already know." He sat down and looked up at me. His glasses perched on the end of his nose. "When a handler turns on their operative it's always bad news. Our group was waiting to see if you made it out."

"If he wanted me dead, he didn't send enough people." I leaned forward, my arms resting on the counter. "Has there been any talk about a hit on an American?"

"The woman someone said was with you? No. Not a hit. I've heard rumblings though." He took his glasses off and wiped them on his robe. "Abduction."

"Abduction?" I leaned back and thought about it. That explained why the squad hadn't taken any good shots at her. "What for?"

"These people aren't all like you, Owen. Most of them don't care the why or what of it. They want the money or the hunt. They don't ask for a reason." He shook his head. "You're a rare card."

"Who put the job out?"

"It came from Marcus." Roger narrowed his eyes. "I don't deal with human trafficking. Nasty business. A good clean kill is one thing, selling a person is another fucking matter. But since it came from Marcus the word got back to me."

"Why her? Why this woman?" It didn't make sense. The connections weren't adding up and I didn't believe in coincidence. Had Marcus turned on me because I'd taken Ava under my wing?

"Not sure. The job was for the American. She wasn't to be hurt, which isn't too unusual. Either they want her as a hostage or a slave." He cocked his head to the side. "You have her?"

"Does it look like I have a woman tucked in my pocket?" No reason to give up any information that I didn't have to.

"Owen, you've always been an odd fit for this job. You still have a heart and most people kill theirs before they reach your age. If you have that woman, you better get her out of the country." The kettle whistled and he stood up to fix the tea. "The game has changed."

"How much has Marcus offered?" I stood up and stretched. It had been a long few days.

"Forty thousand for the girl." He smiled up at me. "But for you, he had to make it worth it, didn't he? People aren't going to go after Owen Walker without good incentive. No, for you, he's offered up five million."

"I need some ammo." What the hell was wrong with Marcus? Why would he set such a high price on my head and then not send a larger squad to mum's old house?

"Well, that I can get you, my boy. That I can get you." Roger led me to a room in the back of the house, his tea forgotten. The room was lined with racks of gun parts and boxes of ammo. I rubbed my hands and smiled at the old man.

Some men liked gadgets, but I was all about the guns.

The smell of the gun oil and hot metal was an aphrodisiac. And the two forty-five millimeter Springfield XDs sitting in the corner were giving me a hard on. I walked over and took them off the wall and gave them a thorough run down. Roger didn't sell shit, but you never took a gun without looking it over.

Roger cackled as he watched me. "You always did like the shiny things."

"These." I set them down on a table. "Do you have anything smaller?"

"For the woman?" Roger opened a cabinet and pulled out a smaller version of the guns I had picked up. "Nine millimeter. Subsonic ammo." He tossed me a box of bullets and I set them on the table next to my gun.

"Do you have any burner phones?"

"How many do you need?" Roger opened the drawer of a work table and pulled out two packages.

"That'll do." I grabbed a bag from the floor and tossed my items in.

"Meh. Take this too." Roger sat a knife and more ammo down.

"What do I owe you?"

"We'll talk after you get this straightened out."

"Five million dollars puts a big target on my head." I watched him carefully. "I might not get it straightened out."

"Always been a bettin' man." He slapped me on the back. "I think you got a good race in you still."

"Thanks." I headed back to the front door and stopped to pet the dog. He barely moved. "You need a better guard dog."

"Bah. He's never been a guard dog. Too fat like his

owner." Roger opened his robe and showed me the Desert Eagle in a shoulder holster. "This is my guard dog."

"That's a lot of gun, old man."

"Get outta here before I decide to show ya what I can do with it."

"Be safe."

"Be smart." Roger slammed the door behind me, but I could still hear him laughing.

I slid the rucksack over my shoulder and headed for a take-away place. Once I had enough food, I headed back to the hotel. I'd been gone for two hours already and would bet Ava was getting fidgety.

I took the stairs two at a time and knocked on the door before using the key the desk had given me.

"It's me." I opened the door slowly, but didn't see her at first. She was on the other side of the room, her gun pointed at the door. She'd picked a good spot to take out someone walking in the room.

"Where the hell have you been?" She didn't lower the gun as I walked in and closed the door. "You've been gone for hours."

"I had to see a friend." I held up the Chinese take-away. "I brought food."

"If you didn't get chicken lo mein I'm going to shoot you in the foot." She narrowed her eyes and I frowned.

"I got lo mein."

"Okay then." She lowered the gun and walked over to me. She snatched the bag out of my hands and started unloading the contents on the little table. "I used some of the soap from the bathroom to clean the table off, so I don't think we'll die from Staph or Salmonella."

"Thanks." I set the rucksack and other bags down on

the bed. It was odd coming back to someone. Weird to know she had been busy while I was gone; to have someone to talk with as I ate. "I got some clothes. I had to guess at your size."

"Thanks. I really want a shower and don't want to put these back on."

"No problem." I sat down and grabbed some chopsticks. "I have some good news and some bad news. Apparently the people in the garage were not trying to kill you."

"Could've fooled me." She slurped a mouthful of noodles and motioned for me to go on.

"They were going to abduct you."

"Are you serious?" She finished chewing her food and took a drink from the bottle of water I'd brought. Her skin took on a green sheen and she took another sip of water. "Why? I mean, why abduct me? I'm not worth a ransom."

"I'm not sure." I stabbed a shrimp with my fork. "Not enough information yet. The contract for you didn't give reasons."

"Who wants to kidnap me?" Sitting her box down, she scrubbed at her eyes. Strain pulled her face into a grim mask. "I've barely been in England for over a week. Why now? Why me? Who did I piss off?"

I didn't have an answer so didn't offer a response. At the house she had said being abducted would be worse than death. Had she meant it? The thought of someone using her as a sex slave froze my blood. She stood up and walked over to the bags and I forced my fingers to unclench before I broke the chopsticks I was holding. Turning toward me she held up a large shirt and gave me a weak laugh.

"Prince Harry stole my heart?"

"It was on sale." I shrugged. "Besides, I thought all Americans came over here to win a prince."

"With all of that family drama? No thank you." She shook her head trying to hide the tears gathering in her eyes. "I'm going to shower and then sleep. I can't think any more."

She closed the bathroom door quietly and I leaned back in my chair. For all of my travel, I actually spent a good amount of time by myself. However, I knew enough about women to know Ava was most likely in the shower crying while trying to be quiet. That bothered me.

A lot.

Fuck.

I ran my hands through my hair and blew out my breath. There was a naked, gorgeous woman crying in the shower and I didn't have a fucking clue how to fix it. Crying women gave me hives. You'd think that over the years I'd be used to it, okay with it even, but it still made me want to kill people.

Standing up, I took off the jumper and threw it on a chair before cleaning up the food mess. I stuffed the leftovers in the tiny fridge next to the tele and looked around the room. There wasn't much I could do in the tiny space. Tomorrow we would do some recon before approaching Marcus. Though I knew he'd be waiting for me. Since the squad in Oxford hadn't worked, he'd know I was coming for him. If he wanted me dead, why hadn't he sent more men? If anyone knew what I could handle, it would be him.

The bathroom door cracked open and I realized I had

been staring off into space. Ava leaned against the door-frame in nothing but the oversized shirt and I felt the blood drain from my head and head south. I hadn't thought to buy her shorts or sleeping pants and I'd never been so glad I had overlooked something. Her long legs went on forever and the image of them being wrapped around me burst into my brain.

"Who gets the bed?" She brushed her wet hair over her shoulder and I had to force myself to ignore the way the damp material clung to her breasts.

"There's enough space for two." I smiled at her dubious expression. "I'll behave if you do."

"Shouldn't someone stand guard?" Her eyes darted to the door and I realized she was genuinely nervous about being caught while sleeping. I moved to the door and slid the old dresser across the floor. I looked back at her to see if that helped but she had moved across the room. I watched as she picked up one of the chairs and carried it across the room. The t-shirt slid up a little higher as she made her way to me and I had to remind myself that she was vulnerable right now. I moved so she could place the chair where she wanted.

Knowing that someone might bust in on you while you were sleeping was part of the job. After a while you learn how to accept it. You take precautions, like picking a secure location, keeping your gun close, and learning to sleep lightly. Ava wasn't used to that and she'd been put through the ringer in the last few days. So, instead of mocking her, or explaining that I'd chosen this inn because of where it was located and how we'd be able to defend ourselves, I moved the other chair to the growing pile of furniture. I unplugged the tele and set it atop the bureau.

Ava grabbed one of the lamps we were using and placed it so it was leaning against the door. The dingy crystals swayed for a moment and I realized she was using it as an alarm. Not a bad idea. The jingle would serve as an early detection sound if someone was messing with the door.

"You think I'm silly." Her mouth pulled to the side and she looked at me with large eyes. "But I know that if someone really wants in, this isn't going to stop them."

"It will slow them down." I pulled my shirt off and made my way to the bed. I sat down on the edge of the bed closest to the door and undid the clasp on my watch.

Ava hadn't come to the bed. She was standing next to the leaning tower of furniture and watching me. Her cheek ticked nervously and I fought my smile. That's right. I wasn't the only one feeling the sexual tension. I swung my legs onto the bed and tucked my hands behind my head.

"Scared you won't be able to control yourself?" I patted the other side of the bed. A blush crawled out of the neck line of her shirt and up to her cheeks. She sputtered and her back stiffened, which is exactly what I had been going for.

"Listen here, buddy. You're no Brad Pitt." Stomping across the room, she ripped the blanket back from the bed and crawled into her spot. "Don't try anything funny."

"I'll try to contain my baser urges." I hit the switch for the light and settled down into my pillow.

Ava fought with her pillow until she had molded it into a shape that suited her. She was on her side facing me. I could just make out her features in the dark and smell the shampoo she had used in the shower. It had been years since I had slept in the same bed as someone else, but with

Ava I didn't worry she would get up and kill me in my sleep.

It was a nice feeling.

"Owen?" Her whisper drew me out of my thoughts.

"Yeah?"

"Thank you for not leaving me." I could barely make out her words as weariness claimed her.

"You're welcome."

CHAPTER
ELEVEN

Ava

COLD AIR CURLED over the skin of my thigh and I snuggled closer to the heat next to me. A soft snore invaded my dreams and I grunted in annoyance. The warm pillow under my head moved, turning me over so I was on my back and immediately yanking me out of my dreams. As my eyes adjusted to the early morning light that poured in around the curtains, Owen rolled into me.

"What the—?" I started to push him away, but his hands closed on my wrists and lifted them above my head.

"It's been a long time since I woke up next to someone." His voice sent goosebumps over my skin and I froze. One of his legs rested between mine and every movement made it deliciously clear how much he enjoyed having a bedmate. "I'm not used to it."

"Wh-why is that?" His lips were so close to mine I couldn't focus on anything else. Flashes of our kiss from the night before ran through my mind.

"Trust." He leaned a little closer, his lips almost touching mine. "Can't sleep next to someone who might kill you."

"That would be difficult." I licked my lips and tried to calm my racing heart.

"But not with you, love." He let go of one of my wrists to run a finger along my jaw. "You're not going to kill me in my sleep."

"How can you be so sure?"

"It's in your eyes." His eyes dipped down to my lips. "The eyes never lie."

I waited for his kiss, waited for the heat that his fingertips promised.

But it never came. Sighing he rolled off of me and stood up.

"Want to grab breakfast?" He stretched without turning to look at me.

Sitting up, I stared after him, wondering what had happened. I hadn't been far from begging him to ravage me and he was worried about pancakes and eggs.

"Sure." I ran a hand through my hair.

"I'm going to hit the shower and then we can head out. I saw a place to get some food on the next block." He grabbed a shirt from the bag and went straight to the bathroom.

"Well." I threw the blanket off and stood up. Muttering to myself I went through the bag and found a pair of jeans that looked like they would fit. He had guessed my size better than I'd expected. "Talk about a let-down. All hot and bothered with nothing to show for it. Big bad assassin. Ha." I slid the pants up and traded my Prince Harry shirt for a black one. It was loose on me, and the v-neck dipped low enough that I worried about the cleavage it exposed. I wondered if he'd chosen it that way on purpose.

"Apparently my eyes didn't say it all, huh?"

I picked up my pistol and stuck it in my pants before pulling the sweater from yesterday over my clothes. Hopefully it wouldn't be too hot today. I needed something to conceal the bulky gun. The thought of getting caught with it made me shudder. An American with no passport, wanted for vehicular homicide, and carrying an illegal firearm —yeah, that would go well for me. So well I'd end up in a cell trading homemade tats for protection.

By the time I heard the shower shut off, I'd gone through all the bags of stuff Owen had bought. He had odd shopping habits. Then again I wasn't an assassin, so maybe he had a perfectly good reason for purchasing duct tape. Maybe it was for something simple, like repairing a ripped bag, not for holding someone hostage. When the door opened I threw the silver stuff back in the bag and sat down in a chair. He was shirtless and his pants were slung low on his hips, revealing those indentions that made my mouth water.

"You can never have enough of that." He nodded. "You'd be amazed what you can do with it."

"Mmm," I mumbled. I couldn't have agreed more.

And then I realized he was talking about the duct tape. Right. I hoped he couldn't see how flushed my cheeks were. Time to move the conversation along.

"I saw a guy on TV make a cup out of it once. A survival show where he could only take one thing with him, and that's what he chose." I rested my arms on the table, trying to snap myself out of the inconvenient attraction I felt. "Never really thought I'd need to know how to do that, but who knows now?"

"If you need a cup made from tape, then we'll have

bigger worries than drinking." Owen pulled a shirt over his head, and I immediately felt the haze clearing from my brain. Disappointment and relief rushed through me as he knelt to open the black bag he had brought back with him last night. "I've brought you another pistol. I thought you'd prefer something a little smaller than the forty-five you're carrying now."

"Will it be easier to conceal?" I stood up and pulled the gun from my pants.

"Yes. I've also got you a real holster." He held up a leather object. "Come here."

I stood up and moved closer to him. I'd never worn a holster so had no idea where it went. I'd seen movies and might be able to guess, but what if I got it backward and couldn't get the gun out when I needed it?

"Lift your shirt."

"Excuse me?"

"Lift your shirt and unzip your pants."

"Where exactly does this holster go?" I narrowed my eyes at him.

"It goes against the small of your back and I'd like a little space to slide it in." I felt myself blushing again, and he smiled. He moved behind me to lift the sweater with one hand. "Now, undo your pants for me."

"Since you asked so nicely." Shaking my head I worked the button loose and pushed the pants open. His fingers grazed along the small of my back and I bit my lip. When he slid the cool leather against my skin I squeaked. "That's cold!"

"Sorry." After a little tugging, he stepped back and I buttoned the jeans.

"Not exactly comfortable." I turned to look in the full

length mirror to see if the holster was visible.

"You'll get used to it." Owen revealed a smaller, chrome and black pistol. "This is a nine millimeter. I think it will fit your hand a little better."

I took the pistol and checked the chamber before leveling it in front of me. It did feel a little more comfortable in my hands, but I wouldn't really know unless I fired it.

"Widen your stance." Owen moved behind me and adjusted my shoulders. "This will give you the best accuracy."

"I look like an idiot." I was standing with my feet shoulder width apart and both arms out in front of me.

"That's because you think you should look like they do in the movies." Owen leaned closer to me as he reached around to adjust my arms. "Strong arms. You don't want the gun to come back and hit you in the face."

"So is this how you stand when you shoot?" I tried to not focus on the way his body wrapped around mine.

"Of course not." He stepped back and I turned to look at him. "I can't look stupid while I'm out killing people."

"Gee, thanks." I reached behind me and tried to put the pistol into the holster. The sweater caught on the gun and I fumbled for a minute before getting it safely put away. Well, safe was a matter of opinion. The gun was loaded, with one in the chamber, and currently pointed down my ass crack.

"You don't want to be comfortable with them." Owen was watching me with guarded eyes. "If you're too comfortable you'll take them for granted and that's when you hurt yourself."

"Or someone else."

"That too." Turning away from me, he loaded another

gun before placing it in a shoulder holster for himself. He also attached a knife to his ankle, and stuck another pistol in the small of his back. He pulled a large gun out from the bag and checked the chamber and I felt my eyes widen.

"I'd love to see where you put that thing."

"I bet you would." He looked around the room for a minute before walking over to the bed. Flipping the mattress over he used a smaller pocket knife to cut a large gash in the fabric.

"There goes our deposit."

"Can't just leave this stuff out for them to find." Kneeling down on the floor next to the bed he began pulling things out of his bags. As I watched the growing pile of ammunition and money, my mouth fell open.

"I don't think all of that is going to fit in there."

"Only some of it." He began arranging things inside the mattress; his entire arm disappearing at one point. "We'll carry some of it in the bag."

"What, are we going to put it in a trashcan at a park?"

"There are worse places." He winked at me and I didn't want to think about where he might have hid things before. "But no. We're carrying this with us for now."

"Don't you worry about someone realizing you're carrying a gun? I mean, it's a big deal here. It's not like back home." The gun on my back felt white hot against my skin. Like a beacon for everyone to see.

"People see what they want to see." He shrugged into his jacket before slinging the backpack over one shoulder. "And most people only see stuff that concerns them."

"What about the people who want to see someone carrying a gun?" I tugged my sweater a little lower and followed him out the door. "There are those out there, always looking for trouble."

"Then you deal with it." He moved beside me and leaned his head down. "Loosen up a little, Ava. Sometimes you just have to roll with things."

"Easy for you to say. This is how you live all the time." I shrugged and tried to calm my racing heart. It wasn't fair that his breath on my ear would send goosebumps over my body.

"True." He stood up straight and put a little distance between us. "This is how I live." His words were firm as if reminding himself. My heart ached for the loneliness that had crept into his voice. It was faint, and I wouldn't have noticed it if I hadn't spent the last couple of days with him, but it was definitely there.

"But you're right. I need to just roll with things a little better." I smiled up at him. "That's what I'm supposed to be doing anyway, right? Stop planning everything out and doing only the safe things."

"What I do is not for everyone." He frowned and looked ahead. "It shouldn't be for anyone."

"Then why do you do it?" The question popped out of my mouth before I could think twice.

"Because I'm good at it." His jaw tightened. "And sometimes it needs to be done."

We pushed out the door and stepped onto the sidewalk. A cool breeze whipped my hair around my face and I pulled out a rubber band to secure it.

Owen led us to an entrance to the Tube, the underground subway that ran through the city. People commuting to work and running various errands rushed to and fro, while a baby cried in the background. An electronic advertisement on the wall flashed images of couples drinking in a pub, with a catchy tagline scrolling underneath. I was jealous of the normalcy all around me, but at least I had Owen by my side.

I stuck close to my new friend, unaware of exactly where we were going or how we would get there. I hadn't ridden the Tube much since coming to London, preferring to walk and take in the city. The maps of different colored lines were like a foreign language that I was slowly learning to decode.

"This way." Owen placed a hand on my shoulder and turned me down a bright hallway.

"You haven't told me where we're going?" We stopped at a platform with only a few people. I scratched at my back in an attempt to adjust the gun into a more comfortable position. It was rubbing a sore spot along my waist.

"Stop fidgeting." He frowned at me.

"I can't. The thing is rubbing me raw." I shifted my shoulder. "I'm going to get a blister."

Stepping behind me he ran his hands over my shoulders, squeezing gently as if massaging me. His hands slid lower in circles until he was kneading my lower back. My eyes threatened to close as he worked. If I'd been a cat I would have purred in pleasure, but I managed to control myself. His hands closed around my waist, while his thumbs pushed at the gun until it was sitting in a different spot.

"Better?" His breath teased the few loose strands of my hair.

I looked up into his eyes and nodded, not trusting myself to speak. Why did he affect me so much? This man, this self-confessed murderer, turned me to whimpering

131

mush. Well, not whimpering. I wasn't whimpering. Yet. But I was starting to feel a bit mush-like.

"Ava, you have to stop looking at me like that." He pressed closer to me, his eyes dipping down to my mouth. The heat of his body washed over my back and I leaned into it, drawn like a moth to flame.

"Like what?" I licked my lips and my breathing hitched.

"Like you want me to kiss you, love." One of his hands left my waist and drifted up to cup my chin, tilting my head a little more in his direction. Tilting his head down, his lips barely brushed against mine as he looked into my eyes. "I'm not the type of man you should want to kiss."

"Why not?" I ached to kiss him, to feel his breath mingle with mine, but it was more than just a physical need. I also wanted to banish the lonely darkness that swirled in the back of his eyes. As much as he was protecting me, I felt this urge to take care of him.

The rumble of the subway car broke our connection and he let go of me like I was a hot piece of coal.

"Our ride." He motioned for me to enter the car ahead of him.

I took a spot near the door and grasped one of the hand rails. I was feeling too antsy from the almost-kiss to sit down; too confused to sit calmly next to him while I waited for our stop. Wherever that was.

"Where are we going?"

"Notting Hill." His voice rumbled close to my ear.

"Oh, good. That was on my list of places to visit." I gripped the hand rail a little tighter. Of course I had wanted to see the Portobello market, not hunt down the man that had tried to kill me. Life certainly had changed my plans.

CHAPTER TWELVE

Owen

I HADN'T BEEN to Notting Hill in years. I hadn't seen my brother in years. I hadn't cared about it for years. We weren't exactly worried about trading presents for holidays or birthdays. Of course, I hadn't realized we'd gotten to the point where we were trying to kill each other. If I'd known, I would have sent a card at Christmas.

When we stepped out of the station, Ava seemed to reenergize. She had been quiet for most of the trip, the wheels turning behind her eyes as she mulled over something. But when she saw the crowds, the bright colors and laughing people, her face brightened. As we passed the pubs and little shops, I was thankful for the crowds. It would make it easier to go unnoticed. I hadn't told Ava much about my plan because I didn't want to worry her.

I knew that my brother would be waiting for me. He may not know when I would be coming or how I would arrive, but he wouldn't doubt that I would make an appearance at some point. Today I was planning on doing research. I needed to know who he had guarding him, because he wouldn't just be hanging around in the sitting room, biscuits and tea at the ready.

Ava stopped at a small stall and looked through a basket of jewelry. She picked up a small broach and asked the craftsman a couple of questions. The old man smiled, all too happy to talk trade with someone interested. I listened while they chatted, but kept a careful lookout for anyone that might recognize either of us. It would be common knowledge at this point that Ava was with me, so they'd be looking for a couple. Still, as a couple shopping, we'd be less likely to be noticed.

"What do you think, Owen?" Ava turned to me and held up the broach. The silver wire was worked into a bow. Smiling she lifted the pin to the base of her throat like a bowtie. "Isn't that brilliant?"

"It's nice." I smiled the gentleman. "How long does it take to make something like that?"

"I've been doing it so long now, it's only a matter of minutes." The salesman winked at me. "Of course, that means you're getting quality workmanship from a true craftsman. Been jewelry making since I was a lad."

"And you can tell." Ava reached for her pocket, but hesitated.

"Let me." I should have made sure that she was carrying cash before we left the Inn. I wasn't used to traveling with another person. Pulling my wallet out I handed the man a fifty note. "Keep the change."

"Thank you." The man smiled and chatted with Ava as he wrapped up her purchase. By the time we were on our way, I had the feeling that if the circumstances had been different, Ava could have spent hours talking shop.

"I'm sorry. I know we're here for a reason, but I

couldn't help myself. What a creative idea! Bowties and fancy collar necklaces are really popular right now. If he shopped his piece, he could sell thousands."

"No, it's good to shop; blend in." Some of her excitement dampened at my reminder of why we were here. Not wanting to derail her happiness, I prodded for more information about something she was obviously passionate about. "So you think he could sell the idea? Make a lot of money?"

"Definitely. There are buyers that look for just that thing. Searching little fairs and markets for gems."

"And is that what you want to do? Search for hidden treasure?"

"You make it sound like pirates." She laughed. "Maybe. It would take a while before I'd get to that point. You have to start at the bottom, show that you know what will sell. Plus I just love the actual work, you know? Making something come to life that had been in my head."

"That takes a lot of imagination." I steered her around a group of people congregating outside of a popular pub.

"I guess so. Sometimes I start something and have no idea how it's going to end up. I'm just as surprised as anyone else." She shrugged. "So, how about that breakfast you promised? I'm starving."

"What would you like? A muffin? Some fruit? Or the full course?" I motioned down the street. "There is pretty much anything you can think of."

"Hm. Let's grab something substantial. That way if we don't get to eat later, we won't be running on fumes."

"Smart." I let myself drape my arm over her shoulders. We were supposed to look like a couple out enjoying the sights, after all. "But I promise to do my best to keep you fed."

"Good. You don't know this, but I'm mean when I'm hungry." She smiled up at me as we wove through the crowds.

"Actually, it was made quite clear when you threatened to shoot me last night over Chinese take-away."

She shrugged. "What can I say? I really like lo mein."

I pointed at a door between two Inns. "It's been a while, but the last time I ate there, it was pretty good."

"Well, let's give it a go." She bounded up the short steps and into the little restaurant. The person behind the counter waved us to a table and Ava greedily pored over the menu. "It smells divine."

I smiled as I sat down. We were here in Notting Hill to stalk my traitorous brother but she was still excited about the smell of bacon and eggs. Then again, the food did smell pretty good.

"I can't believe I'm here." Ava set her menu down and peered out the window. "I've always wanted to visit Notting Hill."

"And why is that?" I folded my hands in front of me.

"Julia Roberts." She shook her head at my blank expression. "The movie? Notting Hill? Julia Roberts, superstar actress and Hugh Grant, the average bookshop owner?"

"Afraid I missed that one." I shrugged.

"You haven't seen it? Are you serious?" Her eyebrows drew together. The little wrinkle along her nose made me smile. "How could you have missed it? You don't even remember the previews?"

"Is it a recent movie? I've been out of the country."

"No. Gosh, it came out when I was young. I grew up

with this idealized vision of Notting Hill and the people that would live here. Blue doors and people with orange hair."

I had no answer for that. Blue doors and orange hair? What kind of movie was it?

An older waitress came over to take our order, but the glimpse of a familiar face distracted me. I tried to peer around the tiny restaurant without being conspicuous, but there wasn't much hope. It was too crowded for me to see anyone without actively standing up and that would give away that I had indeed seen someone.

It wasn't until Ava cleared her throat loudly that my attention returned back to the table.

"Excuse me?" I realized that Ava and the woman were looking at me.

"What'll you have?"

"The same, please." I nodded at Ava and smiled. I didn't want either of them to see the worry that was gnawing at my stomach. When the waitress walked off, I shifted in my seat to get a better look around the room, but it was hopeless. I debated getting up and pulling Ava along with me, but the crowd eating breakfast provided a little security.

"Who did you see?" Ava lowered her voice, but thankfully didn't look around the room as if trying to spot something.

"An old coworker." I ran my finger over the butter knife next to my drink.

"Coworker." Ava leaned forward a little more and her eyes tightened. "You mean another assassin."

"Yes." I saw the swish of blonde hair in my peripheral vision and silently palmed the knife and slid my hand under the table.

"And is this coworker a friend?" Ava's eyes darted out the window.

"Depends on her mood." I shifted in my seat so that I'd be able to get my legs out from under the table quickly. "She's a short-tempered one."

"Now, that's not fair." A warm voice replied from behind me.

"Hm. The last time I saw you, you shot out my tire." I narrowed my eyes, but didn't turn around. The muscles in my body coiled tightly as I prepared to fight.

"You forgot to call." A small hand slid over my shoulder and under my jumper. I wrapped my fingers around her wrist and pulled her closer. Her small knife dug into my back, but it was safer than letting Mavis have a chance at Ava.

"You burned my clothes." I turned just enough so I could angle my blunt knife at her stomach. "I thought you didn't want to hear from me."

"Meh." Her lips moved close to my ear. "I got over it."

"What do you want, Mavis?" I lowered my voice.

"Well, since it looks like you've moved past our fun in Rome, I guess I could collect the money on your head." The knife in my back moved away and she stood up a little straighter. "Or I could settle for breakfast with an old friend." Mavis pulled the chair out next to me. "Would you rather me sit here or across from you? All the better to keep an eye on me?"

"Sit down." I growled the words. I didn't want Mavis any closer to Ava until I knew exactly what she was after. Mavis was an assassin, a very accomplished assassin, but she usually picked cases where her appearance would make it an easy kill. It was much easier to get next to a powerful man if he wanted to fuck you. And Mavis was very fuckable. I knew from experience.

"Would you like a menu, miss?" The waitress sat the plates down on the table and smiled at Mavis.

"Tea, please, and a muffin." Mavis set her black purse on the floor. We'd argued about purses in the past. I thought they would be a distraction, but Mavis insisted that they let you get away with a lot more than trying to conceal a knife in a thigh holster.

"Yes, ma'am." The waitress moved away and I looked at Ava. I tried to reassure her with my eyes, but I couldn't tell what she was thinking.

"You said your name was Jilly." Ava narrowed her eyes at Mavis. "I knew there was something wrong with you."

"Jilly?" I looked from Mavis to Ava.

"She was at the shop in Oxford." Ava narrowed her eyes at Mavis. "I had a feeling she was full of shit."

I paused and looked at Ava. Was she jealous? Hm.

Mavis tsked. "I just wanted to see you for myself. How was the book?"

"Just perfect." Ava's fingers clenched her fork.

"So, this is nice." Mavis folded her hands on the table and smiled.

"What do you want?" She had talked to Ava in Oxford and I hadn't even known about it. If she was going to collect her, that would have been the time to do it. Not here with all of these people.

"God, Owen. You always were bad at small talk." Mavis glared at me. Her perfect lips pursed in disgust.

"Why don't you introduce me to your friend?"

"I thought you'd already done that."

"Well, I wasn't exactly honest."

"Ava, this is Mavis. Mavis, this is Ava." I glared at the little woman next to me. "Mavis, don't kill Ava."

"How have you put up with him these past few days? He's such a grump." Mavis smiled at Ava, but Ava wasn't impressed. "I could only stand a few hours at a time."

"We were doing okay until a few minutes ago." Ava's chin jutted out.

"Ah, I see. Well, he does have his good points." Mavis ran her hand over my thigh and I shoved it away.

"Quit it, Mavis. That was over a long time ago."

She laughed loudly, but it wasn't cruel or mocking. Genuine humor shone in her eyes as she regarded me and Ava. I was struck by their differences. Mavis, poised and polished, radiated self-confidence and sex appeal. Ava, with her large eyes and baggy clothes, looked innocent and trusting. But just as sexy. The t-shirt under her sweater barely clung to her cleavage, threatening to slip too low at any minute. Her heavy bangs shrouded her eyes in a way that enhanced them, making them feel deeper. A natural beauty, one that didn't have to try to be alluring. It was a breath of fresh air next to the perfectly coifed woman sitting next to me.

"You know, when I saw the video of you I wasn't sure. I had to check it out for myself." Mavis turned her smile on the waitress as she took her tea. "And now I know."

"Know what exactly?" Ava narrowed her eyes at Mavis.

"What video?" I asked.

"That he really is protecting you." Mavis poured milk into her cup and I passed her the sugar. "Videos of you and Ava in the parking garage were circulated. There were lots of theories, of course. That you were going to collect the bounty, you were going to offer a trade. Oh, lots of things. But it's much simpler than all that." She winked at Ava. "He's just chasing cute ass. Men are all the same."

Ava went pale and I ground my teeth. I wasn't sure if she even registered the dig about sex, because her eyes had taken on a look of horror at the mention of me stringing her along just so I could collect the bounty.

God damnit. What did I have to do to get her to trust me?

"Mavis." I felt my lips pull back in a sneer. "That's rubbish."

"Relax. I knew you wouldn't do that, but I wanted to see what was really going on." Mavis took a sip of her tea. "And now I know! It's sweet, really. The big bad assassin saving the adorable, clueless American."

"I'm helping Ava. That's it." I said the words flatly. I could guess what Mavis thought she understood, but that was far from the truth. Despite her background and cold exterior, the woman curled up every night and watched romantic comedies. "She's been wrongly targeted and wouldn't last on her own."

"Hey." Ava sat up straighter in her seat. "I can help myself."

"Relax, sweetheart. You should be grateful. He's the best there is. In more ways than one." Mavis smiled over her cup at Ava. "And we all have our skills. Maybe yours are just more...romantic?"

Red washed over Ava's face and before I could tell

her to not let Mavis push her buttons she exploded.

"I don't know what the hell you want or why you're here, but you can take your snazzy British accent and backhanded compliments and shove them up your ass." Ava clenched the table with her hands and I hoped that my mouth wasn't hanging open. "I'm tired of looking over my shoulder, tired of being shot at, tired of *assholes*. And I sure as hell don't want your bitchy attitude ruining my breakfast. It could be my last one."

A heavy silence descended on our table as I stared at the woman across from me. Pride welled up in my chest as I watched sweet Ava stare down the killer next to me.

"She called me bitchy." Mavis raised an eyebrow. "I think I like her after all."

"Figures." I shook my head and leaned back in my chair. A test. Mavis had been testing Ava and apparently she had gotten what she'd been looking for.

"Right. Thanks." Ava rolled her eyes. "I'm going to eat now while you tell us why you're here."

"I'm not out here for you, but I couldn't help the tease." Mavis leaned forward and I could see her playful mood melt away to something more serious. "I'm actually helping a friend and my leads are bringing me back to your brother. I think there might be some connections."

"What the hell is Marcus mixed up in?" It wasn't good whatever it was, that was for damn sure.

"Missing girls." Mavis's lips clamped together for a minute as if she was fighting to not say something.

"No." The word left my mouth, but it was only an automatic response. Despite my denial, there was no flutter of hope that she was wrong. No need to make sure she was right. I knew there was something off with Marcus, with the way he had become greedier over the years. My brother was mixed up in the slave trade; something I despised. Something he should hate just as much as I did. There was no denying that something was really wrong at this point. And all of this time… "How long?"

"Years." Mavis sipped her tea calmly, as if the floor hadn't just been ripped out from under my feet. How long had my brother been dealing with the devil? And how many of the hits I had accepted had been what I thought? My eyes slid to Ava, wondering what she must be thinking, wondering if she had made the right decision in sticking with me. Her bright eyes watched me with sadness— not for herself, I guessed, but for me.

"Right." I cleared my throat and looked out the window.

"I thought that maybe we could help each other." Mavis set her cup down.

"And how's that?" Ava asked. But despite her bravado, she still hadn't touched any of her food.

"Well, I've been tracking down Marcus's workers, but I need to talk to him. There is something that doesn't add up. Marcus is smart and has contacts, but I don't think he fell into this on his own. There is someone else involved and I need to know who it is. I had hoped you might be able to get me in there." Mavis frowned. "Of course, that was before he put out a contract on you."

"Puts a damper on that plan, huh?" Ava sighed.

"Not really." I looked back at them. "Does he know you're on his scent, Mavis?"

"No." She smiled. "I'm good at what I do, Owen."

"Then you're our key inside." I looked at Ava. "Eat up, sweetheart. We're about to get some answers."

CHAPTER
THIRTEEN

OWEN WAS DISCUSSING plans quietly with Mavis as I stuffed my mouth with food and tried to keep up. There was talk about guards, talk about guns, and talk about scaling a wall. I looked down at my now clean plate and frowned. Maybe I shouldn't have had that last piece of bacon.

"Explosives?" Mavis asked calmly.

"Too messy." Owen shook his head. "We need to enter without conflict. We don't want the police involved."

"Too right, that. Blundering bunch of fools." Mavis sniffed.

"What am I supposed to do?" I wiped my hands on my napkin and looked at them calmly. "Sit on my thumbs and count cars?"

"I could take her with me." Mavis wasn't answering me, she was looking at Owen.

"No." The word was harsh and his eyes flicked in my direction.

"Owen, I won't let him have her." Mavis finally

looked back over at me. "I would make sure you were un-harmed."

"Why take me?" I twisted the napkin in my hands. "How will that help you?"

"He's got a price on your head. I can offer you as a trade." Mavis shrugged.

"No." Owens fist slammed down on the table, startling people around us.

"A trade for what?" I ignored him, curious as to what Mavis was thinking. Despite her overt flirting with Owen and her pompous attitude, I could see the wheels turning behind her eyes. There was intelligence there; I just hadn't decided if it worked for good or evil.

"Laura." Mavis's eyes grew dark with anger. "My friend's sister."

For a minute I couldn't breathe. I couldn't think of anything except the horror that the girl might be experiencing and how bad I felt for her sister. The worry and fear would make me sick. Then, with a flash of lightning hot adrenaline, determination filled my veins. Something had to be done. This had to stop.

"Okay—"

"Absolutely not." Owen shook his head. "You are not taking Ava into that place. It is a pen of vipers. I'm sorry about your friend. I'm sorry. But you are not in any way taking Ava in there as a trade." He leaned forward and looked at me. "I won't risk it. End of story."

It was odd, to feel completely calm about the idea of using myself as collateral, and then to compare it to the panic in his eyes.

"You can come in the back while he's distracted." Mavis's words were quiet. "There are two guards at each door and one that stays with Marcus. If I'm at the front door with Ava, you can take out the back guards quietly and slip in. You know the house and how to get in, where to hide. It would be simple."

"No." Owen stood up and pulled his wallet out. He threw a few bills on the table and held his hand out to me. "Ava?"

"We should talk about this." I crossed my arms.

"I promised to never lie to you." The words were a growl as if he hadn't wanted to say them in front of Mavis. "If you go in there you will get hurt."

"I could get hurt walking down the street." I frowned at him.

"I'm not talking about a random drunk driver or tripping on a curb." His green eyes flashed angrily. "These are people that would *hurt* you. They won't hesitate to torture you or even—" He stopped and made a horrible face. "If they are selling sex slaves then you know what they are capable of."

"They're already after me. They've shot at me, Owen. They chased our car through traffic." I crossed my arms. "I want to know why. Why me? Are they after Tess? I can't just hide away. I need to know what is going on."

"Ava." My name came out as a forceful grunt just before he pulled the chair back out and dropped into it. "This is not so simple."

"Sure it is. This is a pretty simple plan that will work." Mavis sat up straighter in her chair as if smelling victory. "Simple is the best. You taught me that."

Owen watched me from under his furrowed brow, but didn't respond. I could tell that he was thinking it over, deciding what could go wrong and what could go right.

"We don't have to do it today," I reasoned. "We could take a look, see if there is anything you don't like and then come back tomorrow."

"We're not doing anything today because we'll have to get you ready." Owen frowned at me.

"What are you thinking?" Mavis smiled.

"She can't carry a gun." He leaned forward. "They'll frisk you. Anything you have on you will be found."

I nodded, but my stomach dropped. The idea of walking into the enemy's base without a weapon seemed like very bad idea.

"And there is no guarantee that they will let you stay with Mavis." Owen watched me closely. "And guards that work for sex slave traders are not to be trusted with the merchandise."

"Stop it," I said. I didn't want to focus on what could go wrong. "We make plans."

"You can't plan for everything, love." Owen shook his head.

"Marcus likes pretty girls," Mavis suggested. "We put her in the right clothes and he'll make sure to show up."

"Won't he suspect there is something wrong if he already knows I'm with Owen?" I fought the urge to chew on my thumbnail. I didn't want either of the professional killers to know how nervous I was.

"That part's easy. You ran away." Mavis shrugged. "You were scared and tried to go it on your own."

"And you were there to sweep me up?" I took a deep breath and looked at Owen. "It could work?"

"It could, but you have to know that no plan ever works just the way you think it will." He shook his head and stood up. "We'll meet back here tomorrow. Mavis,

148

you have my number?"

"I do." She cocked her head to the side. "Do you want to do some surveillance?"

"I know the house. Looking at it again isn't going to change the layout." He walked around to my side of the table and held his hand out. I let him help me stand and took one last drink of the orange juice.

"Very well." Mavis didn't stand, just sipped at her tea. "What time, then?"

"Just after the lunch crowd." His fingers clasped mine warmly as he pulled me to the door. "Bring your purse."

"Of course." Mavis smiled. "Nice to meet you, Ava."

I smiled, not sure if it had been nice to meet her or not. Owen walked quickly down the street, tugging me along with him. From the set of his shoulders and the way people melted out of his way, I knew he was angry. His fingers weren't rough on mine, just firm as he guided us through the crowd.

I didn't say anything, not wanting to turn his ire in my direction. When he ducked into a quiet alley and turned to look at me, I felt my blood pressure rocket. Gone was the gentle man that had offered me sliced apples and teased me about my romance book. I was staring into the eyes of the man that killed people for a living.

"Owen?"

"Why? Why would you agree to go in there with her?" He stepped toward me and I took a step back. "With a woman that is suggesting she use you as bait? What part of that sounds like a good idea? You don't even know her."

"I—"

"You could be killed, Ava. I'm trying to protect you

149

and you offer yourself up as the sacrificial lamb!" He took another step toward me, but I had nowhere to go. Cool brick and the hard edges of the pistol pressed into my back.

"It's—"

"You don't belong in this mess. You're going to get hurt." His eyes bored into mine. "I'm taking you to another safe house and locking you up there. I'll come back in the morning and deal with Mavis."

"The hell you are!" I shoved his shoulder. "You're not locking me up anywhere! I'm in this, Owen! I'm at least going to help get myself out of it. And what about Tess? I still don't know if she's in danger."

"I don't care about Tess!" He growled the words. Slapping his hands against the wall, he barricaded me between his arms and glared down at me. "I care about you!"

My heart thumped hard against my chest as I stared up at him. Cared about me? How had that happened? I opened my mouth and shut it, not sure how to respond.

"Damn it. In a few short days you've turned my entire life upside down. You're everything I've always avoided." His words were quiet, but there was a desperation underlining them. "You're too good for me and I'm the death of everything that makes you perfect. You should be running in the opposite direction and instead you look at me with those big eyes and easy smile and I..." He shook his head as if lost.

"Owen." My stomach clenched tightly as my mind tried to understand what he was telling me. "I care about you, too."

"I'm wrong for you, Ava, but damn if I can help the way I feel." His hands moved to cup my face and his lips touched mine in a fierce declaration of need.

There was no thought, no internal struggle or worry about the outcome. I wrapped my arms around his neck and kissed him back with every bit of me. His mouth begged my lips to open, his tongue a hot stroke of desire. I groaned as the sharp angles of his body pressed into mine. He fit against me perfectly, not too tall, not too short. Everything lined up just right. Letting go of my face with one hand, he reached down to grab my hip, moving me so that he could press closer against my core.

I fisted my hands in his hair, desperate to hold onto his kiss. It was wild and hungry, something that would consume me if I let it. And I wanted to let it. Never in my life had a man kissed me in such a way; as if he was drowning and I was air. I grabbed his bottom lip between my teeth and gently tugged until he groaned. His fingers tightened on my hip and I slid one hand into his jacket to trace the muscles along his midriff.

A loud wolf whistle broke the bubble we had been in, and Owen pulled back to look in my eyes. He was hungry for more, but I could also see the guilt creeping back into his gaze.

"This isn't over." I stared up at him, my chest rising and falling with heavy breaths. I fisted my hand in his shirt so he couldn't move away. Now wasn't the time, but we were going to have to figure out whatever was between us. "And you're not locking me up somewhere to keep me safe."

"What else am I supposed to do?" His eyes flashed with frustration. "You're intent on getting yourself killed."

"Am not." I glared at him. "I want to help."

He leaned back just a little. "This isn't your world,

Ava. People die and they don't come back."

"I know all about death." I frowned. "You don't own an exclusive license on the term. Orphan, remember? I know what could happen, but damn it, it's better than sitting around and waiting for someone to find me. I'd rather go out because I was doing something, rather than flinching in the dark."

He watched my face. "You're tougher than you look."

"That's what I've been trying to tell you."

"I'm sorry." Closing his eyes, Owen rested his forehead against mine. "This is complicated. I don't do complicated."

"Tough."

He chuckled and pulled back. "You're difficult as well."

"Would you have it any other way?" I winked at him as I straightened my shirt. The material hung so low you could see my bra after our game of back alley tag.

"Right." He looked around the alley. "We should head back."

"Excellent. People will shoot at us and there will running. Lots of running." I flourished my hand toward the street. "Allons-y!"

"Did you just make a Doctor Who reference?" Owen raised an eyebrow.

"What? You know about the Doctor? But you don't know about the Notting Hill movie?" I tsked.

"Of course I know the Doctor." He put his hand on the small of my back as we walked. "I'm quite fond of the Daleks."

"You would be." I chuckled.

"Well, I do exterminate for a living." He lead the way

out of the alley and back toward the underground. He was making an effort to relax, but I could still see the tension gripping his jaw.

"So, where are we going now?" I stuck my hands in my sweater pockets and kept pace.

"We're going to see Marcus." He looked straight ahead.

"I thought you told Mavis we were going to do it tomorrow." I stopped walking.

"So trusting." He turned and looked at me with dark eyes. "You are a rare person, Ava."

"Is that a nice way of calling me stupid? Or whatever you Brits say? Daft?" I rolled my eyes.

He snorted. "No, you just aren't as jaded as I am. That's not a bad thing."

"So we're going to Marcus now?" I watched out of the corner of my eye as we maneuvered around people. "And how are we going to get in? Grappling hook? Disguises?"

He looked at me like I had grown an extra head for a moment before busting into laughter. I would have enjoyed the sound if it hadn't been directed at me.

"No. We're going to do as Mavis suggested. You'll be my hostage and I'll offer you as trade."

My feet froze and for a moment I wondered if he would do it, give me to his brother, but then I remembered the look in his eyes. He wasn't going to give me to anyone.

"I thought you said that was a bad idea."

He turned to look at me. "That was before I was the one going in with you."

"But what if they just shoot you?" I didn't move. It

suddenly felt like a horrible idea. "There's a price on your head as well. A much bigger one."

"Marcus is the boss, so no one touches me besides him. And he'll want to talk. He'll know I have a good reason to be there since I could have much more easily waited to kill him when he left the house." He wrapped his fingers around mine and pulled me with him. "We can't stand out in the middle of the street, even with all of these people. It's too risky."

I let him pull me down another road, through the stands and around the shoppers. I was still thinking through how this could possibly work when he stopped next to a small shop. He looked at the table out front, showcasing fresh fruit.

"Are you really hungry?" I asked.

"I didn't eat anything." He tsked over a basket of fresh berries. "But no. However, the house with the dark brown door and large man standing out front is my brother's home."

I fought the urge to turn and look; instead I picked up an apple and stared at the peel. "What now, sneaky one? With your disdain for grappling hooks and fake mustaches."

"Do you trust me?" His eyes locked on mine.

I didn't respond immediately. He'd asked me that several times now. Did I trust Owen? Did I know that he wouldn't do anything to hurt me? My gut told me yes, but it was the sincerity in his eyes that made me respond out loud. "Yes."

"I promised to never lie to you." He looked at another basket of berries before handing them to the shop attendant to buy. "This is going to be dangerous and people will die.

I will do my best to make sure that we aren't among them."

"Okay then." I tried to calm my racing heart.

"I'm not always like this, Ava." He looked between us and I knew he meant how he treated me. "I've never hidden what I am and what I do, but you haven't seen it in action."

"I understand."

The employee handed Owen the basket of berries and his change before moseying off to help another shopper.

"You need to give me your gun."

"Right here, on the street?" I looked around us. "You're the daft one." I smiled. "Ha! I said daft!"

"Not here. Come with me." He pulled me into a small clothing shop and pushed me toward the back. "Wrap it in your sweater and we'll put it in my bag."

Grabbing a shirt from a random rack, I headed toward the back where the fitting rooms were located. I pulled the curtain closed and spun in a circle. There was a full length mirror, a hook, and nothing else. I hung the shirt on the hook, checked the curtain one more time and ripped off my sweater. Throwing it on the floor I reached behind me and tried to pull the gun out of the holster without shooting one of my buns off. It wouldn't budge, so I had to unbutton my jeans. Peeking over my shoulder I tried to pull the pistol and holster off at the same time, but it was stuck in there good. Becoming frustrated, I yanked as hard as I could. The gun and holster came free from my pants and spun in the air. Whipping around, I tried to juggle it between my hands, but was terrified my finger would catch the trigger.

With a loud clunk, the gun hit the floor and I

squeezed my eyes shut. As soon as I realized it hadn't gone off and that I hadn't been shot, I scrambled to pick it up from the floor and wrap it in my sweater. Really, I knew better. Guns didn't just go off when they were dropped, but it was hard to fight that immediate reaction.

I looked in the mirror and took a deep breath. My face was pale and there were circles under my eyes. I had slept well the night before—being exhausted had a way of making sure you did that— but nightmares had made it difficult to truly rest. A tap on the wall next to the curtain made me scramble around and shove the sweater-wrapped gun behind my back.

"Someone's in here." My voice was too high.

"Everything okay in there?" Owen's voice was quiet.

"Yeah. I'm just finishing." Grabbing the shirt from the hook, I tucked my sweater under my arm and pushed the heavy material out of my way. "Didn't fit."

Walking over to the rack I replaced the shirt and turned to Owen. "Ready?"

"Are you?" He placed a hand on my cheek.

"Yeah." Sure I was ready. Why wouldn't I be ready to march into the house of the man that wanted to hold me hostage? Pfft. I shrugged and handed him my balled up sweater. "Here, put this in your bag, will you?"

He took the hidden gun from my hand and stuck it into his bag. "Let's go."

Placing a hand on the small of my back, he guided me out of the shop. "Do as I say. I don't know what Marcus has gotten himself into, but I have a feeling it's ugly."

"Gee, you think?" I fidgeted with my shirt as we walked. It kept falling forward, the neckline revealing more cleavage than I wanted.

"Leave it." Owen's eyes dipped down to the top of my breasts.

"What?" My eyebrow raised in annoyance. Now wasn't the time for him to be telling me how to dress. In fact, never would the perfect time for him to tell me how to dress.

"It'll work to our advantage." His eyes moved up to my face. "It will make you look vulnerable and distracting."

"Vulnerable?" I sneered. "That's the last thing I want to look like!"

"It's always better to be underestimated, Ava." He reached over and grabbed my arm, his fingers tightening enough to make me glare at him. "I'm sorry, but we have to make this look right."

"What the hell are you doing?" I pulled on my arm but he didn't let go.

"I'm taking you to my brother." Without missing a step, he marched directly to the front door of the house he had pointed out earlier.

"Owen." I pulled on my arm a little. "You're hurting me." Being restrained was starting to make me panic, despite my brain's reassurances.

With a quick movement he threw his bag at the feet of the man standing guard on the steps. "I need to see Marcus."

"Yeah, and I want to be King." The man shrugged lazily, but I could feel his eyes sweeping my body. "So what?"

"Tell him his brother is here and that I want to make a trade." Owen pushed me forward, but didn't let go.

I looked up at the man gripping my arm. His eyes

were hard and cold. I swallowed. I liked it much better when Owen was fighting a smile or looking at me with a slightly confused expression. This Owen was distant and rigid as if his stare would cut through metal.

The man spoke into a little piece of plastic attached to his shirt. We stood there, my heart beating so loudly I knew everyone could hear it. I glared at the man on the steps as he leered down at me.

"Come in." The man opened the door and motioned for us to step inside. Owen pulled me along quickly and I sneered at him, continuing with my difficult hostage act. Inside, two men were waiting with guns drawn. Owen let go of me and held his arms out at his sides. One of the men stepped forward and patted him down, taking the weapons he had stashed in his pants and shirt. I had seen him hide all of them, but it still amazed me to see the pile that was growing on the table in the small foyer. His gaze was blank, as if there wasn't a thought in his head.

"He's clean." The man stepped back and looked at the one holding the gun.

"Take the girl downstairs." His gruff voice sent chills down my spine and I froze at the thought of what was downstairs.

"No." Owen's voice brokered no argument. "She's my hostage. She stays with me until the trade is done. Or no trade, and I walk."

"Boss said she gets put in the stables, you can barter by yourself."

"The stables? Are you fucking serious?" The words burst out of my mouth before I could rethink them.

"Shut up, bitch." The man with the gun looked at me. "You'll do as you're told."

"She stays with me until I get what I want." Owen stepped forward until the gun pressed into his sternum. "Or I kill you all and take what I want anyway."

"Yeah right, mate."

There was no hesitation in Owen's movement when he grabbed the gun, breaking the man's hold on it at the same time he delivered a painful, cracking kick to the man's knee. The man crumpled to the floor, his face twisted in pain, and the sound of his neck snapping filled the foyer.

The other man took a step back, but it was too late. Owen moved so quickly there was nothing that could stop him. He slammed his fist into the man's jaw, sending him sprawling.

Owen looked down at the man on the floor and pointed the gun at his head. "Did you think Marcus hired all of you to protect him because I would be easily intimidated?"

"Fuck you." The man glared at Owen.

Owen's finger tightened on the trigger and I was certain I was about to be covered in the man's brain goo. He stopped just before looking toward the people making their way downstairs. Four men with machine guns stopped and stared at us, their faces set in angry lines. My heart dropped as they pointed their guns in our direction. For one beat of my heart I was certain we were about to be mowed down by a thousand bullets. But then a radio crackled, and a voice came over it, sounding steady and also bored.

"Hold your fire. Guns down."

The man that had checked Owen for weapons grabbed my arm and pulled me against his chest. I wasn't sure if he was intending to use me as a human shield or if he thought having control over me equaled control over Owen. If it was the latter thought then our ruse wasn't worth playing any longer. Hoping that wasn't the case I fought against him, but I couldn't break away. Owen's eyes darted to me before lowering his gun. With a few quick movements he dropped the clip and kicked it across the room before flipping the gun over in his hand and bringing the butt down across the kneeling man's temple. The bodyguard crumpled to the floor with no sound. Owen calmly set the gun down on the table next to him before putting his hands on the back of his head.

"Well, you always did enjoy making an entrance." A man stepped down the stairs around the armed guards. His hair was lighter and his eyes were blue, not the bright green of Owen's, but there was no denying they were brothers. They shared the same nose and body build, but there was something softer and more metrosexual to Marcus. As if he had polished off all of Owen's rougher edges. I'm sure he had meant to give himself a more relatable, relaxed businessman vibe, but instead he looked oily and untrustworthy.

"I've always known how to get your attention." Owen lowered his arms. "We need to talk."

"I'll bet you have a lot to say." Marcus tucked his hands into his suit pockets and smiled.

Owen didn't respond, just looked at his brother with a steady gaze, and I wondered what was going through his mind. Regret? Curiosity? Anger? All of those? Maybe remorse? His features were settled into a blank look as if he was completely unfazed and unbothered by everything going on around him.

"Take the girl downstairs." Marcus looked over at

160

me. His eyes ran over my body in a slow perusal. "Contact Maria's people."

"Who is Maria? What the hell do you want with me?" I struggled against the man holding me, my voice coming out in pants. The thought of being taken somewhere called the 'Stables' made my blood freeze. "What are you going to do to me?"

"Relax." Marcus smiled at me, but it didn't reach his eyes. "We're just holding you for a little while. If you're still here by dinner, I'll even invite you to dine with me."

"Who is Maria?" I yelled again as I fought the man trying to take me out of the room.

"She stays until we have a deal." Owen never took his eyes off his brother and I tried to curtail my panic. He wouldn't let them hurt me. He wouldn't, I reminded myself. "I'm not the brother that put a price on the other ones head."

"Fine. She stays." Marcus looked at the men on the stairs. "He wouldn't kill me. Leave us."

"Sir?" The man holding me dropped my arms and I almost fell to the ground. He obviously didn't agree with his boss's decision. I pushed myself back into a standing position and jerked further away from the man. Owen still didn't look at me and I was glad. I'm not sure why I did it. What possessed me to do it. Maybe it was the need to do something, the need to point my fear in some direction. Maybe it was to try and make our cover story look even more real. But no, I didn't give it that much thought. I just took a step forward and slammed my fist into Owen's side as hard as I could.

"You're an asshole!"

He 'oofed' under his breath but barely moved. Marcus on the other hand laughed while the men with the large guns dropped them to their sides and filed out of the room.

Owen still didn't look at me, which scared me. He wasn't angry, or confused. He looked bored, as bored as his brother. Who could be bored in the middle of a situation like this? People were just waiting to shoot us—or worse.

"You really brought her here to trade?" Marcus walked toward me and ran his eyes over my cleavage and down my backside. I turned to keep him in my eyesight, afraid of what he might do if I couldn't see him. There was lust in his eyes, but worse: there was calculation. Like a farmer at market, judging a new cow. He trailed his fingers down my arm and across my stomach. "Had a bit of fun first though, huh? Told her sweet nothings, took her for a ride, and then brought her here to me. I knew you were a cold fish, brother."

I glared at Marcus even though my stomach was rolling. I told Owen I trusted him and I knew he had a part to play. I wouldn't freak out just because Marcus seemed to be buying it.

"Why did you put a price on my head?" Owen stepped away from me as if he thought I might cling to his arm.

"You were in my way." Marcus shrugged. "I needed the girl. And you had her."

"You put a five million pound bounty on my head to collect a forty thousand dollar profit? Not buying it," Owen said.

"Worth it not have to deal with you," Marcus spat.

"You could have called." Owen raised an eyebrow.

"What? And play Russian Roulette with your sweet

conscience? No." Marcus leaned against the wall with one shoulder. "No. I needed something that would ensure you would bring her in."

"Who set up the contract?" Owen kept his hands at his sides as if assuring Marcus that he was harmless.

"Local business woman." Marcus picked up one of Owen's knives from the table and looked it over. "She's quite the entrepreneur."

"How many people did you have me kill for a slave trader?" Something hard glinted under Owen's tone.

"See, there it is. Your annoying conscience. Do you know how much money we've lost over the years because you would only take certain cases?" Marcus set the knife down. "The bad guys pay much better, Owen." He shook his head and took a step toward me. "And she's not a slave trader. She has more than enough women working for her willingly. It's much easier to control someone when they want to make money and you're the one that signs their check."

"Why me?" I said the words quietly. We were here for information and I needed it. I needed to understand why people were after me.

"Why would I care?" Marcus twirled a lock of hair from my pony tail around his finger.

"Maria...this Maria you were talking about. Does she normally tell you to get specific women?" Every muscle in my body tensed. I felt like I was being sniffed by a rabid dog and at any minute he might bite.

"Usually I clean up her messes." He leaned close to my ear. "Though I have helped her fill a few *specific* orders for clients."

"How long?" Owen's voice cut through the room.

"How many did you lie about?"

"I didn't." Marcus looked away from me. "I kept you as far away from my profitable business as I could. In fact, I didn't want you to have the Song case, but Maria insisted." He sighed. "But I knew this would happen. You'd stick your nose into something that wasn't your business and ruin what we had going."

"I made you rich, Marcus. How much money do you need?" Owen's lip twitched in disgust.

"We started out with so little, but there is much, much more out there for the taking." Marcus shrugged. "You know I never was one to settle."

"You knew I would come to you." Owen narrowed his eyes.

"Of course." Marcus turned away from him and looked back at me. "I knew those men wouldn't be enough to take you out, but I knew it would make you bring me the girl." His eyes watched my face carefully. "I had my doubts of course. She's rather pretty. Then again, here you are."

"Are we even, then?" Owen asked. "You call off the hunt for me. I walk away now. End of story."

I knew Owen was bluffing, but his cold words still stung.

"We're even." Marcus touched my cheek and I twitched away from him. His words were for Owen, but his eyes were trained on me. "I called it off when I was certain you were heading to London."

"And the girl?" Owen turned around and started picking up his weapons.

"She is Maria's problem." Marcus turned away from me. "Apparently this one's husband has something that belongs to the woman." He looked back at me. "Though I'm not sure she'll be worth trading if her husband finds out she's been fucking you."

My insides froze and I fought to breathe. They were looking for Tess, not me. I tried to regain my composure, lest I give away the fact that I wasn't who they really wanted. If they found out, they would start looking for my friend and she had no heads up, no one to protect her. No Owen.

"Who is Maria?" Owen tucked his gun into his pants while watching Marcus. From the angle I was standing at, I caught the glint of a knife as Owen palmed the blade.

"Not anyone that concerns you." Marcus wrapped his fingers around my arm and I tried to jerk away. "I'm assuming that this is the end of our work arrangement?"

"I can't trust you." Owen shrugged. "I can't work with you."

"Mum always said to trust no one."

"I don't think she was talking about each other, Marcus." Owen shook his head.

"We'll never know." Marcus pulled me closer to him. "I was certain you'd try to kill me. It's much easier this way."

"Just stay out of my way." Owen turned toward the door, stooping down to grab his bag of weapons.

My heart dropped as I watched him walk away without looking back. He was leaving me; leaving me with the man that wanted to give me to some woman that sounded like the villain in a comic book. I had trusted him, but my faith was starting to waver. What did I really know about him?

"The least I can do." Marcus used his free hand to

reach in his jacket. The glint of metal caught my eye and I panicked.

"Owen!" I balled up my free hand and swung it down and backward into his crotch as hard as I could. He crumpled behind me.

"Bitch!" Marcus shoved me to the ground and my head slammed into the table as I fell. Pain exploded behind my eyes, but I scrambled to get upright. I couldn't afford to be on the floor right now. Unfortunately, my legs weren't working quite right.

I could hear people running through the house, shouting from upstairs, and Owen said something, but I couldn't make out the words. I push to get off of the floor, adrenaline pumping through my veins, but my feet still wouldn't support me. I caught a glimpse of Marcus pulling a knife out of his shoulder, blood dripping down his linen jacket.

Owen grabbed my hand and pulled me up, pushing his bag into my arms and me toward the front door. Just as I reached for the handle it turned and the door swung open. Owen moved like quicksilver, and his fists flew, rendering the new man impotent. Spinning around he pulled his gun and shot the first guard that came down the stairs.

It was like watching an action movie, but in slow motion. My ears were ringing and I couldn't focus on anything. I pushed forward, trying to get out. After stepping on the man Owen had incapacitated, I was almost out the door when Owen's voice ripped through the air.

"Ava!" There was so much anguish in his voice I turned in midstep, just in time to see the gun pointed at my head. My body froze, every muscle, every cell, every atom just stopped.

Something large and heavy slammed against me,

knocking the wind out of my lungs. I fell face first on the cement stairs and for a moment wonder if I'd been shot, but the person on my back rolled off to the side. Slick fingers wrapped around mine, urging me to stand, and I looked up into Owen's face. Once I was on my feet, he let go of me and pushed me toward the street.

Pulling one of his guns from his holster, he fired behind us. The sound was so loud it felt like a bomb going off in my head. Or maybe I had a concussion. I wasn't really thinking straight. I reached to rub the sore spot on my head where I'd hit the table, and my hand came away red. Was that my blood, or someone else's? But there was no time to think about it as another volley of gunshots rang out.

People were watching from behind cars and trash cans, afraid to move. A black car skidded around the corner and came to a screeching halt in front of us.

"Bloody hell." Mavis rolled down her window and fired two quick shots past us. "Get in."

I grabbed the door handle with still-bloody fingers, and the sight made me dizzy. I turned around in a panic, looking for Owen, but he was right behind me.

"Get in, Ava." His eyes were calm, despite the red that stained his shirt.

Hurrying, I opened the door and threw myself across the bench seat, leaving room for Owen. He fired two shots before ducking into the seat. He reached for the door handle and winced, but made no sound. He almost didn't get the door shut, but luckily when Mavis hit the gas, the door swung backward and latched.

"Oh my God." I ran my hand over his arm but he shooed me away. "Stop that! You've been shot!"

"I noticed." A little of his temper peeked through his calm façade.

"Let me look!" I reached for his shirt but he gave me a stern look.

"I'm fine. Right now we just need to get out of here."

"I should kill you for going in there without me." Mavis's cool voice floated from the front of the car. "And if you lost my lead, I *will* kill you."

"You wouldn't have saved us if you were going to do that." Owen shook his head. "And you're looking for a Maria. She's local."

"Right then. Try to not bleed all over the seat." Mavis responded calmly as if she wasn't dodging cars and pedestrians, her anger dissipating.

"Where are you taking us?" I asked as I opened Owen's bag and pulled out my sweater.

"A safe place."

"Right. I don't believe in those anymore." I ducked lower in the seat and noticed Owen's eyes snap shut in pain when the car hit a large pot hole. "So where is it?"

"It's fine, Ava." He turned to look out the window.

"No one is following us," Mavis told him. I could see her bright eyes watching us in the rear view mirror.

"Don't go straight to your place."

"Thank you, Owen, but I've done this once or twice on my own." I could practically hear her rolling her eyes. "If you want to drive next time, don't go into the bad guy's house without back up, and don't get shot along the way."

I pulled at his sweater, trying to find the wound. I knew he was feeling bad if he wasn't complaining any more. When I found the source of the blood, my stomach rolled. It took a minute before I could actually make sense of what I was seeing. I leaned close to try and see if there was any bullet, but couldn't see anything.

"It's a flesh wound." I looked up into Owen's calm eyes.

"How can you know?" I looked back at the wound.

"Would have made a bigger hole otherwise." He took a deep breath.

I made him lean forward so I could wrap the sweater around his shoulder to try and slow the bleeding. As I held my hands pressed against the injury an ugly thought began to fill my mind. He had been shot from behind and in the top of his shoulder. As if he had been running.

Running to tackle someone.

"That bullet was meant for me."

CHAPTER FOURTEEN

Owen

BEING SHOT WAS never fun. I'd been shot once before, in the leg. That hadn't been fun either. The weird part was that it had happened before my current occupation. There was a reason becoming an assassin had seemed like a logical job choice. My childhood hadn't been a picnic.

However, having Ava look at me with those big eyes while her tiny hands pressed against me almost made it worthwhile. Almost. Bruises were already developing along her cheekbone and above her left eye. They hurt me more than the damn gun shot.

"Marcus said a woman is in charged. Her name is Maria." I frowned as I went over the details of my meeting with her. "She's the one that hired me to kill Song."

"Why did you take his case?" Mavis asked. She knew I was picky when it came to hits.

"He was a sex slave trader."

She didn't respond and I knew from the way her shoulders stiffened she was thinking about her friend.

"It looks like she's into a lot of different things."

"Then we need to find this Maria and get her to tell us where Laura is and why she is trying to kill Tessa. And me." Ava's voice was firm.

Mavis hit another pothole and Ava's tiny little hands felt more like hot irons as they pushed against me.

"Oy, pay attention, woman!" I growled.

"Sorry," Ava winced.

"I didn't mean you." I looked at her and tried to smile. It probably wasn't as comforting as I had intended because her face blanched.

"It's not my damn fault there are potholes on this road." Mavis growled from the front seat. "Take it up with Parliament."

"I'll send a letter with my taxes." I closed my eyes and breathed deep through my nose.

Mavis barked a loud laugh. "Right."

"We should take you to a hospital." Ava pressed her hand against my shoulder. "You're losing a lot of blood."

"No hospitals." I opened my eyes and looked at Ava. "Besides, it's not that bad. Mavis can fix me up."

"Aren't you lucky?" Mavis asked.

"But you need medicine, and to be checked out." Ava shook her head.

"I'm fine." I touched her cheek. I couldn't remember the last time someone had been worried about me. It was…nice and a bit frustrating, but in a good way. "This is an easy fix."

She narrowed her eyes and sucked her bottom lip into her mouth. I hated seeing her so upset, but I'd known this was a possible outcome going in there. It could have gone much worse, to be honest. However, we weren't going to get any answers without some risks. And I wasn't willing to let Ava pay the dues.

"No one has followed us. I'm taking us to a house." Mavis turned down a small road. "Can you walk?"

I curled my lip. "I was shot in the shoulder, not my foot. Of course I can walk."

"Good, because you're too big to carry." Mavis slammed the car into park in a tiny spot behind a building. The other buildings were so close I wondered how I was going to open the door wide enough to get out.

My fingers slipped on the door handle and Ava reached over me to push it open before hurrying out of her side.

"Are you okay?" Mavis asked quietly. She turned in her seat and let her eyes roam over my bloody shirt. I knew she was asking while Ava couldn't hear on purpose.

"Bloody hurts, but I'll live." I kept my voice calm. No jokes. She needed to know where I was, because we were in trouble. Marcus would send men out looking for us and by now he would know that Mavis had helped us.

"Good."

My door opened and Ava stood there with her hands out like she was going to help me stand. Part of me wanted to laugh, the other part of me felt weird and gooey. That had to be the blood loss. Her cool hands wrapped around my uninjured arm and she looped it over her shoulders. My eyebrows rose and I felt the twitch of my lips.

Mavis was watching us with an amused expression that she quickly schooled into one of boredom when Ava looked her way.

"Where are we going?" Ava asked.

"This way." Mavis turned around and climbed a short set of stairs.

"Lean on me if you need to." Ava placed a hand on my stomach as she urged me forward.

"You know, I've been shot before." I smiled down at her as she tried to push me up the stairs. I wanted her to understand that I was really going to be okay.

"Yeah, but this time it was for me." Her eyes welled up and I reached to catch a tear with my thumb. Her cheek was puffy under my fingers and I wished I could go back and beat all of those guys again.

I didn't know what to say, so it was best if I kept my mouth shut. Seeing the gun pointed in her direction had sent fire like panic through my veins. I had acted on instinct, not worried about anything but getting her out of harm's way. When we hit the ground I had been more worried about checking on her than concerned with my shoulder.

"Are you two going to stand there all night?" Mavis stuck her head out the door. "If you pass out, I'm not hauling your sorry carcass in here."

Ava sighed and pulled me the rest of the way up the stairs. It was an older building, riddled with hallways and tiny rooms. Mavis was at a small kitchen table going through a bag of medical supplies. I took a seat next to her and pulled off my jumper and shirt. The wound wasn't pretty, but would be easy to clean up and stitch. I could do it myself, but it would be easier if someone else did the sewing. Thankfully, Mavis was a pro.

"What can I do to help?" Ava looked pale.

"Do you have any medical training?" Mavis looked up at her.

"No." She shook her head. "But I can get stuff. Or boil water. I don't know. What the fuck do you do for a

173

gunshot wound?"

I was relieved to hear her cursing. It meant she wasn't going into shock. At least I thought it meant she wasn't going into shock. I didn't exactly have a lot of medical training myself. I just stepped over bodies on my way out.

"Sure, boil some water." Mavis twisted my arm, making me grimace. "I could use a cup of tea."

"Tea?" Ava stood there looking at Mavis with a strange expression. "Bloody Brits and their tea." She muttered as she turned around and rummaged through the cabinets.

Mavis went to work on my arm, squirting cool liquid over the wound, before giving me a numbing shot. I let my mind wander, trying to not focus on what the woman was doing to my arm. Ava provided a good distraction as she moved around the kitchen muttering to herself. She was favoring her left leg, but not enough that most people would notice.

"Where the hell do you keep the cups?" She looked over her shoulder at Mavis before quickly turning away.

"How would I know?" Mavis didn't look up. She was threading her needle and getting ready to stitch.

"It's your house." Ava said it so calmly I knew she was forcing the words through her teeth.

"No it isn't." Mavis replied.

"What do you mean it isn't your house?" I watched Ava turn around and look at us.

"I mean, I don't own it. Don't live here. Don't stay here." Mavis looked over at Ava in exasperation. "I'm kind of busy, if you haven't noticed."

"But—you knew there was a first aid kit." Ava twisted the rag in her hand. "Whose house is it?"

"An old man that now lives in assisted living. I knew there would be medical supplies here, because he's been sick for a long time." Mavis started stitching, her attention on the wound, her words an afterthought. "I saw him being helped in here by nurses one day and then out in an ambulance another day."

"There might not have been a medical kit here." Ava frowned before turning around to search for cups and I let myself be distracted by the view of her ass as she bent over. "That was a big gamble. What would you have done if there hadn't been anything?"

"Made do." Mavis stuck one end of the thread in her mouth as she tied off one knot. "Here, come over here and try one."

Ava set a cup of tea next to me and one next to Mavis. I saw the liquid splash over the rim as her hand shook. She closed her eyes for a moment and took a deep breath. After a second she moved closer to me and peered down at the wound.

"What are you doing?" she asked.

"Cleaning out the foreign debris." Mavis squinted at my arm. "I missed some earlier."

"That's just great." I felt my eyebrows draw together.

"Shut up." Mavis snapped at me before turning to Ava. "Here, when you're stitching someone, you want to use the smallest needle possible."

Ava took the needle with shaking fingers.

"Maybe you should just let Mavis so this." I watched the needle with apprehension.

"I trust you, you trust me." Her hand stilled and she glared at me.

"Fine." I let out a slow breath. Her fingers were cold

175

on my arm as Mavis coached her through where to place the stitch and how to tie the knot before cutting the thread. If I wasn't mistaken, they were using a thin fishing line.

"Move over a little bit to the right."

"Here?" Ava touched a spot below the wound.

"That's good." Mavis nodded.

I closed my eyes as they worked, making no sound when Ava pulled the stitch a little too tight. When it was completely closed Ava bandaged the area with gauze and white tape. Her hands had been steady as she'd stitched my wound, but they were shaking again now that she was finished.

"Are you okay?" I asked her quietly.

"What?" She opened her eyes and looked at me. "Sure I am. Why wouldn't I be? It's not like people don't get shot every day; or break into houses to use medical equipment. Totally normal. All of this." She took a sip of her tea. "Every bit of it."

"It really is for me. Thanks, Mavis." I rolled my shoulder when Mavis finished dressing the wound. Grabbing my bloody clothes I got up and put them in the trash bin. If I took the trash out before we left then no one would even check to see if there was a bloody shirt inside.

"I know." Sighing she turned around and poured the rest of the tea in the sink.

"Not good?"

"No matter how much I try, I just don't like it. Tea should be sweet and cold." She smiled sadly.

"I tried sweet tea once in New Orleans. It was like drinking a cake through a straw." I wrinkled my nose. She laughed and the tension between my shoulders loosened a little.

Mavis was cleaning up the mess quietly, her expression blank. I knew from experience that a blank expression was a bad sign. She was worried.

"Are we safe here tonight?" I asked her.

"Should be." She shrugged. "I was careful, but you never know."

"Okay. We recoup and strategize." I headed out of the kitchen.

"Where are you going?" Ava asked.

"To find a new shirt." I offered her a weak smile.

"You're going to steal an old man's clothes?" She raised an eyebrow.

"Would you rather me run around naked?" My smile grew. "I could do that."

Red filled her cheeks and her eyes darted toward Mavis before coming back to me. She waved her hand in the direction of the stairs. "Do what you have to do."

I chuckled as I turned a corner and took the stairs slowly. At the top I leaned against the wall and took a deep breath. I'd lost more blood than I realized if walking up the stairs winded me. Looking around I saw the door that led to the bathroom slightly ajar. Pushing through I turned on the sink and splashed water on my face.

Blood was smeared along my jaw so I used a wash cloth from the shelf to scrub it away. There was a small cut that would heal pretty quickly. I rinsed the rag carefully before cleaning off the sink and throwing it in the trash. There were two other doors on this floor and one led into a small bedroom.

I checked the bureau and pulled out a white shirt. It smelled a bit like mothballs but it was better than nothing. It was tight but didn't pull at the bandage which was good.

I sat down on the edge of the bed and let my head fall back.

Marcus.

My brother had tried to kill me. Not just ordered someone to kill me, but was going to pull the trigger himself. I in turn and pinged him with a throwing knife. Then again, considering our family, I guess I shouldn't have been so surprised.

He'd run his hands over Ava because he knew that I wouldn't like it. He was selling hostages to people. He had been using me until I wasn't necessary.

It wasn't that it surprised me that he would do it. It surprised me that it hurt.

A soft knock on the door made me open my eyes.

"Owen?" I could see Ava's bright blue eyes through the crack in the door.

"Come in."

"You okay?" She closed the door behind her and put her hands behind her back like a kid told not to touch things in a store.

"I'm fine."

She took a couple of steps to close the distance between us. With a slow hand she reached out and touched my jaw. "What happened here?"

I fought my desire to close my eyes as she touched me. "It's a little fuzzy."

"Can I do anything to help?" Her words were quiet. I looked up to see the concern etched on her face. Concern for me.

"Sit with me?" The words exited my mouth before I could rethink them. It was fucking weak, but I wanted to have her near me.

She didn't say anything, just sat down next to me. Our arms brushed against each other and she played with the hem of her shirt. I took a deep breath and closed my eyes. It was nice to know that she wasn't going to try to hurt me. To use me for something. Wasn't that how I should have felt about my brother? About my mother?

"Marcus is a year older than me." The words were hard to say. For so long I'd kept every little detail about my life locked away in a vault. It felt weird to even say Marcus' name out loud. "He was always the brain, the schemer. I thought he knew everything."

Her hand moved and she threaded her fingers through mine, but didn't say anything.

"It was just us and our mum. She was a whore." I wasn't trying to make her upset, but I'd promised to tell her the truth. "We didn't see her often and when we did we wished that we hadn't. She wasn't horrible. She didn't beat us and we had food, but she always looked close to death. Like she had given up her will to live."

Her fingers tightened on mine, but I just felt hollow as I explained my life to her.

"By the time I was seventeen I'd followed in Marcus's footsteps and was running with a bunch of thugs. Underground fights, that sort of thing. I didn't visit my mother often. I barely came home. When I did, it was to give her some of my prize money. I had a pocket full of cash that day I found her on the front porch. She was unconscious. Her face was beaten so badly I wasn't sure if it was her at first. It was... bad."

"I'm so sorry."

"She was hemorrhaging from her kidney. It was touch and go for a while." I shrugged. "The police came, but there wasn't much to report. They said it could have been a john, not her pimp, so without her testimony there wasn't much they could do."

"That's bullshit."

I snorted. "Yeah."

"Did they ever find out who did it?" Anger laced her words. Anger for my dead mother, a prostitute she had never met.

"No. They didn't." I closed my mouth at that point. I wasn't a saint. I wasn't an avenging angel like Mrs. Abernathy thought. I was just a murderer.

"But you did." Her words were calm.

"Her pimp came to the hospital and wanted to know when she was going back to work." I looked at her so that she would understand I had no regrets about what I'd done. "He said she'd been late with her money. Called her names and threatened Marcus. I would have killed him there if a nurse hadn't come in."

Tears glistened on her cheek, but if I stopped now I'd never finish the story.

"He laughed as he left. When they told us there was nothing else they could do for my mum and pulled the plug, I went straight to his place."

"Didn't he have bodyguards or something?"

"One of them managed to shoot me in my thigh."

"What happened? How did you get away?"

"I killed them all."

She swallowed.

"There were five." An image of the room flashed through my mind, the thick stink of smoke, and dreary lighting. "They'd been counting their take for the day. I remember some of the women grabbing stacks of bills off the table before they ran out."

"Did the police find you?"

"Marcus did. I was sitting at the table, staring at the blood. He tried to get me to leave, but I wouldn't move. Probably shock." I shrugged. "When he realized I'd been shot, he called Edgar to help get me out of there. I don't think I said anything until they started shoving money in their pockets. Marcus told me we had to run and we'd need the money."

"There are a lot of people out there that would have done the exact same thing, Owen." She turned toward me so that her legs pressed against mine. "I'm not sure I wouldn't have killed him after watching my mom die."

"I didn't just kill him, Ava. I killed all of them." Her eyes met my stare without flinching. "I enjoyed killing them, felt satisfaction when they were dead. I knew they wouldn't be able to kill those other women the way they had my mum. All of that adrenaline had added up to five dead bodies, but it hadn't brought my mother back."

Ava looked down at our joined hands before tracing the line of words tattooed on my arm.

"Find what you love and let it kill you." Her fingers were cool against my skin. "Who said that?"

"Charles Bukowski." I looked at my arm. "I was young and thought it made sense, given what I do."

"But not anymore?" Her bright eyes met mine.

"The meaning changed as I grew older." I shrugged, unsure I could explain how I felt.

"What does it mean to you now?"

"Not what I thought it did yesterday."

CHAPTER FIFTEEN

Ava

MAVIS WAS TAPPING her spoon on the table and I was debating if I was fast enough to snatch it out of her hand. I had a feeling I wasn't and that she'd end up killing me with it instead. My head was throbbing and the bag of ice I was holding to my cheek didn't seem to be helping at all. As the adrenaline left my system, I realized I hurt pretty much everywhere.

"Can you please stop?" I looked pointedly at the spoon.

"Sorry." Mavis sat the spoon down and returned her gaze to the clock above the kitchen sink. Within seconds her foot took up the same rhythm against the table leg.

"Ava, did you use my phone?" Owen walked into the kitchen, his expression blank.

Busted.

"Um, yeah. I sent an email the other day."

"No, no. Say it like you aren't guilty." Mavis perked up. "Make him feel bad for asking. You've got to mean it. 'Of course I sent an email. Did you expect me to sit around and do nothing while evil henchmen stalked me?'"

"Um." I looked back at Owen who was staring at me. His blank expression was slipping into one of frustration. "Did she respond?"

"No." His voice was calm.

"Oooh. He's mad." Mavis sat back in her chair and crossed her arms.

"Would you stop it?" I glared at her.

"Yes, just like that, but to him." She jerked her chin in Owen's direction.

"I'm serious. You're making this worse." I chewed on my bottom lip. I felt like I'd betrayed him. And he found out just after his brother had tried to kill him.

"Oh, good." Mavis smiled and I pictured punching her face. Maybe I'd get in one good hit before she reacted. Her smile wilted and she rolled her eyes. "Okay. Fine. I'll go. But I'm going to listen from the other room."

She took her time extracting herself from the table and walked slowly across the linoleum. She had taken her tall shoes off and she seemed even smaller next to Owen. Her hand darted out and she rubbed his good arm. He leaned down and listened to something she said. Jealousy bubbled up my throat and I squashed it. He wasn't mine. I had no real claim to him, just a fictional story to hide behind in public.

When she walked off he sat down in her chair and watched me.

"I emailed Tessa. I used our old email addresses. She probably hasn't even gotten it." I lowered my voice, certain that Mavis would follow through with her threat to listen from the other room.

"I thought you agreed to not contact her." He sat his

183

phone down on the table.

"I figured that no one would look for email addresses we used years ago, but if Tessa thinks I'm in trouble she will go through everything."

He sighed and looked up at the ceiling. "I'm trying."

"Trying to what?" I cringed a little.

"To not lose my temper. Mavis reminded me that you aren't like us. You don't know how to handle this." He lifted his good shoulder. "You're normal."

I narrowed my eyes. "Thank you for that glowing compliment."

"I just meant you were bound to do something like this."

"Like what?" I leaned back in my chair and crossed my arms. "Like worrying about a dear friend and trying to warn her that she was in trouble?"

"Exactly." He leaned forward. "These people are the real thing. If your parents kept journals, they will find them. An active email account you don't use anymore? That's just a few minutes of work. If she responds, they will know exactly where she's staying."

"So I was just supposed to sit back and let her blunder into this mess? She's family. She's all I've got left and I'm going to try to keep her safe." I stood up. "I might be normal, but I'm not stupid. I knew if I asked you again, I would get the same answer. So I took an opportunity when I saw it."

"That's not—"

"No, it's okay. Go yuk it up with Mavis. I don't know how to hogtie a three hundred pound man. I can't speak Mandarin or German. I don't know how to disassemble and reassemble an assault rifle in twenty seconds. I'm just a boring old normal person, scared out of my mind and trying to keep my only friend and myself alive." I wasn't making sense but I didn't care. I thought I'd been pretty calm considering everything that I'd gone through. Apparently the word normal was my secret trigger.

For the first time since I'd met him, Owen looked frightened. I checked over my shoulder to see if someone was standing behind me, but there was no one there. Go figure. The man could kill people with a punch but my meltdown scared him.

Turning on my heel I stomped out of the kitchen. Mavis was sitting in an old wingback chair next to the stairs. She gave me a thumbs-up and I growled at her. She was not nearly as funny as she thought. There wasn't much upstairs, but I couldn't go back downstairs. What was the point of storming away if I just went right back?

I picked the room Owen had used earlier and slammed the door.

I'd like to say it made me feel better, but it didn't. I could go open and slam shut the door another forty times and I still wouldn't feel better. I wasn't pissed at Owen.

No, I was sort of pissed at Owen. I was pissed at how he and Mavis seemed to have a connection I'd never understand. I wasn't stupid. I knew they'd slept together. That wasn't why I was mad at him.

Was it? No.

I was pissed at this whole situation. Every single bit of it. I hated feeling lost and out of my element. I didn't even have the gun Owen had given me anymore.

I stomped back to the door and flung it open.

"And I want my damn gun back!"

I slammed the door again.

I was really tired of feeling helpless. I kicked the little table next to the bed.

It fell apart as if it was made of paper. The lamp and picture frame fell to the floor with a crash, the glass scattering across the old carpet.

"Oh, shit." I stepped carefully through the glass and tried to pick up the table. One of the legs fell back to the floor. "Well, fuck."

"Ava?" Owen knocked on the door.

"What?" I leaned the rest of the table against the wall and kicked some of the glass under the bed.

"Are you okay?" It sounded like he was leaning against the door and listening.

"I'm having a discussion with the furniture." I picked up the remains of the picture frame and set it on a shelf. I picked up the lamp and sighed. It was in three pieces all held together by the cord that ran through the center. It was a lost cause. There was nothing to do for it but sing some hymns and bury it. If only I had a roll of Owen's duct tape.

He cleared his throat outside the door. "I brought your gun."

I walked over to the door and pulled it open with my free hand, letting the lamp dangle from the other.

He was standing in the little hall, both hands by his side. A smaller gun was in his left hand, his larger version in his right.

"And you brought yours. Are we dueling? Pistols at sunset?" I held out my hand and took my gun.

"I didn't mean to upset you."

I looked at him. How was I supposed to explain that I'd just thrown a spectacular temper tantrum without sounding pathetic? I'd broken some sick old man's lamp.

"I'm sorry, Ava." He stepped a little closer and lowered his voice.

Tears welled up in my eyes and I looked down at the floor. Damnit. Now was not the time to angry-cry.

"I'm not mad at you." I took a breath and tried to will away the tears.

"You were rather convincing downstairs." He stepped into the room and closed the door behind him.

I turned around and put the lamp on the table and it crashed back to the floor. I stared at the mess on the floor and sniffed.

"Stupid table." I covered my face with my free hand.

"Are you crying?" Strong hands closed on my shoulders and turned me around. "Did you hurt yourself?"

"I'm not stupid!" I meant I wasn't stupid enough to hurt myself, but at this point I wasn't so sure. I might win a stupid award tonight.

"Of course you aren't." Owen's voice took on a soothing tone. It should have been weird to hear it come from his mouth, but it wasn't. He took my gun out of my hand and set it on the dresser next to his.

"I mean, I didn't hurt myself. I broke the lamp."

"I noticed." His hands rubbed my shoulders. "I'm sorry for what I said downstairs."

"Don't be. I'm not mad at you. You just made a good target." I wiped at my face. "I'm scared. I've been in scared mode for days now and it's starting to wear on me. And I'm worried about Tessa. And Mavis's friend that I've never even met. Maybe I shouldn't have sent the email, but it was killing me to feel like I was doing nothing. I feel like dead weight. I'm useless."

187

"You are not useless." He lifted my chin and I hoped there wasn't any snot on my face.

"Don't patronize me. I can't contribute. I have no money. I can't kill people. Well, unless it's with a car. My last job was as a receptionist at a place where they build planes. Knowing how to deal with rich customers and answering the phone isn't exactly helpful right now. I can make a killer pair of earrings but they aren't going to actually kill anyone." I sniffed. "I'm just trying to stay alive. You—you got shot because of me. And now—now I'm crying which isn't helpful either."

The tears were coming now and there was no stopping them. He pulled me against his chest and tucked my head under his chin. He didn't say anything, just held me while I cried.

When I finally got myself under control I pulled back and scrubbed at my face with the palms of my hands.

"I'm sorry I unloaded on you."

"I think you've earned it." He pulled me over to the bed and sat down. I sat next to him and stared at the broken glass on the dirty carpet. "You shouldn't have sent that email and I should have understood why you did it. I've been in tight spots before, but this is… pretty bad. I've been in worse, but this one isn't a cake walk either."

"You've accidently run over a man, been shot at by strangers for no reason, run away with a hot assassin, and let someone shield you from bullets like a pathetic non-warrior before?" I glared at him.

"You know, if you keep calling me hot, I'm going to start to think you like me." His green eyes twinkled in the dim light.

"Shut up." I shook my head but couldn't help the giggle that escaped. "I think I got snot on your shirt."

"It'll just mix in with the blood from my heroic act today." He smiled and my heart sped up.

"It goes nicely with the mothball smell."

"I didn't have many options." He lifted his arm and sniffed the sleeve. "It is pretty strong though."

"What do we do now?" Some of the tension had seeped from my shoulders and I realized I was exhausted.

"Mavis has contacts looking for a Maria. She's the one that wanted you, so that's our next step."

"You could go, Owen. Your brother won't keep looking for you." I brushed some of the hair out of my eyes.

"You're really throwing some mixed signals. One minute I'm hot, the next you're trying to get rid of me."

"I'm not joking. Your part in this is finished. There's no reason to get dragged any further into this mess." I needed him to understand. "I don't want you to get hurt because of me again. I can't—you can't jump in front of all the bullets pointed in my direction. I'm not worth that."

"We're in this together." He leaned forward. "You think you're useless, but you aren't. For the first time in a long time I don't feel toxic. You do that. You make me feel human. And for that, you're worth more than you'll ever understand. You're worth everything."

My heart stopped. If I lived long enough to look back on this moment one day, I would swear that time stopped. His barriers were down, his eyes earnest. I couldn't imagine how difficult it must've been for him to admit something like that.

"Owen..." I wanted to say something. But I didn't know how to explain the feeling in my chest. If I didn't know better I'd think I was having a heart attack, but I was

NICHOLE ● CHASE

sort of happy about it.

"Don't say anything." He shook his head. "I just wanted you to know that you are not useless. You are not worthless. Not to me."

Again, I was left speechless and close to tears.

He stood up and I realized the room was dark. Where had the day gone?

"It's late." Well, that was lame. High-five Ava. Way to follow up his beautiful words with an obvious comment.

"You should get some sleep. Mavis is downstairs and I'll take the room next to yours. Nothing will get past us." He moved toward the door and ice snaked through my body.

"No." I stood up. "Stay."

He turned to look at me and I wondered if he could see my blush in the dark.

"I'll sleep better if you're in here with me." I bit my lip and forced my breathing to stay even. "Like at the hotel. That was the best sleep I've gotten since I arrived in England." At the time I'd been nervous, but I'd also felt safe. And when I woke up that morning I'd felt good. It had felt right. Normal.

Maybe normal wasn't such a bad word.

I kicked off my shoes and undid the button on my jeans. Carefully I slipped them down and stepped free. Without looking at him I pulled the blanket back on the bed and climbed in. I lay on my side, facing the windows, and counted my breaths.

"Please."

He didn't move for five more breaths and I almost turned to check and see if he was still there. After a moment I heard the sound of fabric shifting and the mattress dipped under his weight. His arm snaked out and pulled me against him. He'd taken his shirt off and his skin was warm against mine. So maybe not just like at the hotel. I shifted so that my head was resting on his good shoulder.

"How's your arm?"

"Good." I liked the way his voice rumbled out of his chest. Carefully I slid my hand across his stomach. He covered my hand with his as if to show me it was working just fine.

"Thank you."

"You don't have to thank me, Ava. You never have to thank me."

CHAPTER SIXTEEN

Ava

SOMETHING WAS BEEPING near my head. Owen shifted, reaching for something on the shelf above the bed.

Owen.

My eyes popped open like I'd been electrocuted. He slid back into the bed and molded to my back, his arm around my waist.

"Go back to sleep. It's still early." His whisper sent a thrill through my body.

"What time is it?" I was scared to move. I didn't want him to pull away from me.

"Four thirty." His voice sounded groggy and I smiled. Sounded like he'd gotten some good sleep too. "Old bugger must've been an early riser."

"How's your arm?"

"Stiff." Hm. An honest answer. I'd have to remember to save my questions for early mornings.

"Do you want me to get you some ibuprofen?"

"No." His arm tightened around my midsection. "I want you to stay where you are."

"It'll only take a minute."

"I'm really okay." He lifted his head so he could look down at me. "But thank you for offering."

I let my eyes travel over his face. "Any time."

His eyes dipped down to my mouth and I licked my lips. This was the second time I'd woken up in this man's arms. There was no way I could let him go now without even a kiss.

I saw the doubt flash through his eyes, but I was ready for it this time.

I rolled over so that my body was flush with his and he had to look at me.

"Owen."

"Yes?" Tension wove through his voice.

"Kiss me."

His eyes flashed and I saw just a hint of his wild side peek through.

"You shouldn't want me. I'm not—"

"Don't you dare say you aren't good enough for me. I get to make that decision." I tilted my head and whispered, "And I decided that I want you."

His lips were feverishly warm when they touched mine. He fell back on the bed and dragged me onto his chest, never breaking the kiss. I cupped his face, kissing him with everything I had and I never, ever, wanted to stop. His hands tangled in my hair before running over my back and making circles just above the edge of the cotton panties I'd bought in Oxford.

He bent one jean-clad knee up and I settled between his legs. With one hand, he tilted my head up and ran his mouth down my neck before lightly dragging his teeth across my shoulder. I shivered and pressed closer. There was no way I'd ever be able to get enough of him. I ran one of my hands down to touch the warm skin of his chest, enjoying the way he seemed to shift so I could touch more of him.

When the hand on my lower back moved to cup my ass I sighed into his mouth. He shifted me so that I was pressed against the hard length straining through his jeans and I moved against him. The groan that escaped his mouth was an aphrodisiac. I sat up and pulled my shirt over my head, tossing it and my bra to the floor. Before I could lean back down to kiss him, he captured one of my breasts in his mouth. I let my head fall back while his tongue drew circles over my skin. My fingers fisted in his hair, holding him to me. When he raked me with his teeth I moaned loudly and had to bite my lip to stop.

His masculine chuckle filled the tiny room. "Is that what you like, Ava? Tell me again."

He pulled away, swapping one breast for the other. This time he was a little more firm when his teeth touched my skin and I gasped.

"I…like…you." I could barely get the words out. His hand had found the junction between my legs and my vision blurred. I wasn't sure how much longer I'd be able to stay upright on my knees.

"Good."

For a moment I felt like I was flying. My head touched the pillow just as his hands made quick work of my panties. I strained under him, wanting him to touch me again, but instead he pulled away.

I opened my eyes in time to see him outlined against the early morning light streaming through the curtains. The sound of his zipper was quickly followed by the whisper of his jeans hitting the floor. He set something on the shelf above the bed and then slid in beside me.

I turned to him, hungry. His hands slid over my bare skin, his callouses rough in a pleasant way. I wanted more. Needed his hands everywhere. I tried to get closer but he grunted.

"You're going to have to be on top, love." He ran his lips down my throat.

"Did I hurt you?" I froze.

"I'm fine." He dipped his head down and lazily traced my nipple with his tongue. "I just don't want to have to rush."

I'd gotten so carried away I'd forgotten about his shoulder.

I moved carefully so that he was settled against the pillow and I was perched above him. His hand ran down my stomach and found that spot I'd wanted him to touch again. When his fingers dipped inside, I could barely keep it together.

As I neared my peak he pulled his hand away and cupped my hip.

"Not yet. I want it all, Ava." His husky voice slid over my skin like velvet. "I want to taste you first and then I want to be inside you when you finish."

He gripped my hips and pulled me over so that I was straddling his chest. He urged me further up and I found myself face to face with the wall when his tongue moved against me. I let out a ragged breath and gripped the head-board. He was agonizingly thorough, dragging it out until I was panting, my hips bucking, but still he held me firmly in place.

When my breathing became too fast he'd move to a

different spot. It was sweet torture. When he touched his teeth against my inner thigh I whimpered and my knees gave out.

He held me upright, waiting for me to collect myself. Slowly he brought his lips back to my center. This time he didn't fight the rocking of my hips against his face. His tongue moved faster, and his fingers pulled me closer. I knew I was moaning, but I couldn't stop. I was close to the edge, so very close when he pulled away from me. He was breathing heavy and seemed to be fighting himself, trying to slow things down.

"The condom is on the shelf." He spoke the words against the skin of my leg. I pushed the hair out of my face and reached up.

Once I had it I moved back down his body until I was between his legs. I took him in my hand and watched as his muscles tensed. When I bent to put him in my mouth his eyes never left mine. My hair fell between us and he gathered it at the back of my head so he could still watch me. His breathing was heavy and his hips strained underneath me, I pulled back and brought my mouth to the juncture of his thighs and bit gently just as he had done to me.

"I can't take much more, Ava." My name came out on a hiss.

He found the condom and ripped the package open. When he was ready, I straddled his waist and guided him inside.

His groan was worth all of the torture he had put me through. I moved slowly, getting used to him. His hands gripped my hips, urging me to move faster. He strained under me and I let all restraint go.

This might be the only time I had with Owen and I

was going to enjoy every bit of it. This beautiful, broken man, who told me the most beautiful things. The man that had taken a bullet for me and didn't even want my thanks. But I could thank him in other ways.

As I neared the peak I let my head fall back and closed my eyes. I wanted to remember this. All of it. Even the smell of mothballs.

He clutched my hips at the same time that I fell over the edge, his body slamming into mine as he found his finish. I collapsed against his chest, my body still rocked with aftershocks of pleasure.

His hands stroked my back and hair.

"Thank you." He pressed his lips to my temple.

"You don't have to thank me, Owen. You never have to thank me." I repeated his words against his shoulder.

"I'll try to remember that next time." Humor laced his words and I smiled even though he couldn't see it.

"You do that." I gathered my strength and rolled to the side so I wasn't squishing him.

He swung his legs over the side of the bed and took a minute to clean himself off. I watched as his naked rear walked across the room to grab a towel from a small cabinet I hadn't noticed on the far wall. He brought it back to me and straightened the blanket. When I lay back down, I felt sated and happy.

Which was an unfamiliar feeling after the days filled with anxiety. He slid in beside me and pushed some of the hair out of my face.

"I think I'm starting to remember why it's nice to wake up next to someone." His face was relaxed, a content smile curling his lips.

"Only when they aren't trying to kill you, of course."

"I dunno, love. I wanted you so bad I thought it might kill me."

Heat flooded my cheeks and I rolled my eyes. "Geez. You're mushy."

"I've learned a lot of new things about myself in the last few days." He picked up a lock of my hair and rubbed it between his fingers.

"Like what?" Curiosity had me watching his face carefully.

"Apparently I'm a sucker for brunettes with big blue eyes and an American accent." His gaze was thoughtful, his eyes distant as he really contemplated it. "I've been all over the world, seen lots of things, met so many different people, but I wasn't really living. Like you, I was just existing. Doing the only thing I thought I was capable of."

"That's pretty deep." I tilted my head. "Between the running and the gun fights, when did you have time to come to that conclusion?"

"While I pretended to be busy doing things on the internet in Oxford." He tugged my hair gently. "I also decided that I really hate soup."

I laughed loudly and covered my mouth with the back of my hand.

"No, really. I hate soup. Hate it. If I never eat another bowl of soup again, it would still be too soon." His smile was infectious. "I do, however, really like your smile."

"Yours isn't so bad either."

I reached up and touched the bandage on his shoulder. We'd knocked it askew. "Did we hurt this?"

"I'm fine." Amusement rippled across his face.

"You think we can just hide in here for a few days and pretend the rest of the world doesn't exist?" I leaned back on the pillow.

"I'd settle for a few more hours, but I doubt we can spare that. You'll always be running if we don't deal with Maria. You deserve a life better than that." He settled down next to me and I snuggled up against his chest.

I must have drifted off, because the next thing I knew someone was pounding on the bedroom door. I jerked awake and clutched the blanket to me.

"Put your clothes on and come downstairs. I've got information." Mavis hollered. She pounded on the door a couple more times for good measure before I heard the clap of her high heels on the stairs.

CHAPTER SEVENTEEN

Owen

MAVIS HAD A laptop set on the kitchen table. Video footage of a woman getting into a black car played across the screen.

"You can't see her face," I said. "But that doesn't look like the same Maria that I met for the hit on Song."

Ava shook her head. "I think I would have remembered meeting someone like her."

"She might have been traveling incognito." Mavis sat back in her chair and cupped her tea with both hands.

"No, people with that kind of money have a way about them. It's not something they put on and take off like a jacket." She leaned closer to the screen. "If she was wearing a tattered wizard cloak, she would still hold herself differently. That isn't a humble woman, that's a woman that fought for her success, and won't let anyone forget it."

"You get all that from ten seconds of a black and white security clip?" Mavis looked Ava over the rim of her tea.

"Look at the way she expects people to be where they're supposed to be. She never breaks stride when heading for a door; she knows someone will open it in time. She knows everyone will be doing their jobs, because they can't afford not to. Anyone higher up in her business would be kept on a short leash, though. She'd want to make sure they didn't forget who was in charge."

I looked at Ava in surprise. I knew she was insightful, but hadn't realized just how much she picked up on.

"Organization, not business." Mavis sat forward. "She has her hands in anything that will make her money. It's broken up and scattered amongst her people, but it all goes back to her. Her biggest money makers are the casinos and the girls, but she also dabbles in fine art."

"She collects antiques?" Ava slumped back in her chair.

"My information just mentions that she collects fine art. I don't know if that's oil paintings, statues, pottery, or pictures of boogies."

"Boogies." Ava raised an eyebrow.

"From your nose." Mavis looked away as if the whole idea was distasteful and she hadn't brought it up to begin with.

"She's worked really hard to keep a low profile." I rubbed a hand along my jaw. I needed a shave. "I've never heard of her."

"Neither have I." Mavis reached forward and pressed a button on the computer. A different video started playing. "She's good at weeding out who will get her what she wants but still be controlled. Marcus only cares about money. Unless she stops throwing jobs his way, he'll be content."

"No, eventually he'll set his sights higher." My stupid big brother. This woman would mop the floor with him.

The woman walked on the screen flanked by a well fed man and well-dressed woman—obviously a subordinate by the way she stayed one step behind Maria at all times.

"Can you freeze that?"

"That's Mr. Song." Ava pointed at the screen.

"That's the man you were supposed to kill?" Mavis paused the video. "Your contact was named Maria?"

"Yes. She was a tall brunette woman."

Mavis snorted. "A coincidence?"

Owen shook his head no. "You and I both know those don't happen. I couldn't get a bead on her. She never stated that she was the person that was paying me, but if that was someone's secretary, I'd hate to meet her boss." I looked at the profiles of both women. "A real cold fish. If I had to pick one of them, I would say that Maria really was named Maria. I wouldn't bet that she wasn't one of the women on that video though. They have similar traits."

"What do we do now?" Ava looked at me and then Mavis.

"We find a way to get close to her." I nodded my head at the screen. "That's the hardest part."

"Then what?"

"We ask nicely what the hell her problem is." Mavis narrowed her eyes. "And what she's done with Laura."

"And when you say 'ask her nicely'…"

"We don't take no for an answer." I met her eyes and waited as she processed what I meant. I wasn't in the business of harming women, but if I thought I had to kill Maria to keep Ava safe, I wouldn't hesitate.

Someone knocked on the back door and I slid out of my seat and pulled Ava with me. I pushed her against the wall and stood in front her, my gun in my hand.

"Relax. It's Kenny." Mavis stood up and walked to the door. She was holding a forty five in her left hand. Where she had been hiding that I wasn't sure.

"And Kenny is?"

"Someone with a very promising future in electronics." Mavis opened the door and a skinny lad walked in. He nodded his head at me and handed an envelope to Mavis.

"This is the list?" She looked at him.

"There isn't a list. They pick them one at a time." His voice was high, but I'd judge him to be at least eighteen. If he managed to bulk up, he'd be someone people would avoid.

"An algorithm?" Mavis opened the envelope and flipped through the pages.

"Not that I can find. No random generator, no algorithm, not an employee with any sort of preferences." He shrugged. "Maybe they throw a dart at a map."

"Helpful as always." Mavis closed the envelope. "They won't be able to tell you were in there?"

"No." His chest puffed out a little. "I hacked harder stuff than that before I was ten."

"This is serious, Kenny. These are bad people."

"I'm not an idiot, Aunt Mavis. I looked through all of their stuff. I know they're bad people."

Aunt Mavis? I felt Ava peek around my shoulder to watch the family reunion.

"Damn it, Kenny. I told you not to call me that in public. It makes you a target. How am I supposed to believe you're taking this seriously if you can't remember that simple rule?" She stood on her toes and poked his shoulder. He backed a step away. I didn't blame him. I'd only seen Mavis lose her temper once and that time she had calmly told the guard she was pissed before putting a bullet in his chest.

"Do we gotta kill them now?" He looked over at us and I felt my eyebrows rise.

"I swear that if I ever see my sister in the after-life I am going to strangle her." She threw the envelope on the table and put her hands on her hips. "No. We don't 'gotta kill them.' They're good people. If you need help and you can't find me, you find Owen. And if we were going to kill them, we wouldn't want to announce that and start a panic."

"Yes'um." His cheeks turned red and he looked anywhere but at his tiny aunt.

"Just go in the living room." She shook her head.

The boy made feet for the front of the house.

"Aunt Mavis?" I holstered my gun and moved so Ava could escape the tiny corner I'd stuck her in. She rolled her eyes at me and went back to her seat.

"Shut up, Owen." Mavis sat back down and opened the envelope. She started separating the pages into stacks.

"Any other siblings?" Ava sat down and craned her neck to look at the pages.

"No." Mavis ground the word out.

"How long?" In the five years I'd known Mavis I never would have guessed she had a kid tucked away somewhere. I guess in my world you never truly knew anyone.

"Eight years." She sighed and looked up at us. "Do

we really have to do this?"

"Yes." Ava answered the same time I did.

Ava's voice took on a kind tone. "Obviously, Owen didn't know about him. We need to be able to trust you."

"Fine." She lowered her voice. "My sister died and I got the kid. Et cetera, et cetera. The end. Stop prying."

"I'm sorry you lost your sister." Ava was smart enough to not reach out to touch Mavis. I could see all of the muscles tensed along her neck and shoulders. "It must've been hard to lose her and find yourself in charge of a ten year old."

"Eight year old." Mavis looked up. "He's only sixteen. His father was the bloody Green Giant. He's been taller than me since he was nine."

"How did you manage to take care of a kid?" I tried to keep the disbelief out of my voice. "Our job isn't exactly something you can list on the contact form for his school."

She cocked her head to the side, almost like a bird. "Assassinating people isn't my only business. When things were bad I didn't need to work. I only took the occasional job when I needed to let off steam. Now that he's older it's easier."

Huh.

"You can tell you two are close." Ava smiled. "He might be taller than you, but he still looks up to you. And it must have been nice to have someone to come home to."

Mavis smiled a little. "Sometimes. Other times I'd come home to find out he'd done something stupid, like getting kicked out of a private school."

"Being a parent would be hard." Ava shook her head.

"You have no idea." Mavis cleared her throat. She

handed me a stack of papers. "Previous places the casino was held. Illegal gambling never goes out of style."

"You think this is the best way in?" I glanced over the list. Geneva, Moscow, Hong Kong, Singapore, Morocco, Samoa, Quebec. It didn't look like they avoided any particular countries.

"It's invite only. Everything else we would have to infiltrate slowly over a couple of years." She looked at me. "We don't have that kind of time."

"And how do we get an invite? And how do we know Maria will be there?" Ava leaned forward. Her hair fell in her face and she shoved it out of the way. I had flashback to this morning, when all of that hair had been hanging in my face while she moved on top of me.

"Maria is always there. And they seem to send the invites out to prominent businessmen and women. People with connections. Though it looks like those people are allowed to bring guests with them as well." Mavis slid some photos of people dressed in finery walking out of an abandoned building. "'Hey, come with me to an illegal casino that's full of sex slaves and expensive drugs.'"

"They're compiling blackmail." Ava pursed her lips.

"Exactly." Mavis's eyes flicked in my direction. She wasn't easily impressed.

"Why would they go?" Ava looked from me to Mavis.

"Brains." Mavis shrugged. "They lack them."

"Are they really all that stupid?"

"No. Some of them don't care. Some of them are shady anyway. For a lot of them, it's pride. Something to boast about." I spread out the pictures. "A lot of them are bored. They've seen it all, done it all. This is exciting.

Forbidden."

"What? They don't watch reality TV like everyone else?" When she smiled it lit up her face.

Fuck, I had it bad. I couldn't remember the last time I'd felt like this. Maybe as a teenager, but no, even then it wasn't more than overworked hormones. Ava was different. I liked the way her facial expressions changed as she'd read that stupid Christmas book. I enjoyed watching her think, for fuck's sake. Who sat around and watched someone else think?

"Owen, dear, we're not in remedial health class. There's a lot more at stake than your GPA right now." Mavis slapped a paper down in front of me.

It was a list of flight numbers.

"Zone out on your own time." She tapped the paper. "Do you notice anything about the numbers?"

"I'm going to guess they correspond with the list of casino locations," I said. Mavis rolled her eyes. She was brilliant, gorgeous, and clearly missed out on a career as an angry librarian.

"Oh, you're awake now. I thought I was going to have to ask Ava to step out of your line of sight."

"Get on with it." I frowned.

From the corner of my eye I saw Ava look down at the table with a small smile. God, I didn't deserve to be in the same room as her, but she'd let me love her this morning. I'd fallen asleep with her in my arms and I wasn't sure I could go back to not waking up next to her.

I looked back down at the paper and cleared my throat.

"They keep track of all the flight records for their guests. Why?" Mavis tapped the table excitedly.

"I haven't a clue." It wasn't that I didn't do my research like a diligent little assassin, but I didn't derive the same amount of satisfaction out of it that Mavis did.

"Me either." She smiled.

"And this makes us happy because…"

"This could be how they go through customs, or how they arrange for the guests to arrive at the casino. If we figure this out, we're a step closer to weaseling our way in."

"Then I'll be happy when you figure it out." I shuffled through the paperwork. "What do we know about their security?"

"Guards, cameras, the works." She turned back to her list of flight numbers.

I found a picture of the interior of one of the casinos. It was a lavish setup with enough guards to start a small war. Cameras were all well-placed, exits were monitored, and plainclothed guards were placed strategically around the room. Whoever was handling their security knew what they were doing.

"Is there footage from the security cameras inside?" I set the photo down.

"Hm. Ask Kenny. He can help you." She chewed on the end of her pencil, dismissing me from thought. "Ava, why don't you look at the guest lists, see if you notice anything."

"Like what?" Ava picked up a stack of papers.

"Recurring names. Important names. If they're compiling blackmail material, maybe we can use the same tactic to get in."

"Okay." Ava peered down at the pages and sucked in her bottom lip.

"Highlighter, dear?" Mavis pulled a marker out of her laptop case.

"Thanks." Ava tucked her hair behind her ear and narrowed her eyes at the paper.

I stood up and went to the living room. This was good. Ava was doing something she would feel was useful.

Kenny was sitting on the sofa, his boots up on the table in front of him. He bobbed his head at me when I walked in the room and turned back to the television.

"Mavis said you could get me footage from security cameras inside the casinos." I leaned against the doorframe and crossed my arms.

"Sure." He stood up, his lanky frame bending in sharp angles. "My stuff's in the car."

I followed him through the house and out the kitchen. Ava was now in possession of three different highlighters and Mavis was humming to herself. If I didn't know they were trying to figure out how to break into an underground gambling ring, I would think they were catching up on work or doing a word puzzle.

The black car Mavis had used to save us yesterday was gone and a silver minivan sat in its place. Kenny pulled out the keys from his pocket and hit the unlock button. It beeped twice and he pulled open the back door.

"You should disable the noise." I watched as he shuffled through bags and tossed around computer parts.

"Huh?" He looked up at me with a disc hanging out of his mouth.

"I said you should disable the noise on the unlock feature." He took the disc out of his mouth. "No need to draw attention to yourself."

"I never thought about that." He looked at the van in interest. Probably deciding what else he should do.

"If you can't figure it out, let me know."

"Thanks." He handed me a black duffle bag full of cords and other bits and ends. "It'll take a while for me to set up here. Do you know what the internet is like?"

"No." I looked down at the stuff in the bag. This wasn't typical teenage game gear. Kenny was well funded.

"Do you help Mavis often?" I held my arms out for another bag. My shoulder pulled a little, but it wasn't bad. Nothing that would stop me if I needed it.

"Just tracking bank accounts." Translation: she didn't let him do anything cool. "This is the first time I've gone out with her and it's only because of Laura. She knows I'd go looking for her on my own if she didn't let me help."

"She must trust you or she would have locked you up somewhere and come back for you later." I wondered who this Laura was to Mavis. I hadn't thought she kept many close connections. Then again, I didn't know she was raising her nephew.

He picked up a big box and managed to push the van door closed with his shoulder. If he hadn't looked like he was about to trip over his own feet it would have been impressive.

"She wants me to attend university. Doesn't want me to muck up my chances."

"Not a bad idea. You obviously have a talent for computers." I opened the kitchen door and we slipped back into our stolen bat-cave.

Ava was laughing at something Mavis had said, her face slightly pink. She shot me a guilty look before highlighting something on the paper she was holding, her smile

210

never leaving her face.

Maybe I shouldn't let them work together. There was no telling what Mavis might be sharing with Ava.

"Can you put that black bag over there?" Kenny dropped his box on the table and I winced. There was a small fortune contained in within that cardboard.

It took two hours to get everything set up the way the kid wanted. He might throw the stuff around, but it had to be just right before he could do anything. By the time I was scrolling through videos it was late afternoon. My stomach growled and I set the laptop down so I could stretch.

"You going to the kitchen?" Kenny looked over at me.

"Looks that way." I raised an eyebrow.

"Cool. Bring me something back. I haven't eaten since breakfast." He looked back at his computer and I cocked my head to the side. I could see why Mavis lost her temper with the boy.

"Did something happen to your arms and legs since we carried the stuff in from your van?"

"No." His face was schooled into an innocent expression, but I could see in his eyes that he knew he had overstepped.

"If you want them to keep working, you'll get up and find your own food."

He set his keyboard down and stood up. "I brought groceries this morning."

"Right. Then you should know what to cook."

His eyebrows drew together. "Cook?"

"You heat up food in a pot or pan." I mimed stirring a pot.

"I don't know how to cook." He scratched his neck.

"You're telling me that Mavis leaves you without any way to feed yourself?"

"I can make sandwiches and we have a microwave. Plus there's always take-away." He shrugged.

"If you want to go out in the big bad world, you've got to learn how to take care of yourself. Mavis spoils you." I turned and headed for the kitchen.

"I heard that." Mavis didn't look up from her work.

"I can always buy something to eat." Kenny followed behind me.

"No you can't." Ava piped up from her seat. She looked up at us. "If you can't cook, you could end up stuck in a house for days with nothing to eat but canned soup."

"What's wrong with soup?" The kid opened the tiny refrigerator and poked around inside.

"Just say no to soup." Ava smiled at me.

"Try eating it and nothing else for a while." I took the milk from him and poured myself a glass. I looked at Ava and lifted the carton.

"Please." She smiled and then looked back down at what she was working on. She was drawing lines between highlighted lines. I handed her a glass and looked over her shoulder.

"Have you found something?"

"I'm not sure." She hesitated.

"Talk it out."

"It's probably nothing. I worked for aircraft engineers, so maybe I'm reading too much into this." She chewed on her lip. "Most of these flights are on private jets. I can tell from the call signs. They're a little more complicated here than in the States, but there are a couple that show up very often."

"Gambling addiction?" Mavis looked up.

"Maybe. Or it's people that charter a private jet."

"You mean the owners of the charter." Someone that had connections to a group of people that had more money than most small countries. "They're feeding guests to Maria."

"I've been wondering how Maria could just approach all of these wealthy people with invitations and not worry about being sold out. Yeah, a lot of them are bored, but there's gotta be a portion of them that are uptight and not willing to step out of line. She needs someone to gauge who is right and who isn't." Ava shook her head. "I'm betting that Maria is the owner and has a hooligan managing it for her. Someone charming that can get away with passing out an invite."

"Makes sense." Mavis tapped her chin with her pen. "She hides behind a face and they funnel even more money into her bank accounts."

"So, how do we find this person?" Kenny leaned against a counter and looked at us. He was holding a cucumber in one hand and a spoon in the other. I wasn't sure what he was going to do with either, but he had a good question.

"We need to figure out which companies seem to be feeding customers. Then pick someone to target." Mavis leaned back in her chair and pulled the clip from her hair, letting it fall down her back.

"And force them to take us?" Kenny brightened. "Impersonate them?"

"Yeah, because no one would notice we're not the person they normally worked with," I snorted.

"Forcing someone to take us would backfire the moment they got a chance to rat us out." Mavis was watching the cucumber in her nephew's hand with concern.

"Not if we kill them afterward." He mimed using the cucumber as a knife.

"How can you be so smart and so stupid at the same time? It seriously boggles my mind." Mavis rolled her eyes. "We convince them, Kenneth. Make them want to help us."

"What if it's a woman?" The teenager sat the cucumber on the counter and bent back to the fridge, looking for something to go with his vegetable.

"Not a problem." Mavis raised an eyebrow. "Not that I'm going to explain it for you."

"Not to doubt your skills, but not all women are going to like you. Or find you attractive," her nephew pointed out as he pulled bread from a bag.

"Then Owen can seduce them." She said the words as if this plan was completely normal, nothing more than a job, but I saw Ava tense from the corner of my eyes. Usually I wouldn't mind that job. It took little effort and usually worked better than killing everyone. But after last night I really had no desire to ply anyone else with my charms.

I shrugged, but couldn't meet Ava's eyes. I would do whatever I had to, to keep her safe. Even if it made her hate me in the process.

CHAPTER EIGHTEEN

Ava

WHAT THE HELL was I? Chopped liver? Had last night not meant anything to him? He was all set to go seduce some rich woman.

I hoped she was eighty-five and on oxygen.

And had an ingrown toenail that he would have to massage.

He could apply her anti-fungal cream.

With his big, manly hands.

Ugh.

I took a deep breath and looked back at the papers in front of me. It was much more likely that it would be a man and Mavis would be working her thing instead of Owen. Yet, he had just agreed to do it if he needed to.

Needed to. He'd do it if it meant we'd get to meet Maria. God damnit. He was willing to do it for me. That was fucked up so many ways I couldn't count them.

I looked back up at him. He wasn't looking at me. Instead he was frowning at Kenny as the boy used a spoon to try and peel a cucumber.

"What are you doing?" I stood up and moved toward where Kenny was bludgeoning his cucumber.

Heh. I needed to remember that for a joke someday.

"I was going to make tea sandwiches." The boy looked over at me, his wide eyes dipping to my cleavage before meeting my gaze. A slight blush filled his cheeks and I fought to not shake my head. Hormones. "I'm hungry."

"And you're using a spoon because…?" I reached over and took the utensil.

"Couldn't find a knife." He licked his lips and stepped away from me as if I was dangerous.

"They're in the block over there." I pointed at the counter near a small toaster oven.

"Oh." The faint red tinge of his cheeks darkened.

Mavis snorted, but was smiling at her paperwork when I looked over my shoulder at her. Owen, on the other hand, was watching me with sad eyes. I knew in that moment in his mind, he'd already resigned himself to sleeping with someone to get us where we needed to go and had said goodbye to whatever we had. That stupid fucking idiot. Like I was going to let him go now.

Wait a minute. Was I contemplating keeping Owen? Owen, the hot assassin? The Owen that-had-driven-me-to-brink-of-insanity-with-pleasure-Owen? He was a human being with a mind of his own. He might—no scratch that —wouldn't like the idea of being kept by anyone.

This morning had been spectacular, but it didn't mean I got to keep him.

Maybe it had only been spectacular to me. I was a little rusty, after all.

Nope, I wasn't going to think like that. This morning

had been awesome and he was going to refuse to sleep with the eighty five year old woman with toe fungus.

At least that's what I would tell him.

Sighing I took the knife from Kenny's fingers. "What else do you have in the fridge?"

The boy folded his lanky frame in half and started pulling out other odds and ends from the tiny refrigerator. I was well aware of Owen's eyes on me but I ignored him. No reason to give him more ammo for his brooding session.

I really shouldn't be upset at this point.

"Here's the butter." Kenny slid a small bowl toward me.

"Okay. Where's the cream cheese?" I looked up from the cucumber.

"Cream cheese?" Kenny wrinkled his nose.

"Americans." Mavis snorted. "They put cream cheese on everything."

"The stuff some people put on bagels? That's disgusting." Kenny shivered as if I had suggested slapping crunchy peanut butter on the sandwiches.

"Hey, now. This American doesn't appreciate all of the hate she's getting. I could have left you to poke at the cucumber with your spoon." I flourished the stumpy vegetable in his direction.

He held his hands up in surrender. "Sorry. Please don't beat me with the cucumber."

"I thought you were going to make the food." Owen stepped closer and Kenny backed further into the counter.

"She took my spoon!" He pointed at me.

"I'm hungry and it was going to take him years to do anything with a spoon." I rolled my eyes.

"Cucumber sandwiches are not real food. They're for old ladies at tea." Owen's eyes took on a more amused look.

"I like them." Kenny muttered under his breath, but he turned around and rummaged through some bags.

"I'll take whatever I can get. I'm starving." I looked at the little tub of butter. "So, if you don't use cream cheese do you add anything to the butter? Or just slap the butter on the cucumbers?"

"For the love of God." Mavis pushed back from the table. "Just move. I'll fix the food."

The slender woman slipped between me and the counter. She held her hand out for the knife and I quickly placed it in her palm. Stepping back I bumped into Owen, who slid his hands around my waist and spun me so I was facing the hallway.

"Oh. Um, do you need any help, Mavis?" I leaned around Owen and looked at the back of her blonde head.

"No thank you." Mavis had already finished slicing the cucumber and was cutting the crusts off the bread. "You're not very good with a knife. I'll be much quicker without you in the way."

I blew the hair out of my face and then stuck my tongue out at her. Owen chuckled and his chest vibrated under my fingers. I looked up at him, still unsure if I was pissed at his selfless decision to seduce some faceless rich woman.

"While we wait for food, we should find you some more clothes." His hand slid along my waist, urging me toward the staircase.

I looked down at my shirt and grimaced at the blood. The jeans were scuffed but otherwise serviceable, but the shirt had to go.

"I have a bag in the living room. You can use one of my shirts." Mavis offered. "Just don't take the cashmere."

"I don't think your Barbie clothes fit normal-sized humans." Take that, you knife-wielding, pint-sized assassin!

"That's what I get for trying to be nice." Mavis huffed. "Why do you think I told you not to touch my cashmere? I don't want you stretching it out."

I rolled my eyes and bypassed her small suitcase by the couch. Wearing her clothes would make me look like I was wrestling to climb inside doll clothes. Instead I'd look at the shirts in the dresser upstairs. Maybe I could find something that would work.

Owen followed me up the stairs and into the tiny bedroom we had claimed the night before. The sheets were still scattered from our morning tussle and I felt the heat creep up my neck and into my cheeks. It was followed by a small smile of pride which I tried to hide while poking through the chest of drawers.

I certainly had tried something new today.

Owen closed the door and walked past me to look out the windows that faced the street. He tucked his hands in his front pockets, the dwindling sun casting shadows across his jaw and sharp cheek bones. His eyes were scanning the street, but I could tell that his mind was elsewhere.

I stacked a wife-beater tank top and a blue button up shirt on top of the dresser. The top drawer was filled with neatly rolled socks and folded boxers. The thought of clean socks was more tempting than a chocolate cake, but I couldn't bring myself to wear the old man's.

"You might as well take the socks." Owen's voice cut through the quiet room.

I looked at him and frowned.

"It just seems so… disrespectful." I shivered. "And gross. What if he had toenail fungus?"

"You had sex in his bed." Owen pulled his hands from his pockets and moved toward me. His whole body language shifted as he moved gracefully in my direction. "I don't think wearing the old man's socks would be any more disrespectful."

"You have a valid point." I ignored the heat that was suffusing my cheeks and igniting in much lower places.

"I really enjoy the way your cheeks turn pink when I mention sex." He dragged out that last word and moved so close that I had to look up to meet his gaze. "Like just now. Just the word makes you blush."

"You're making fun of me." I tried to control my breathing, but my lungs refused to behave.

"No. No, I'm not." He cupped the back of my head, forcing me to look up even higher. "I like the way you blush when I say sex because I know you're thinking about having sex with me. Isn't that right, love?"

I wanted to be coy, to rattle off some sort of sophisti-cated answer, but my mouth betrayed my brain.

"Yes." I licked my lips.

"And if I said I wanted you right now, here, against this dresser, moaning my name, what would you say?" He backed me against the wooden furniture so that my rear was pressed against the top ledge.

"I would say that there are people downstairs who would hear us." My body was screaming something else entirely, though. I bit my lip and managed to not squeak

220

when he lifted me so I was sitting on the dresser.

"Do you find it hard to be quiet with me?" He leaned down and nuzzled my neck.

"Hm." I tilted my head back so he had better access to my neck.

"What if I do this?" He dragged his teeth across the skin at the base of my neck.

The moan that fell from my lips couldn't be helped. Having his mouth and teeth against my skin was an aphrodisiac that set my body on fire.

"That's it." He ran his lips back up my neck and nip my earlobe between his teeth and tugged. "That sound. I love when you make that sound for me."

I ran my hands up his arms and fisted them in his hair, tugging gently so that he pulled back and met my gaze. His eyes were swirling with desire, half lidded, and looking at me as if I was the most delicious thing in the world.

"I love making those sounds for you."

His eyes flashed brightly before his lips came crashing down on mine. His tongue wasn't soft when he demanded entrance; his mouth wasn't tender as it moved over mine. Raw, ragged need pulsed off him in waves that made my head spin and set my body alight.

I grappled to get closer to him, desperate to press the hot ache between my legs against him, to feel him move there. I needed him like I needed air. Now.

"Ava, I'm not in the mood to be gentle." He breathed raggedly in my ear and began pulling at the button on the top of my jeans. "I need you."

"Thank God." I clawed at his shirt, desperate to have my hands on his skin.

We were in a mad race to get each other naked. He pulled me off the dresser and yanked my jeans down to my knees. Wasting no time he stood back up and peeled my shirt off, throwing it to the floor. I kicked at my shoes and jeans until I was free, working his pants undone so I could reach in and grasp him. As I slid my fingers down his length he hissed in my ear. Squeezing, I slowly jacked my hand up and down until I could feel his excitement run down over my fingers.

He ripped my bra off, throwing it across the room and knocking something off a shelf before dipping his head to catch my breast in his mouth.

"Owen." My head fell back and I groaned loudly as he teasingly bit me before tracing my nipple with his tongue. My panties disappeared with the sound of popping seams and torn cloth. They were replaced with his hand, his fingers playing in the slickness between my legs.

His deep growl filled my ears and I bucked against his hand. He worked me with talented fingers, his mouth ravaging my breast as my cries grew louder. When I neared my peak he didn't stop. Instead, he pulled back to watch my face as pleasure exploded in my body. I bit my lip to try and control my groans of pleasure.

Slowly he pulled his hand away and brought his fingers to his mouth. Deliberately he ran his tongue over them, tasting my orgasm for himself.

"You taste so good, love." Slowly he trailed his tongue down one of his fingers. "I could eat you every day and never get hungry for anything else."

"I like that plan." I panted, trying to catch my breath, my head still spinning from the pleasure.

"Good, love, because it wasn't up for discussion. I

222

need you." His green eyes were dark with desire and something else. Something much more serious.

I ran my hand over his shaft, enjoying the way his breath whistled out between his teeth. Carefully I let my nails drag along the tender skin, cupping his balls, and enjoying the way his eyes drifted shut.

"Are you ready, love? Or do you want to keep touching me?" He braced a hand on either side of me against the dresser. "I love the way your hands feel on me."

"Ready for what?" My breathing hitched and moisture began to gather between my legs once more.

"It's my turn." He looked at me with hooded eyes. His hands slipped down to cup my ass and lifted me to the top of the dresser. "I want you hard and fast, screaming my name."

I wrapped my legs around him and pulled his mouth to mine. "Then take me, Owen. Now."

He wasted no time. Sliding home in one hard thrust he groaned loudly and dropped his head to my shoulder, breathing heavily.

"God, you feel like heaven," he whispered against my neck. His hips began to move, pulling back so that only his swollen head rubbed along my clitoris, before filling me again with a powerful thrust.

He wasn't gentle. His movements were greedy, hungry for me and what I could give him. One of his hands grasped my hip while the other massaged my breast. I met him thrust for thrust, leaning back to brace against the wall behind the dresser, and watched him as he moved.

The muscles along his chest and abdomen constricted tightly with effort, his biceps rigid as he held me, sweat gathering on his brow. His green eyes watched me, drinking in my details as I did his. Despite my earlier orgasm, my body responded to him willingly, as if I had been waiting for this moment—the moment he took me without hesitation. Reaching between us I massaged my fingers against the spot that would push me over the edge. His eyes widened and his jaw clenched firmly.

Arching my back I groaned loudly, nearing my peak. I had never been pushed over the edge just watching a man enjoy my body, but that's what Owen did to me. The way he looked at me, as if I was a goddess, made me feel sexy and powerful.

His movements came faster, his hand on my breast tightening as the dresser slammed against the wall, again and again. I met him thrust for thrust, wanting to give him all that he needed. Knowing that this was more than physical need and desire. It was so much more.

"Owen, please… there. There. Owen." I gasped the words.

I climaxed the moment he stiffened, my body grabbing at his hungrily, milking him dry. He half grunted, half groaned before leaning forward and pressing his head between my breasts.

I'd never felt so satisfied.

CHAPTER
NINETEEN

Owen

BREATHE. I HAD to remind myself to breathe. With my face pressed between Ava's delicate breasts it seemed more like a suggestion than a necessity.

"Ah, fuck, love. That was perfect." I took a ragged breath and looked up at her. "You're perfect."

"You're not so bad yourself." She brushed the hair out of her eyes and smiled at me. She wiggled a little and I stood up, removing my weight from her. "But I think there is a model airplane stabbing my back."

"Can't have that." I scooped her off the dresser and deposited her perfect bottom on the bed before climbing in to wrap her in my arms.

She wasted no time curling into me, her hand on my chest, her leg thrown over mine, her sweet face looking up at me with smiling eyes. She looked sated, satisfied, and pride welled in my chest. I'd put that smile on her face, that dazed, groggy look in her eyes. She sighed, content.

"I love those sexy little sounds you make." I leaned in so I could nip at her ear. "Especially when you're loud and

225

telling me what you want."

"I think we may have been more than a little loud." She whispered, her cheeks darkening.

"Good." I shifted so I could pull her even closer. "Teach that boy not to look at what's not his."

She snorted. "You've got to be kidding. Jealous of a pimply teenager?"

"Not jealous. Just asserting my claim."

"Your claim?" She arched an eyebrow.

"Damn right." I kissed the creases on her nose. God help anyone that tried to get between me and this woman.

"And what about the geriatric woman on oxygen? I'm supposed to just be okay with that?" Her eyebrows drew together.

"What's that?" Had she hit her head on the wall while we made love?

"You said you'd seduce some woman if we needed her to get into the casino." Hurt flashed in her eyes before she tucked it away. "You're not the only one with a claim, Mr. Assassin. I don't fuck random people on dressers. You're mine, too."

MINE, my mind screamed. Yes, she was mine. The thought of her with someone else sent a surge of rage through my system and I took a deep breath. I had no right to claim this beautiful woman, but it was too late. She had found a place in my heart and I would kill anyone that tried to take her away.

She propped herself up on her elbow and looked down at me.

"Look, I know you're used to working in this under-ground world by yourself, but you said we were in this together." She touched my chest above my heart. "Together. And you aren't the only one with anger issues. I punched Julie Sage in eighth grade for kissing Tommy Bend. She knew I liked him, but kissed him anyway. I'm not sure what I would do if you took someone else to bed." Her fingers clenched on my chest and I was shocked to see the fierceness in her gaze.

She constantly surprised me with these darker little bits of herself and I had to admit it turned me on that she would want to inflict violence on someone over me. I tried to get her to meet my eyes, but she jerked her chin up so I couldn't see her expression.

"I don't want to seduce anyone, Ava." I tilted her face so I could see her better. "But I will if it means getting us into the casino. I'd do it so I could keep you safe."

She looked down at me with hard eyes. "I knew you were going to say that." She sat up and pulled the sheet over her breasts. "That's fucked up, Owen."

I shrugged. I was fucked up. What did she expect?

"So, I'd possibly be safe, but my heart would be ruined. Is that what you want?" Her expressive eyes made my stomach clench. "How do I just pretend like I'm okay with that?"

"I don't want to hurt you," I whispered.

"Then don't seduce anyone. Seduce me instead and we'll figure something else out for the casino." She looked at me and I could see her fighting to keep her composure. "I'll play hard to get so you'll have to really work for it. Make it more exciting."

"I like you willing, love. You get me more than excited." I brushed the hair from her eyes. "It probably won't come to me seducing anyone. We'll most likely need Mavis's talents."

"I don't really feel any better about Mavis seducing people to get us information." She fell back on the bed with a huff.

"Should I be jealous of the short blonde woman downstairs?" I rolled over on my good side and looked down at her. Her lips quirked and I found myself memorizing the planes of her face.

"I think I have a better case for being jealous of Mavis." She narrowed her eyes.

Shit. I'd walked right into that. Look at me, being an emotional dumbass, blundering around like a teenage boy.

"You don't need to worry about Mavis." I cleared my throat. "That was a long time ago and it wasn't what we have. It was one time and we just used each other to scratch an itch."

"I don't want details." She shook her head vigorously. "Don't want to know about the scratching. I like Mavis. Mostly. I think and I don't want to picture the two of you—"

I captured her chin with my finger and thumb so she'd stop shaking her head and look me in the eyes. She had turned pale and it made my chest hurt. Perhaps seeing her jealous wasn't as amusing as I had originally thought. "Don't."

"I know I don't fit in your world." Doubt clouded her eyes and that was the last thing I wanted to see. She was right: she didn't fit in my world. I should be keeping her as far away from me as I could, and yet here I was, my naked skin pressed against hers. I couldn't seem to help myself. And I didn't want this dream to end.

"Don't say that," I said.

"It's true—"

I shifted my weight, rolling on top of her delicious body. Her breath caught in a gasp, but at least she had stopped talking. I wasn't good at the talking part. I sounded daft every time I tried to explain myself to her. I'd stick to showing her.

Her legs spread for me, accepting me without question. I nestled against her warmth, letting her feel just how much I liked being tucked against her skin.

"Seems to me that you fit. Here." I ground against her, enjoying the way her body responded. Taking her hand I placed it against my chest, just under the bandage on my shoulder. "And here."

"Owen." Her eyes sparkled brightly and she trailed her fingertips over my skin to the bandage on my shoulder. So much emotion rolled across her face I didn't know where to start to decipher it.

"Shh." I leaned down and kissed her softly. "Don't try to make sense of what's happening with us. I don't want to think about it, I just want to experience it."

She let me kiss her again, her hands tracing my jaw, before twisting in my hair. When she tilted her hips upward in invitation, I slid inside. Just like before she took my breath away. Her warm body held me, moving with me, as I took us toward the end.

Earlier I'd needed her fast and hard, but right now I needed to treasure every inch of her body, taste every breath that escaped her, and commit her soft sounds to memory. I needed this just as much as I had needed to make her groan and claw at my skin. And she gave to me no matter what I needed, no matter what I demanded. I had no idea why she did, but I couldn't turn away from it— from her.

She was heaven and I was headed for the darkest pits of hell. If this was my only chance for bliss I was going to savor it before the angels kicked me out.

The fall was going to hurt and I was going to make sure it was worth it.

As her movements increased I let myself drown in her. I had been drowning in her blue eyes, in the way she moved, in the way she thought, from the moment I'd first laid eyes on her. Now I'd drown in the way she made me feel.

"Owen." Her harsh whisper drew my gaze. I watched her face as she fell over the edge, her blue eyes almost electric as she came under me. It was one of the most intimate moments I'd ever experienced and it sent me crashing after her.

I pressed a kiss to the crook of her neck, resting my head next to hers as we caught our breath. Something powerful stirred in my chest, wrapping my heart in hot bands. I didn't want to ever let her go.

I was a selfish bastard. I'd fight the angels to keep her, because Ava was worth all that hell could throw at me.

"Let's shower." I lifted her in my arms, glad that my hurt shoulder barely gave a tug of pain.

"We're naked." She whispered and wriggled against me.

"Makes showering much easier." I let her down before twisting the door knob.

She threw herself at the door. "There are people downstairs. We can't just waltz out there naked."

Turning around I snatched the blanket from the bed and wrapped it around her shoulders. "Better?"

"What about you?"

Rolling my eyes I lifted part of the blanket that trailed on the floor and wrapped it around my waist.

By the time I'd coaxed her into the shower her face was pinched in thought. I would have paid to know what she was thinking about, but I didn't feel that I had the right to ask. We were all entitled to our meditations. Instead I focused on getting us clean, taking my time to enjoy the way the water ran over her breasts and down the planes of her stomach.

"I'm not sure how I can go downstairs and look them in the eyes." She had one foot propped on the tub and was drying her leg with a towel I'd found. "They have to know what we were doing."

My dick jumped as I watched her bend further over to dry her foot. You'd think three times in one day would be enough to keep him satisfied, but I was quickly learning it wasn't possible to get enough of Ava.

And she had a killer ass.

"Earth to Owen." She straightened and pushed her wet hair behind her ears. "Are you listening to me?"

"Of course."

"Really? Because it looked like you were busy staring at my ass, not listening to me."

"Your ass is worth appreciating." I smiled at her wide eyes. "But I did hear what you said. Who cares if they know what we were doing?"

"I'm serious, Owen." Her scowl would have worked better if she hadn't been fighting so hard to keep from smiling. "It's embarrassing."

"Mavis could care less and the kid will be jealous. No judging. Put on your old man clothes and let's go get some food." I pulled her against me, kissing her quickly. "I'm starving and we need to start planning."

She grumbled but pulled her jeans up over her naked rear. "I can't believe you tore my panties. I don't have anything to wear now."

"You didn't seem to mind when I did it." I pulled my own pants up before grabbing the clean shirt from the sink ledge. I grabbed her bra and held it up. "At least this doesn't seem any worse for the wear."

"I really need to get some new things. Or at least a washing machine." She snatched the lacy black thing from my hands and slid it on before grabbing a white tank top.

"I don't think we'll be here much longer." I hung our towels on the rack and picked up the discarded blanket. "We need to move on. We've been here too long as it is."

"Where will we go?" She chewed on her bottom lip. It seemed to be her tell for when she was nervous.

"That depends on what kind of information Mavis and the boy wonder have found." I opened the door and motioned for her to walk out.

She took a deep breath and squared her shoulders before marching down the stairs. I kept my chuckle to myself. I could care less who knew that I'd just spent the last two hours inside Ava. In fact, I was feeling quite proud about it.

Downstairs was a mess of computer cables. Kenny was sitting on the floor, leaning against the couch as he stared at his computer, pointedly ignoring our entrance. Mavis was on the couch, papers spread in her lap.

"Food's in the kitchen." She didn't look up as we walked past.

"Thank you," Ava said as she walked past. In the

kitchen she found two plates and set about spooning pasta for us both.

"Milk?" I opened the fridge and lifted the jug.

"Thanks." She smiled at me before turning back to the plates.

We moved around the kitchen, getting the food ready with little talk. When we sat at the table, the silence was comfortable, and the pasta was good.

"Cucumber pasta salad. Much better than tiny tea sandwiches." She smiled at me.

"Better than soup, anyway." I wasn't sure either really counted as a meal.

"Ava? Can you look at some of these?" Mavis's voice drifted back to the kitchen.

"Sure." Ava stood up, taking her plate with her.

I finished the food on my plate and washed it quickly before following her out. She was sitting on the couch arm and reading over Mavis's shoulder.

"Those planes are from the company I worked at." Ava leaned forward.

"Do you remember who bought them?" My pulse quickened. This could be our link.

"Not really." Ava frowned. "I mean, these aren't painted in a way that makes them stand out. Some people have crazy paint jobs and it's easy to remember who picked out the pink and leopard print plane. These aren't meant to stand out in any particular way. They're fancy on the inside and used to carry self-important people back and forth."

"So, corporate planes?" I shrugged. "That should be easy to figure out."

"It could be a charter company." Ava looked up at

me. "Someone that hires out planes to people that don't want to fly commercial."

"Or to people that can't fly commercial." Mavis tsked. "People that don't want their every movement tracked and documented."

"They still have to fill out paperwork and go through customs…" Ava snorted. "After the last few days I should realize that it would be easier to skip customs forms and security checks on a private plane. They probably just hand over cash with whatever clipboard the official gives them."

"Have you seen any of these people before?" Mavis pulled up a file of headshots on her computer and scrolled through them. "Maybe you can tell us about the company owner."

"If you recognize one, I can get files on them from the company you worked for," Kenny offered.

Ava watched as Mavis clicked from one picture to the next. There were corporate headshots, images of people in the plane or about to board a plane, a few were of the owners doing an inspection as the plane was being built.

"I'm sorry. I don't—stop!" Ava touched Mavis on the shoulder and leaned forward. "That's one of the hangars owned by my company. Can you zoom in?"

Mavis touched the screen of her laptop with pinched fingers and then spread them so that the image enlarged. It was fuzzy, but I could make out a tall man talking with several people in uniforms. He seemed to be laughing.

"Oh my God." Ava leaned back. "That's Captain Horny."

CHAPTER
TWENTY

Ava

IT FELT LIKE it had been a lifetime ago that I had last seen the pilot that had a running reputation where I once worked. He was infamous for hitting on any available woman. Tall with brown hair, blue eyes, and a Scottish accent meant he'd been pretty successful in his attempts.

"Excuse me?" Owen's eyebrows pulled together. "Captain Horny?"

Mavis threw her head back and laughed. It was loud and honest.

"I meant Patrick. He's a pilot for a charter company. The girls started calling him Captain Horny over the years. He was always hitting on someone." I blushed. He'd hit on me more than once, but I'd always turned him down. Despite whatever was going on between me and Owen, I didn't usually bed hop. One night stands were fine, they just weren't really my style.

Or I hadn't met anyone that had inspired that kind of lust. At least not until Owen. If I was going to risk my heart being broken in a fling, it had to be worth it. My heart tightened. And I was definitely headed for a broken heart. No matter what happened between me and Owen, I knew that I didn't fit in his world. I couldn't be sneaky or kill bad guys and he would never be happy in routine job.

"I bet he had a good track record." Mavis looked at Ava and smiled. "Did you give him a go?"

"Um, no." I bit my lip.

"Why not? Were you in a relationship?" Mavis cocked her head and frowned at me. "I know he had to hit on you. You're blushing."

"If you weren't wearing a ring he considered you fair game." I shrugged. "Some of the other girls enjoyed his company."

"So, you just told him no and that was it?" Mavis raised an eyebrow.

No. Captain Horny was also Mr. Persistent. He'd shown up with a different flower every time I was working. Which I assumed meant that he showed up on the days I wasn't there with a flower for whoever else was at the front desk. Another reason that made it easy to tell him no.

"Pretty much." I nodded.

"You're a terrible liar." Mavis looked at Owen. "We need to get her ready."

"What? Ready for what?" I looked from Mavis's amused face to Owen's tight jaw.

"I'm out." He looked at me with dark eyes. "You and Mavis are in."

"In what?" A sinking feeling filled my stomach. "I really don't have any way to get in touch with him and I don't remember ever meeting his boss. A lot of buyers send their pilots in to handle things."

"We already know who his boss is," Mavis said. "Captain Horny is our way in."

"I have a feeling I'm not going to like what you're suggesting."

"Owen doesn't." Mavis laughed. While she rattled out information for Kenny to start digging into, I looked up at the man standing stiffly behind me.

"What is it?"

"You and Mavis are going to tag team Captain Horny." His voice took on a distant note.

"Whoa. I don't want to know about my aunt's freaky business." Kenny looked in my direction and blushed.

"Um, I'm not sleeping with Mavis." His face clouded and I rushed to clarify. "Or Captain Horny. I mean Patrick. I'm not sleeping with anyone."

"That's not what I heard." Kenny muttered loudly enough to carry through the house.

"You know what I mean." I fought to not sound exasperated.

"Relax, dear. I'll do the heavy hitting, but you can be my way in." She shrugged.

"How am I supposed to do that?"

"Well, like I said. We're going to have to work on your lying." Mavis turned back to her computer. "Can you remember his last name?"

"Van Horne." I sighed.

Mavis started laughing so hard she snorted. "Oh, that makes it so much better! Hullo, Captain Van Horne. How's it hanging?"

I tried to not laugh, I really did, but watching the serious faced assassin on the couch giggle like a school girl was contagious. Even Kenny couldn't keep from smiling.

Owen sat down in the chair next to the couch and propped his elbows on his knees. "Okay. Van Horne is our gatekeeper. What else do we know about him?"

His voice was calm, even, and completely fake. I cringed. This wasn't exactly how I thought this kind of thing would go.

"He dates a lot of models," Kenny offered. He turned his laptop around to show a picture of Patrick standing in front of the Victoria's Secret Plane, his arms around several of their popular models. "Maybe I should rethink the computers thing and become a pilot."

"Not happening." Mavis responded.

"Any idea where he's based?"

"Edinburgh." Kenny and I answered at the same time.

Owen's eyes locked on mine for a moment before looking over at Kenny. "Can you get us more information?"

"That's what I do." Kenny's fingers danced across the keyboard.

"I have a place in Edinburgh. Will that work for you?" Mavis looked over at Owen.

I zoned out as they discussed locations and logistics. I had no idea where the streets were or the buildings they were discussing.

"Yo, incoming." Kenny sat up a little straighter as he looked at his computer.

"What's wrong?" My muscles tensed and I looked over my shoulder thinking someone was about to burst through the back door.

"Three of the planes have chartered trips to Paris three days from now." Kenny licked his lips and leaned forward.

"Captain Horny?" Mavis looked around her computer.

"Not yet." Kenny looked over at his aunt.

"Get me the number. Now."

Kenny called out the number and I watched as Mavis deftly dialed and waited for someone to answer.

I would have sounded like I had a stutter or would have accidently pressed a button while trying to answer a simple question. Mavis did none of those things. As soon as someone picked up, her mouth curled into a small, calm smile.

She booked a trip for her imaginary boss and assistant to Paris. When offered flights she asked the right questions to narrow down the possibility that we would get a pilot other than Patrick. By the time she hung up, I was in awe.

"And that is how a professional does it." She tossed Owen the phone and wiggled her hips.

"Pack up." Owen stood up and looked around the room. "We need to go."

I looked around the little old living room and felt a bit of sadness. I'd started to feel comfortable in the place.

Okay, maybe not exactly comfortable. I wasn't wearing any panties and jeans without panties wasn't exactly as sexy as it sounded. Denim just wasn't meant to rub against certain points on the body for prolonged periods of time.

And it smelled of mothballs.

But so far, no one had shot at me here. Which a definite improvement compared to some of the last places I had been staying.

"You and Kenny go together. I'll take Ava on a separate train with me," Mavis announced.

"Ava stays with me." Owen crossed his arms, his chin

tilting upward as if preparing for a fight.

"Hello. I'm right here." I waved my hands in the air.

"People are looking for you to be traveling with an American woman. It makes more sense for her to go with me." Mavis stood very still, obviously aware that she was walking a tight rope. "Besides, I need to get some things together, and Ava needs to go shopping."

"It's like I'm invisible." I looked over at Kenny who just shrugged.

"You get used to it," he said.

"I don't think I will." I frowned at Owen.

"I'm trusting you with my family, Owen." Mavis let her hands hang by her sides. "He's all I've got left and I wouldn't let him out of my sight if I thought there was a better way to do this."

Owen was quiet, his jaw tight as he looked from me to Kenny to Mavis. Even without Mavis explaining it, I understood that she was offering Owen her trust, which wasn't something to be taken lightly.

"I won't let anything happen to her." Mavis voice was so quiet I barely heard it.

"I'm not a child, guys." Slapping my hands on the chair arms I stood up. "I'm going with Mavis. It makes the most sense. Your brother is probably still looking for us and it will be easier for Mavis and I to arrive in Scotland together in case anyone from the charter service is watching for her. It'll look like we work together. I'll be her assistant and carry her bags so her gun hands are free."

Owen looked at me, his calm expression in place. I waited for him to ask me if I was sure, to ask me if I really trusted Mavis, but he didn't. Instead he nodded his head.

I sighed in relief. He trusted my judgment and that

meant more to me than a suitcase full of money. This was important. All of our lives were at stake. Including Kenny, Mavis, her friend, and Tessa.

"Have you heard from my friend?" I knew he would have told me had he heard from her, but I still needed to ask.

"No." He watched me carefully.

"Do you think they have her?" I took a breath and held it.

"I don't know. She hasn't responded which could mean she hasn't checked her obscure email, or she knew better than to respond. It's impossible to say at this point."

"What's her name?" Kenny asked from where he was bundling up computer pieces to put in a box.

"Tessa Myers." I took a quick breath. "Tessa and Danny Myers."

"Danny Myers?" Mavis stopped and looked up at the ceiling trying to remember something. "That sounds familiar."

"We think that the original ticket was meant for Tessa, Ava's friend. However, there wasn't enough information and they went for the first female American they saw staying in that flat." Owen cocked his head. "You think you know a Danny Myers? Is he in the same line of work?"

"Danny is an assassin? No. I can't believe that." I shook my head. "He's a contractor. Everyone likes him."

"That's the best cover." Mavis shook her head. "But I don't think he's an assassin. I'd remember that for sure."

"Someone connected to an assassin?" Owen lifted one of the boxes of computer parts.

"Not sure." Mavis flipped through her bag, pulling

out a scarf and sunglasses that she tossed to me. "I just know the name rings a bell. He must be into something on the shady side of things."

I looked around the room and frowned. Danny was into something that would make him the target of a criminal mastermind. Did Tessa know? Did she realize that people would be looking for her because of her new husband? She was in danger. People had tried to kill me because they thought I was his wife.

Anger boiled under my skin.

"That fucking asshole!" I turned around and kicked the chair. "I trusted him! I let him marry my best friend. I gave him my blessing!"

I kicked the chair again and again, sending it backward a foot at a time. It was a heavy chair.

"I've been shot at! And you! You've actually been shot because of me!" I turned and pointed at Owen. "What if he's hauling Tessa around while he does shady stuff?"

"She might know that he's into shady stuff," Mavis offered. She was looking at the chair I had kicked across the hallway. "Maybe she doesn't care."

I turned to give the tiny woman my full attention. "You think my best friend would marry some kind of—of —of criminal?"

"You're shacking up with an assassin." Mavis arched an eyebrow.

Point for Mavis.

"That—that's not the same thing," I sputtered.

She just looked at me.

"Okay. Fine. It's the same thing." I flung my arms in the air. "I'm going to get my gun. Wait, how am I supposed to take a gun on the train? Aren't there metal detectors and stuff? I hope Tessa has a gun. If not I'm going to give her mine so she can shoot Danny if she doesn't know about his extracurricular what-evers."

"Traveling with your firearm is the easy part," Owen said. "We need to get you new identification first."

"I already took care of that." Kenny stood up and brought over paperwork and a passport.

I looked at the picture and frowned. "Is that my Facebook profile photo?"

"I had to put it on a different background, but you can't tell." Kenny stood up with a box of stuff in his arms and looked over my shoulder. "Turned out pretty good."

"Huh." I ran my finger over the picture and then the shiny seal claiming dual citizenship. Funny how I had hoped to move to England and find a job so I could stay. Now I had fake paperwork giving me that very thing. Not exactly what I had planned on. "Thanks."

"No problem." He turned around and exited the back door, kicking it shut behind him.

I went upstairs, slipped on the men's button up shirt and wrapped the scarf Mavis gave me around my hair. I looked in the mirror and put on the giant sunglasses.

Yep. I looked just like me in sunglasses and someone else's clothes.

Eat your heart out, Ava Gardner.

"You'll be careful." Owen's voice came from the bedroom door.

"Fine, I won't run down the street screaming my real name." I turned to look at him. "What do you think?"

"You're wearing sunglasses."

"Thank you, Captain Obvious." I pushed the sunglasses up on top of my head.

He grunted. "Well, not everyone can be Captain Horny."

"And I can't tell you how thankful I am for that." I tried to not wince. Way to remind him about my new role in this game. "I much prefer Captain Obvious."

"Let's keep it that way." He grabbed me and pulled me to his chest. His mouth covered mine in a deep, lingering kiss.

"You're not saying goodbye to me, are you?" I pulled back and tried to catch my breath. I didn't want to say goodbye. Saying goodbye implied that I might not see him again...and I couldn't think about that. It made my heart ache.

"Just giving you something to look forward to when I see you in Edinburgh." His eyes ran over my face. "I don't like this. I don't like leaving you."

"Me either." I pressed my face into his shoulder. "But we've got to man up and do what's best."

He chuckled and tightened his arms around me before letting go. "I'm leaving with the kid. We need to stagger our exit."

"Okay." It wasn't really okay. Owen and I had been through everything together so far. It felt weird to separate from him. It wasn't that I didn't trust Mavis. She wouldn't have suggested Kenny go with Owen if she was going to pull something horrible. And...

I trusted her.

That brought my total trusted assassins up to two. I might need to get my sixth sense checked at this rate. I never even suspected Danny was a criminal.

"I will see you in Scotland." Owen tilted my chin so I was looking up at him. "And I promised to always tell you the truth. Do you believe me?"

"Yes." The word left my mouth without hesitation.

"Thank you." He lifted my hand and pressed his lips to it.

"Don't kill Kenny." I tried to keep my lips from wobbling. "He's just a kid."

"I promise to not leave any marks." His lips quirked. "But I can't promise I won't rough him up a bit."

"I guess that's all I can ask for." I stepped back and looked at the room we'd used.

He pulled me in for one more kiss. His warm lips made my knees weak and for a moment I let myself forget that this was goodbye, that we were about to run head first into danger, and enjoyed the kiss of the man I was falling in love with.

A loud honk blared from behind the house and I jerked, but not because of the horn. Was I really falling in love with Owen? The sexy assassin that brought me to my knees with just a look?

"Go. Before he starts hollering your name." I gave him a gentle push. His eyes tightened and I could tell that he was worried. His lips pressed firmly and I wondered what he was fighting not to say. "Go. I'll be fine. I've always wanted to visit Scotland. Maybe you could pick up a kilt while we're there."

"Kilt?" The skin around his jaw loosened and one side of his dashing smile tugged upward. "I'm an Englishman, not a Scotsman."

"I wouldn't care if you were from Mars. Having sex with a man wearing a kilt is on my bucket list. If you wear one I'll have my wicked way with you until neither of us can walk." I winked at him before bending over to pick up the sheets that had managed to make their way onto the floor.

Large hands grasped my hips, pulling me against his large erection. I stood up quickly and he caught my ear with his teeth before kissing my neck. "I'm not promising a skirt, but I'm going to hold you to that other part anyway, love."

I shivered. "I certainly hope so."

The horn sounded again and he growled. "I'm going to bloody kill that boy."

"Go. Get out of here." I walked to the other side of the bed to put distance between us. Part of me wanted to throw myself at him and beg him not to leave me. Not because I was scared for myself, but because I was scared something might happen to him.

"Tomorrow." He stood there for a second watching me before turning and hurrying down the stairs.

I found a small linen closet and chose new sheets for the bed. I was switching the pillow cases when Mavis knocked on the door frame. She had a trash bag in her hand.

"You should throw those blankets away and the towels you used to shower. I've cleaned up all the medical supplies and figured I'd take those with us rather than throwing them away."

"Uh, thanks." Talking about throwing away the sex-soiled sheets was a bit uncomfortable. "Did you happen to check Owen's shoulder before he left?"

"You do realize that unless he's actively bleeding he's not going to let anyone know if he's hurting, right?" Mavis leaned against the wall and crossed her arms. "He's stubborn."

"I think most men fall into that category." I tossed the last pillow on the bed.

"He wouldn't have gone out there if he thought it would hinder him. He wouldn't risk not being in top form." She tilted her head and smiled. "He wouldn't want to put you at risk. Because of an injury."

"Oh, I don't know. I'm sure he thinks he could take out an entire army with only one arm." I shrugged and tried to go through the door, but she didn't move.

"Actually, he probably could take out an army with one arm. The man is deadly. I'm more worried that he will be distracted and get himself killed by a lone gunman hauling around a bazooka twice his size."

"You think I'm a distraction." I let the bag I was holding rest on the floor. "I want Owen to be safe, I only want what is good for him."

"You're a double edged sword. You are great for Owen. I can't remember ever hearing him talk so much or laugh so quickly. You light him up from the inside out." She paused, her eyes never leaving my face. "But you're also the number one thing that will get him killed. He'll do anything to keep you safe and to ensure that you spend as much time with him as you are willing."

Forever, I wanted to shout. I wanted to spend forever with him.

"I don't have a claim on Owen. Despite what happened in the past, we were nothing but friends." She took a step forward and somehow managed to grow a foot, and the aura of a pissed off tigress. "But if you bail on him after all of this, or push him away because this was just a heat of the moment thing, I'll make sure you're sorry. Owen is a rare man. Don't break him."

"Right." I nodded my head, sarcasm far from my mind. "I'm not going to hurt him. I can't. It would be like trying to stab myself. I need him. I need to know that he's okay each morning. That he's still alive and whole."

Gulping in air I frowned down at the short woman.

"Trust me, I'm the one that will end up broken." I closed my eyes. "I'm in love with him, but I don't fit in his world. At some point he's going to realize I'm holding him back." It had taken a week, maybe less than a week, for me to fall in love with the sexy assassin that had rescued me.

"You love him." Her entire face broke into a grin. "I thought it would take you a lot longer to realize it. Good. I'm happy for you both. He needs you as much as you need him."

I watched her, a little shocked. She really didn't mind that I'd fallen in love with Owen. There was no resentment or anger that I had encroached on her territory. She looked genuinely happy. There wasn't a hint of dishonesty or sarcasm.

"We should get ice cream while we're out to celebrate." Mavis smiled before turning and skipping down the stairs.

I'd just poured my heart out, admitted I was in love with a man that I couldn't possibly keep, and she wanted to get ice cream and gab like teenagers.

Okay, then. I guess a little ice cream wouldn't be amiss considering the week I'd had.

As I made my way down the stairs with a trash bag full of dirty sheets I wondered if the giggly assassin bouncing down the stairs would order sprinkles on her ice cream sundae.

CHAPTER TWENTY-ONE

Ava

A DOUBLE SCOOP of ice cream may have not been the best idea right before clothes shopping. I could practically hear the mirror in front of me laughing as I tried on the pencil skirt and blouse Mavis had picked out for me. The teal shirt was tucked into the black pencil skirt which left nothing much to the imagination. Cool air touched the large swatch of cleavage exposed by the shirt.

"Try this next." A tiny scrap of black material was flung over the dressing room door. "But come out here first. I want to see what you've got on."

I took a deep breath and brushed the hair out of my face before opening the door.

"My, my." Mavis tapped her chin before motioning me to spin in a circle.

I held my arms out and tried to keep from looking like a sullen teenager. It wasn't that I didn't like the outfit, I just didn't like having it approved by the tiny woman across from me.

"You look like Kenny when I make him wear a suit."

I frowned down at my clothes. I wasn't a model, but I owned my curves and they were quite obvious in this ensemble. Which I'm guessing was the idea.

"I'm pretty sure Kenny doesn't have boobs."

"God knows if he did I'd never get him out of his room." Mavis sighed.

A sales associate nearby laughed and I smiled.

"Shoes. You need tall, sexy shoes. How are you in heels?"

"That depends on how tall they are." I narrowed my eyes. "So, this outfit passes inspection?"

"Oh, yes. Definitely." She looked at the employee. "We'll take this one as well. What other colors does that shirt come in?"

"Peach, gray, and white."

"One in each color, please." Mavis tapped her fingers along the back of a chair. "And the skirt. We want the pinstripe one as well."

"Yes, ma'am."

I headed back to the dressing room to change so I could give the clerk the pieces I was wearing. I pulled the black fabric down from the top of the door and frowned.

"What is this?" I held it up.

"A cocktail dress." Mavis looked at me over her shoulder.

"That's nice." I lifted a layer of black lace that covered the tiny skirt and looked at her through it. "Where's the rest of it?"

"Seriously? You had sex so loudly with Owen that I had to put headphones on and now you're a prude?" She put her hands on her hips.

"Mavis," I hissed. Heat flooded my cheeks and I

250

looked around the dressing room. "I'm not being a prude. The skirt is barely going to cover my butt cheeks!"

"That's the point, Ava." Mavis walked over and gave me a gentle push toward the dressing room I was using. "We want Captain Horny distracted and eager to impress."

"I thought you were the one that was going to be distracting Captain Horny! I'm just your introduction." I waved the microscopic dress at her.

"If he is led by his dick the way you say, it won't hurt to have two scantily clad women." She pointed at my tiny room. "Go try it on. And I've got a couple more things for you afterward."

I jerked the door shut and pulled the pencil skirt and blouse off. I held up the dress and frowned. There was a tiny zipper in the back. Sighing, I held the dress open and stepped into it. It took a lot of wiggling, but I managed to pull it up over my hips and slide my arms into the lace sleeves before grappling with the zipper. I looked at the mirror and froze. I stood up a little straighter and pushed my hair out of my face.

Oh, I couldn't wait for Owen to see me wearing this dress.

"Does it fit?" Mavis asked.

I opened the door and stepped out. The skirt was definitely short but it stayed in place as I walked toward the triple mirror at the end of the hall. I took inventory of myself and actually wasn't unpleased. My legs looked longer than normal, which was great. I stood on my tiptoes miming wearing high heels.

I looked at Mavis's reflection, surprised to see her smiling smugly.

"What?"

"I was right. It's perfect." She crossed her arms. "I missed my calling as a personal stylist."

I rolled my eyes. I could just imagine her with a pin cushion strapped to her wrist, a throwing knife tucked behind it. She could sell and market little gun shaped charms and handcuff earrings. That wasn't a bad idea, actually.

"Okay, so we can head out now?" I tucked my hair behind my ear and bit my lip. Shopping was great, especially with Mavis. She knew all of the great spots to hit. But it had been hours since Owen had left and I was nervous about boarding a train.

"Would you stop worrying? Our train doesn't leave for a few more hours." Mavis handed me another dress. This one was just as short but had fabric that draped from one shoulder. "Try this one too. It'll be easier to carry."

"Carry?" I eyed the red fabric.

"A weapon? Guns, knives, ninja throwing stars."

"Ah. That type of carrying." Blowing out a deep breath I took the dress to my tiny changing stall.

"So, what else do we need to do before we leave?" I slipped the red dress over my head, letting the fabric fall into place.

I looked over my shoulder at the dress and tried to not wince. The material basically cupped my ass. How was I going to sit down in this thing?

"Oh, that's good." Mavis stuck her head in the door and looked me over. "You can wear black heels with that as well. That'll save us a little time shopping. Here, go ahead and put this on." She handed me a bag.

"What is this?"

"If you're going to be my assistant, you can't run around wearing an old man's shirt. I went ahead and bought the clothes. You need to be polished." She pursed her lips. "We're going to a hair stylist down the road and getting spruced up. You could use a trim."

"Gee, it's like I have a sugar mama." I opened the bag and looked in.

"You can thank me later." She winked at me and I chuckled. "Our car will pick us up when we're done with your hair."

"Right, get out of here so I can change." I flapped my hand at her.

"I can't believe you're so prudish after all that noise you made with Owen." She sniffed. "I'm not really into women, you know."

"I'm sorry about, er, the stuff with Owen." Heat rushed up my neck. "This is, uh, really awkward."

"Relax. I just enjoy pushing your buttons. I knew you two were going to be going at it like rabbits when I saw you in the café." She shrugged. "I really didn't hear too much. I'm not an idiot and knew what was going on and chose to ignore it. I was busy doing research."

"Still, it wasn't very thoughtful." I cleared my throat.

"Look, in our world, you have to take what you need when you can get it. Tomorrow isn't guaranteed." Where her eyes had been teasing before, they were dead serious now. "If you're worried about what happened between me and Owen, you shouldn't. We trusted each other enough to let our guard down for an hour or two. That's all it was. I mean, he's attractive and all, but…it wasn't the right fit."

"I…thank you for being understanding." Giving up on the thought of privacy, I slipped out of the red dress and carefully hung it back up. I picked out the black pencil skirt, blue sweater, and black heels. I wasn't wearing any

253

jewelry, but most people wouldn't notice that right away.

"Before you tuck in the sweater, here is a discreet holster. It wraps around your waist." She passed me a black stretchy strip that closed in the middle with bra hooks. "You'll have to untuck your sweater to get to your gun, but it's better than nothing."

I wrapped it around and managed to stick my small pistol in without shooting myself in the butt crack. I tucked the sweater in, making sure to fluff it in the back.

"Here," she said. She dug in the bag and pulled out a small black cardigan. "This will help."

I pulled it on and stepped into the shoes she'd chosen for me to wear. There was also a pair of pearl earrings stuck to a small cardboard card. I popped those in my ears and checked my reflection. My hair was disheveled, but the rest of me looked ready to be a sex-pot on her way to a job interview. Not bad at all.

"Let's go." The little woman picked up one of my new bags. "We need to get you a briefcase and small travel bag, but first we should get your hair done. It looks like you tumbled out of bed from a one night stand."

"Gosh, you know how to make a girl feel good about herself." I rolled my eyes before tucking the money Owen had given me into my bra. My lips pursed as I fought a scowl. I didn't usually stick things in my bra for safekeeping, but this skirt didn't have any pockets and I couldn't just carry it around in my hand. Lots of women thought it was a perfectly acceptable place to store things, but in high school I had worked at a grocery store. When you have a woman dig sweaty coins and soaking wet bills out of her bra to pay for her frozen pizza and beer, you just couldn't think of sticking stuff in your bra again. Boob sweat wasn't something that should be shared.

We stopped by a small boutique where I purchased a purse, travel bag, and briefcase. From there we hurried to get my hair cut. The stylist was not impressed with my hair care routine. I was lectured on the damages of putting your hair up while still wet, moisturizing, and hair masks. By the time she had passed me on to the makeup artist I'd promised to never skip a mud treatment for my hair. Once they had deemed me acceptable, I was released from the chair that I'd been trapped in, and staggered to the front desk where Mavis waited.

"What do you think?" She eyed me critically.

"I feel like a plucked chicken." I touched my forehead gingerly.

"Excuse me?" Mavis cocked her head to the side.

"Never mind." I shook my head. "Am I satisfactory?"

"Yes." She handed money over to the woman at the register. "Our car is out front. Are you ready to leave?"

"Yes, ma'am." I reached and took her large purse so that I could carry it to the snazzy black sedan waiting for us. I was careful to stay half a step behind her as we exited the building. Practicing for our time in Scotland.

"So much for keeping a low cover. This is rather ostentatious," I muttered under my breath.

"People will be looking for an anxious American woman wearing giant sunglasses and a hoodie. They will look right past the business woman and her assistant." She smiled over her shoulder. "People see what they want to see."

"That's what Owen said." I frowned. "But if people are looking for me, won't they see me?"

"Not if your nose is buried in your phone or tablet as I

255

give you work to do. They will only see an overbearing boss and an overworked lackey. The key is to be your part. If you play it right, no one will notice you."

"I'm a terrible liar, Mavis." I shuddered. "And I doubt I'm a much better actress."

"That's why you have me. Relax."

A man with a black hat opened the back door for us. Our bags were already in the car and once inside, I started stuffing my new clothes into the carry on we'd just bought, careful to remove all the tags.

"Right then. Here are our tickets." Mavis opened an envelope that had been in her seat. "Refer to me as Ms. Thomasino."

"Won't you need to hand them your ticket?" I looked over the paperwork she was handing me.

"They won't fuss if you hand it to them and I'm there with you. We want them to think that you are used to doing everything for me. My personal lackey." She opened her briefcase and brought out a tablet and phone. "These are yours. Georgie procured these for us while you were getting your hair done."

"Georgie?" I looked up at the driver. He was an older man, nondescript, his little black hat covering short gray hair.

"Georgie has done odd jobs for me for a very long time." She smiled at the man watching us in his mirror. "Isn't that right, Georgie?"

"Aye, it is. Long time now." His accent was so thick I could barely make out the words. "Ever since I caught her trying to steal my wallet."

"It wasn't your wallet, Georgie." Mavis pretended to frown. "I'd watched you nick it from the mark talking to a

PC. Fair game."

"A'ight then." He smiled the way a grandfather would at his favorite grandchild. "I've not been able to shake her since. Somehow ended up on her payroll."

"You know the most interesting people, Mavis." I put the tablet and phone in the briefcase. Careful so I wouldn't bend anything, I put the tickets and my new identification in the purse. Both bags looked obscenely empty.

"You have no idea, dear." She smiled. "But Georgie is useful."

"Aye, and trustworthy." He winked at me through the mirror.

"As long as I'm paying the best." Mavis glowered.

"Ah now, you never let me down," Georgie announced. "I printed out the papers you asked for and picked up the little things."

I wasn't sure exactly what Georgie had said, but looked through the bag and smiled.

"Chapstick!" I pulled a tube from the bag and held it to my chest. "Oh, I've missed having my Chapstick."

"It's the little things in life." Mavis held her hand out for the bag and passed out the pens and mints. She handed me the rest of the stuff, which consisted of toiletries, and I put them in the overnight bag.

"Where are we headed now?" I looked out the window, watching as the city rushed by. I'd barely scratched the surface while touring the last week. There was still so much more to see.

"Kings Cross." Mavis was playing with her cell phone.

"Are we taking the Hogwarts Express?" I couldn't help my grin. Kings Cross was one of the places I'd been planning on visiting. "Will you take my picture at platform 9 ¾?"

"Sure, we'll stop and take selfies pushing the pretend cart through the wall." She leveled her gaze at me, her best you-are-an-idiot look firmly in place.

"C'mon. It's Harry Potter! I need my picture taken there." I leaned back in my seat. "This whole being on England's most wanted list has put a real cramp into my tourist plans."

"After this is all over I'll take your picture wherever you want." Mavis closed her purse and clasped her hands. "And think about it. You're about to ride a private jet all the way to Paris. I bet you didn't plan on that when you decided to move to England."

"True." I shrugged. "Of course, I won't be me on the flight, and I'll be praying that no one tries to kill us the whole time."

"Focus on Paris. We'll make time to stop at a bakery. Nothing smells quite as good as a Parisian bakery first thing in the morning. The fresh bread, the sweet fillings, candies. You have to experience it." She looked over at me. "I'm sure we'll be able to make time for that at some point."

"So we can make time for éclairs, but not for the Hogwarts Express?" I pouted.

"You know, I thought it would be easier to travel with you than with Kenny."

"Funny." I rolled my eyes. "It's Harry Potter. Shouldn't you have some sort of British pride when it comes to the Boy Who Lived?"

"Of course I do, but I'm not going to take your picture while you pretend to run through a brick wall. We need to look professional and dignified. Have Owen bring you back."

Right. I was going to ask Owen to take me to Kings Cross just for a picture. I sighed. I'd love to do normal things with him, like traveling, picking out where to eat, or apartment shopping. Hell, I'd love to know that I could yell at him for not replacing the toilet paper. And was I really considering finding a place to live with him? Like the big bad assassin would be happy to settle down and have plants. Or pets? A little puppy, maybe. Not to mention I'd sort of like to have kids one day which would definitely send Owen running for the nearest assassin bunker.

Thinking about him made my chest hurt. What if something had happened to him and Kenny? What if they didn't make it to Scotland? Would I go through with the plan without him? Just me and Mavis?

No. We were in this together. If he didn't show up, I'd be hell bent on finding out why. For some reason I had this horrible feeling that he was just waiting to die, waiting to go down in a blaze of glory, and it made me sick to my stomach. I wasn't sure how I was supposed to go back to being normal after all of this, but I knew I wouldn't manage even a fake normal without Owen to lean on.

"Have you heard from the guys?" I managed to keep my voice calm. Maybe she wouldn't even think it was odd to ask.

"We'll see them when we get there." She didn't say anything else, which I took to mean she hadn't heard from them, not that she thought they were dead.

I watched the scenery as we drove, taking in the sights, trying to memorize street names. I'd learned that seeing distant places in movies and television shows rarely conveyed the reality of the location.

When you got to this place that you had built up in your mind from television shows or movies, you were either let down or overwhelmed. Your reaction rarely hit in the middle. Unless you went somewhere you'd never thought about visiting before. When I'd been in high school I'd gone to Ottawa. It wasn't a place I'd ever daydreamed of traveling to, but I'd enjoyed it. There hadn't been any big shock and awe moment and no real letdowns.

London had a lot of places that were everything that I had pictured and very few places that had been a disappointment. I'd really enjoyed most of my time in the city. Well, until I was being shot at.

Or accidently killing people with my car.

Kings Cross was another one of those places that I'd looked at online, read about in travel magazines, and looked forward to seeing. This place was in movies, books, television shows that I adored. I'd imagined a massive hub, where people were always coming and going. I'd grab a train to go see different things, maybe meet new people.

I wasn't disappointed. People on forums had complained that the station was dingy and not very attractive, but thankfully, they had just finished a major refurbishment. The bricks looked fresh and there was a ton of natural light streaming through skylights.

Georgie had dropped us off and I'd followed behind Mavis like a good little employee. We had exactly zero problems getting on the train, which I found a bit worrisome. Either they were very lax or Mavis had greased some palms. I was willing to bet on the latter.

The pistol strapped to the small of my back felt like a

blinking beacon to everyone that looked in my direction.

"Keep up, dear. I don't want to lose you in the car. I'll need my laptop once we're settled." Mavis's voice carried back to me.

"Yes, ma'am." I picked up my speed and stopped looking around like an idiot. I wasn't here as a tourist today. I was here to play the part of adoring assistant.

It was unlikely that anyone was watching for us, but it didn't hurt to be in character. The more I practiced, the easier it would become. Plus, Mavis enjoyed the charade, which made it hard to stay peppy and adoring. When she'd thrust her jacket at me to carry, I'd thought about stomping her into the ground.

She'd make a little squish sound.

Instead, I kept my head down and followed the clicking of her heels as we walked. It was difficult to keep from looking around to see if we were being followed.

The train was what I expected. Mavis had bought First Class seats, so we weren't crowded or stuck with someone else's arm in our ribs. We were on the single side of the car, which meant our seats faced one another and there was a small table in the middle. A window lined up perfectly with our seats and I was excited to watch the countryside slip by before night fell. We wouldn't be making it into Edinburgh until late tonight.

"Why don't you sleep?" Mavis set her laptop on the small table. "I have a few things to take care of and you look tired."

"Really, Ms. Thomasino, I look tired? That's so odd after my week at the spa." I rolled my eyes. "I'm sorry I didn't roll out of bed looking like a female hygiene commercial."

She rolled her eyes. "You know what I mean."

"I think I want to watch the scenery for a bit." I settled back into my chair. "Unless you'd like me to help you with anything."

"No, I'm working on stuff that has nothing to do with our current trip." She leaned closer to her computer. "I have a book in my bag if you'd rather read."

"No thanks, I'm good." This conversation was eerily normal considering that we were traveling under aliases and in possession of illegal weapons.

Instead of focusing on my current situation, I let my mind drift as the train began to move. Being in another country made even the simplest things seem foreign and exotic. I was going to enjoy watching all of the green grass and trees before the crap started to fall.

CHAPTER
TWENTY-TWO

Owen

PACING WAS NOT making the waiting any easier. Stakeouts had never been a problem in the past; I enjoyed the solitude, the peace, gleaning information from my mark. But this was not peaceful. Worry ate at my stomach and my nerves were shot.

"Are they here yet?" Kenny looked up from his plate. A very solemn looking maid had placed food for us at the kitchen island before returning to wherever she had appeared from. When Mavis told me she had a safe place in Edinburgh, I hadn't thought there would be a household staff. It made me itchy to know there were people skulking around the house with feather dusters and brooms. A butler had opened the door for us when we arrived. A butler.

What was the woman thinking?

"No." The word came out in a growl and I stopped to scrub my chin with my fingers. "Have you seen anything online?"

"No, but I don't expect to. Aunt Mavis knows what she's doing." Kenny shrugged and took another bite of his food.

I'd fed the boy an hour before we arrived at the house because he was starving. He'd wolfed down every bit of the food, even asking if I was planning on finishing mine. Now he was tearing into the sandwich as if he'd not eaten in years.

"You should slow down or you could choke." I leaned over and braced my arms on the marble top of the island.

"I'm not a baby." The boy rolled his eyes and I fought that urge to smack him upside his head.

That impulse had become more frequent the longer I was stuck with Kenny. It wasn't that I didn't get where he was coming from, but taking care of a teenager was turning out to be similar to taking care of a toddler, only the teenager was certain they knew what they were doing, even as they drove off a cliff. And he would need absolutely zero help retrieving his car from the bottom of a ravine as he complained about strong winds and an unstable road.

Hormones did that to people. Thankfully age smoothed most of that out.

"I'm frustrated," I explained as way of apology. It wasn't his fault that I was all twisted up inside.

"I get it." He took a long pull of his bottled drink. "Your girl's out there without you. Freaks you out."

My girl. Huh.

"I don't like not being in control." I looked down at the counter. I didn't like not having Ava by my side. "So, this Laura that you and Mavis are looking for. Is she your girl?"

"Nah." That one word spoke volumes in the quiet

kitchen. She might not be his girl, but he would have liked it that way. Suddenly I had more patience for his behavior. A little more. Not a ton.

"Women." I frowned. "They're a lot of trouble."

"Worth it." He looked over at me with dark eyes. "At least you know she wants to be with you."

"Maybe." I stood up and walked to the window over the sink. I wasn't really in the mood to discuss my relationship with Ava. It was still too new, too confusing. If I'd been a stronger man I would have kept her at arm's length. She didn't belong with someone like me.

"She's the real thing, man." Kenny's eyes glazed over a bit and the urge to smack the back of his head returned. "She's hot, but with a brain. And funny. You shouldn't let her get away."

"Life isn't that simple." I frowned. Where were they? It was almost midnight.

"Yeah, sometimes it really is that simple." He looked at me with eyes that were much older than his sixteen years.

I looked at him, really thinking about what he was saying. I wanted to hold on to Ava; wanted to wake up next to her every morning that I possibly could. But was that a real possibility? With her I didn't despise myself, I didn't hide away from the world, and she didn't look at me as if I was broken. I felt whole with her around. Or I would…if we weren't constantly running for our lives.

That had to stop. I couldn't see all of the possibilities while dodging bullets, only focused on keeping us alive.

"I suppose simple doesn't mean easy." I raised one eyebrow.

"You wouldn't want it if it was easy," he replied.

Out of the mouths of babes…

"Besides, her rack is so worth fighting for. I mean, damn." He dragged out the last word and I didn't fight the impulse this time. Reaching out I boxed his ear, sending him leaning in the opposite direction.

"Have some respect, boy." I leveled my gaze at him, letting him see the anger simmering just under the surface. "Next time you'll hit the floor. I don't care who you're related to."

"Ow. Damnit! That hurt!" He covered his ear and ducked away from me. "I'm sorry. It was just a compliment."

"If you think that was a compliment, then it's no wonder Laura doesn't want to date you." I pointed at him. "Being in this business doesn't give you a right to be a perv. In fact, if you follow in your aunt's footsteps the way you intend, you need to walk the straight and narrow in every other way. Otherwise you'll get yourself killed."

"Right. I'm sorry." He pulled his hand away from his ear before tracing it delicately with his fingertips. "Damn, that hurt. Can you show me how to do that to someone?"

"Sure, turn your head and pay attention."

"Never mind. I'll figure it out myself." He took a step further away from me.

"You need to learn how to fight." I shook my head. "You're going to be slaughtered if you can't protect yourself."

"My aunt won't let me take classes. She thinks I'll get myself in trouble."

I looked pointedly at his ear.

"Okay, she's probably right." He frowned. "Or I would have been quick enough to avoid you. You caught me off guard."

I reached out and cuffed his other ear. Keeping my face blank I waited for his reaction. Part of me was willing to fight, not that I'd really hurt him. The other part of me wanted to see if he would be dumb enough to try it.

"Jesus Christ! What is *wrong* with you?" He hopped out of my way and glared at me. "You're a sadistic fuck! I need my ears!"

I just stood there with my arms by my sides. "I am a sadistic fuck, but I wasn't being one to you. I merely pointed out that you are really not ready to take anyone on. If I'd had a knife, you'd be bleeding to death on your aunt's floor."

"That's why I need to learn to fight." He stood there covering both of his ears. "I want to be able to take care of Aunt Mavis and myself."

"And Laura." I kept my face blank.

"Yes, and Laura. She barely knows I'm alive! I'd just left her house after our tutoring session when they took her. If I'd stayed I might have been able to stop them. Especially if I knew how to fight." He glared at me with so much defiance I actually felt a twinge of pity.

"If you can find time to stop eating, I could teach you some things." I shrugged. "But if your aunt finds out and says no, I'm going to back off."

"You'll teach me?" His expression was skeptical.

"I have some ground rules." I held up my hand. "One, you do what I say without question, without arguing. Two, you don't use what I teach you until I say you're ready."

He started to open his mouth and I just looked at him until he snapped it shut.

"Good. Three, even if I'm not around, you practice

what I teach you. If you don't then it's all pointless." I waited for a response but he didn't say anything. "If you can abide by that, then I will teach you what I can. I'm not going to promise that you'll make an amazing boxer or win medals at a tournament, but I promise to try and make you the best fighter you can be."

I fought the urge to suck in a breath at my words. I'd just offered a string to tie me to this boy. I didn't do things like this. I could have told him to find a gym or martial arts studio, but instead had offered to teach him myself. I'd basically bound myself to him. If he took me up on my offer and ended up dead, I'd be the one responsible.

"Agreed." Kenny held his hand out and I shook it. There it went. I'd tied myself to him now. First Ava and now the gangly computer whiz. Life had turned fucking upside down.

"And you need to learn some respect." I pulled him a little closer, not letting go of his hand. "I'm not your aunt. I won't put up with your smart ass mouth. If you cop an attitude or insult your aunt or Ava in my hearing, I'm going to take it out of your ass. Understood?"

"Yes sir." His smile grew. "When do we start?"

"Tomorrow." I let go of his hand and pushed him toward the kitchen door. "Go shower and get some sleep. You stink."

"Let me know when they get back?" His eyes focused on mine. The nonchalant teenage shrug didn't hide his need to know his aunt was safe.

"Yes."

He nodded before leaving. I could hear him taking the stairs two at a time. I sat down on the stool he had vacated and ate some of the chips he'd left on his plate. Agreeing to take care of Ava had been thought-free. It was an immediate knee-jerk reaction to the fear on her face. Offering to tie myself to Kenny had felt similar. I'd offered without thinking about what it would mean for me.

I didn't do things without thinking. What was wrong with me? It was as if someone had flipped a switch in my head and I suddenly had protective instincts.

And I was pretty sure I knew who was to blame.

If anyone else had seen me, I would have denied it, but the thought of how Ava had influenced me made me smile. Everything felt a little more real, a little more survivable. Since I'd met her, I hadn't felt like I'd sold pieces of my soul to be alive.

The sound of tires outside of the house had me on my feet. I moved close to the door and looked out the side of the curtain. The driver opened the door and I felt like I'd been punched in the gut.

Ava took the driver's hand as he assisted her out of the car, one long, bare leg at a time. The skirt she was wearing must've been painted on and the blouse showed off all that cleavage Kenny had thought was worth dying for. Her hair swung around her shoulders in long waves, her bangs pushed to the side, showcasing her giant blue eyes. She was sex and innocence rolled into one perfect package.

Most importantly she was here, safe, and didn't look scared.

I took a deep breath and tried to remember that I was watching to make sure nothing was wrong, not to stare at the gorgeous American. Ava slipped a bag over her shoulder and shifted a coat to her free arm. Her eyes ran over the house, but she didn't make any move to go up the steps.

Mavis slid out of the car next, her blond hair twisted at the base of her neck, her outfit just as revealing as the one Ava wore, but she didn't hold a candle to my girl. Ava held out the jacket for Mavis who waved it away. Her eyes met mine through the edge of the curtain and she smiled.

They were safe.

I stepped away from the window and ran a hand through my hair. It took a lot of will power to not open the door and go swoop Ava into my arms.

Ava used a key to open the front door, moving to the side and holding it open for Mavis. Her eyes darted around the room, looking for something. I stepped out of the shadows and drank in the smile that curved her mouth.

Mavis shut the door behind them and took the coat out of Ava's hands. She said something I couldn't hear before disappearing into the kitchen after a small nod in my direction.

I tucked my hands in the pockets of my pants. The need to hold Ava against me was so intense I was worried I'd hurt her. What if she had decided that everything between us had been a mistake? She'd been left with Mavis and her own thoughts for most of a day.

"Did you guys have any trouble?" She tucked some of her hair behind her ear and licked her lips.

"Other than Kenny eating as much as his body weight, we're fine." I let my eyes roam over her curves, the way her hands twisted together in front of her. "Did you?"

"Eat my weight in food?" She raised an eyebrow and a half smile pulled at her mouth.

"Trouble. Did you have any trouble?" I took a step

toward her, caught in the gravitational pull of her eyes.

"No. It was actually really easy, which worried me more than anything. I kept expecting something to go wrong." She took a step closer to me. She was wearing heels that almost brought her eye to eye with me. "No one even looked at us."

"I guarantee that people looked at you."

A blush rushed up her neck and I felt my own smile grow.

"The clothes were Mavis's idea." She looked down at the skirt and leaned over to look at her shoes, giving me a hearty glimpse of her cleavage. "I feel awkward."

"You shouldn't." I took another step in her direction and took my hands out of my pockets. "You look like sex in heels."

"I think that was her idea, but I'm not really the sexy type." She bit her lip and I couldn't help myself.

It took five large strides to close the distance between us. I tangled my fingers in her hair and enjoyed the way her lips, slick with lip gloss, moved against mine. That was new and unexpected. Her hands weren't gentle either as she pulled at me. Her breathing was fast, her body fitting perfectly against mine, and I knew I was lost. Being away from her had been like holding my breath for hours on end.

"You are definitely the sexy type." I pressed my mouth to the pressure point just below her ear. "Very, very sexy."

"You like the clothes." If I hadn't already been stand-ing at attention, her throaty laugh would have pushed me there.

"Yes." I slid my hand to the nape of her neck so I

could look deep into her eyes. "Very much. Now you should take them off."

"Mavis said we could have the room downstairs. She was going upstairs to check on Kenny." She threaded her fingers with mine and pulled me through a formal parlor to the back of the house.

I followed her, my eyes glued to the way her ass swayed as she walked in those mile high heels. She opened one door, but it was just a toilet. She closed it and opened the door next to it. There was a large four poster bed and other furnishings, but the only thing that really mattered was the bed. She tugged me into the room before leaning against the door and making sure it was locked.

I pressed behind her and let my hands roam up her body. I started to pull at her shirt but she turned and pushed my hands away.

"Nuhuh. You can't tear these." Instead she moved out of reach and slipped the black sweater off that she was wearing and laid it on a chair in the corner. When she began to unbutton her blouse, coherent thoughts fled my mind leaving behind nothing but anticipation and greed. Underneath that satin was a black lace bra that perfectly cupped her breasts. She let the shirt fall to the floor behind her before reaching to undo the zipper on her skirt. After it floated to the ground, she was standing there in nothing but the black lingerie and heels. It took a second for my mind to register just what my body saw.

She was a goddess and I felt totally inept. Which wasn't something I had experienced since I'd been sixteen. This woman was a gift to be treasured and I was sweaty palms, unable to move.

She bit her lip, nerves showing in her eyes, and that

was when it hit me. As she stood there, bare and willing, offering herself to me, an emotion I'd never fully appreciated smacked me in the chest.

This was what love felt like.

I loved Ava.

Nothing would ever be the same now. That thought seemed to align my brain and body. I walked toward her slowly, enjoying the way her pupils dilated as I neared. Tomorrow we would prepare for our trip. We'd have to make plans and I'd have to watch other men salivate over the sexy clothes. But not tonight.

Tonight was for us.

Trailing my fingers down her side I hooked them in her panties, sliding them down her legs, and helped her step out of them. As I stood back up I ran my hands along her skin, reveling in the goosebumps that erupted along her arms. With my thumbs I pushed the straps of her bra down her shoulders to press a kiss where each had just sat before wrapping my arms around her to undo the clasps in the back.

Her warm mouth sought mine, her lips tender as she kissed me. With soft strokes of her tongue she explored my mouth. I pushed the bra off, exposing her perfect breasts to the cool air around us. Her hardened nipples pressed against my shirt and she deepened our kiss, eager for what we could do together.

With gentle fingers she undid the buttons of my shirt and pushed it off my shoulders. Delicate hands trailed over my skin, touching everywhere she could reach. When her breasts brushed across my chest in teasing strokes I growled deep in my throat.

When we finally parted to breathe, she slid down to

the floor in a graceful cascade of skin and dark hair. Her bright eyes sought mine as she undid my belt and pulled me free from my pants. Every muscle in my body tightened in pleasure as her warm mouth enveloped me. The wet sounds coming from her lips and the soft moans that reverberated along my cock made it almost impossible to stay standing. Just the image of her kneeling in front of me while wearing those fuck-me shoes and her lips wrapped around me was enough to push me to the edge. I clenched my fists and fought to not lose it yet. I wanted to enjoy it for as long as possible.

I leaned back against a dresser when my legs threatened to give out. She moved with me, never losing her rhythm. Clutching at her hair, I took a ragged breath, and tried to think of anything but her mouth and the sounds she was making. My thighs burned from trying to stay still but my hips slammed forward, wanting to go faster. Needing to finish.

"Ava," I growled. "If you don't stop I'm going to come."

Instead of slowing, she wrapped her hand at my base and her mouth picked up pace. I groaned and my hips moved with her. My orgasm was building, ready to break the dam at any minute. When I tried to pull her back, she pushed my hands away. Instead she circled my head with her tongue and I felt my eyes roll back.

"Ava, love, it feels too good."

She pulled back from me, her mouth making a little popping sound.

"I want to do this." The vision of her face next to my wet dick made me groan. "Let me take you there."

She didn't wait for my answer. Her hot mouth slid

back over my shaft, taking in as much of me as she could before pulling back and then returning. Her free hand massaged my balls and that was all I could handle. My fingers clenched in her hair, holding her in place as I spilled into her mouth. The world seemed to explode around me and stars floated behind my eyelids. There was an eager need in the way she drank me down, her mouth hungry to taste everything I had to offer, and it was intoxicating. It was as if she thought she might never get to do it again.

When I was finished I swept her up in my arms and took her to the bed. She lay back, spreading her legs, and trailing a hand down to her warm center. Those damn heels were still on and I could already feel my dick tightening again. Watching as she touched herself was the hottest thing I'd ever seen. Her fingers played with the tender spot at the top before dipping lower and then inside.

Her hips lifted off the blanket and she moaned before biting her lip. I slid onto the bed and pulled her hand away from that tender spot. I lifted her fingers to my mouth, licking them clean while she watched me with hooded eyes. Moving between her legs, I lifted her hips up and placed my mouth where she had just been touching.

"Heaven." I murmured against her skin. "You're my heaven, Ava."

I used my tongue to push her on, taking my time to enjoy all of the sounds that escaped her mouth, the way her hips struggled against me. When her breathing sped up and her groans grew louder, I pulled back.

Her whimper of disappointment made me smile. I crawled up her body, paying attention to each breast before looking down into her eyes.

"I want you moving under me Ava." I kissed along

her jaw as I slid inside her. "I want to feel you come."

She rolled her hips against me and we groaned at the same time. When I matched her movements, I knew it wouldn't be long before we reached the end.

I tilted her chin up so I could see her eyes. "I missed you."

Her groan of need was loud as her body shuddered with pleasure. Her finger nails bit into my ass as she pulled me in deeper and despite my turn earlier I couldn't hold back any longer. I came hollering her name, a sort of prayer to whatever god was listening. A plea to keep her, to never have to let her go.

"I missed you, too." She looked up at me with satisfied eyes. "I didn't like being away from you."

I leaned my head down so it touched hers. "Me either."

"Let's not do that again, hm?" Her voice was tired but warm. Content. I would give my arm to be able to make her always sound like she did in that moment.

"Deal." I lifted myself off of her and rolled to the side, keeping her tucked against me.

"Pinky promise?" She held up her little finger with a smile.

"Pinky promise?"

She took my hand, hooking her little finger with mine before kissing her thumb. She watched me expectantly and it took my sluggish brain a moment to understand why she was waiting. Leaning forward I mimicked her and kissed my own thumb.

"You can't break a pinky promise." She tucked her head against my good shoulder. "It's serious stuff."

"I've never made a pinky promise before." I ran my

hand over her shoulder and closed my eyes. "But I won't break my promises to you."

"It's something I used to do with my parents." Her voice took on a sad, thoughtful tone.

That was the first time she had mentioned her past. I didn't want to push her for information. I knew how hard it was to share the darker parts of our memories.

"They died when I was in middle school." I felt her draw in a deep breath, but she didn't stop. "They were killed by a drunk driver. A hit and run."

"I'm sorry." It was such a useless phrase, but what else could I say? I hated hearing the grief in her voice.

"The worst part was that if the driver had stopped and called for help, they would have had a fighting chance. They might still be alive, working, sending me emails about their crazy clients. They'd owned a catering business that was pretty popular." She shrugged, but I could tell it still hurt her. "But he didn't and they died there, in the middle of a dark intersection. It was hard, but I had my grandmother. I moved out of Atlanta and onto her farm. It took some adjusting, but I was so angry at the world, it was probably the best place for me. She put me to work and eventually I found a sense of calm, a different type of happy."

"You don't have any siblings?" I'd had Marcus, even if he hadn't been the best role model. At least I'd had someone to turn to.

That is, before he'd decided I was better off dead.

"Only child. But I had Grandma. She was more than enough family." She chuckled, but it sounded a little wet. "So much personality in such a tiny woman. Mavis kind of reminds me of her. Nothing phased Gram. She was barely over five feet tall, but was larger than life."

"You said she passed, too?" I remembered her mentioning inheritance money.

"I was in college then. I'd moved farther south to go to an art school, but we were still close." She looked up at me. "At some point after my parents died I realized I could begrudge the world for taking the people I loved from me or I could be thankful I'd had any time with them at all. Not everyone gets that."

I tightened my arm around her. My heart swelled. She was too perfect for someone like me. She was too perfect, period.

"Not everyone would be able to move on the way you did." I turned my head so I could kiss her temple. "For example, you could have turned into a vigilante and hunted down the drunken driver. I know a few people like that."

A sleepy chuckle floated up to my ears. "I don't think our stories are exactly the same thing. But if I could have found that drunk driver before the police I probably would have tried to kill him. As it is, he's still in jail, hopefully sharing a cell with someone stinky that likes to cuddle."

"I can't imagine you killing someone on purpose, love." I closed my eyes, happy to have her next to me.

She didn't respond for a while and I thought she had drifted off to sleep. It wasn't until she moved her hand up to the stitches on my shoulder that I realized she was still awake.

"I would kill to protect the people I love." Her voice was so soft I almost didn't hear it. She slid her hand lower, over my chest, and paused, her fingers brushing my bandage.

I closed my eyes, my heart pounding under her palm. I'd give anything to be someone worth that kind of love. Gritting my teeth, I berated myself for even thinking about it. I didn't deserve Ava, and the closer we became, the more I realized it was true.

I just wasn't strong enough to push her away. I knew eventually she would see the monster I was and wouldn't think twice as she ran away. These moments with her would be memories I'd treasure for as long as I lived.

"Point me in the right direction and I'll kill them for you." Gathering her in my arms, I pulled her up so that she was resting on my chest, and tucked her head under my chin.

Something warm dripped onto my chest, but I didn't say anything. I wasn't sure why she was crying, but I wrapped my arms around her a little tighter. Words weren't my best skill, but holding her was rapidly becoming my strong suit.

CHAPTER
TWENTY-THREE

MY FINGERS TIGHTENED, digging into my hips. The urge to poke Owen in the chest was so strong I didn't trust my hands away from my body. He made stubborn an art form.

"If you're going to teach him, you might as well teach me. He's not even going in the casino! I am! I should know how to defend myself." My foot tapped against the concrete of Mavis small back patio.

"I'm teaching him the basics, the very bare basics, so we can build from there. This isn't the kind of stuff you'll need to escape those pros. It's completely different." He held his hands in the air, his eyes trained on me like I was predator.

Two days. Today and tomorrow was all the time I had to prepare for the casino. Nightmares had haunted my restless night as images of Owen and Mavis dead circled around me. I couldn't stop it from happening, couldn't keep the bad guys away. I wasn't enough...of anything.

"You can work with me." Mavis took the last few

steps and gave me a welcoming nod. "Go grab some workout clothes from my room and meet me back down here. I have a routine. Stretch, run, stretch, katas, and then sparring. Work for you?"

"Hell yes!" I took the stairs two at a time, ignoring the angry tone Owen was using to address Mavis. The master suite was on the top floor. Ceiling to floor mirrors covered one wall and I realized that her closet lay just behind those doors.

Once I'd found clothing that actually fit, I headed back outside. The pants were capris on me, but I didn't care. I wasn't trying to look good.

"Stretch first." Mavis tossed me a water bottle before slipping into a deep lunge.

Flexibility had never been a strong talent of mine, but I'd be damned if I wasn't going to give it my all. I'd managed to follow Mavis with a few alternate stretches until she announced it was time.

She took off, heading for the sidewalk in front of the house, and I followed quickly behind her. Part of me wanted to stop and kiss Owen goodbye, but the other part of me wanted to punch him in the nose for treating me like I was some sort of breakable object.

"He's going to hurt Kenny," Mavis said. Resignation laced her words. "I should have already taught him."

"What? Why?" I kept pace beside her despite my longer stride.

"It happens." She shrugged. "Part of the learning process. He won't do it to be mean, but that's why he refused to teach you. He wouldn't forgive himself if he hurt you, not even on accident."

"But I'm part of all this and I want to be able to take

care of myself." I shook my head. "Men are so stupid."

"They have too many heads." Mavis smiled. "Means their thoughts don't know where to go."

I laughed, drawing the attention of some neighbors exiting their front door. Mavis raised her hand and smiled at them. They waved back in acknowledgment.

"Let's go before they walk over to say hello." Mavis took off with ease and I was left pounding the pavement behind her.

She might be a tiny woman, but there was an un-tapped well of energy hiding inside. I wasn't that out of shape, but I eventually stopped seeing anything around me except the next few feet of ground. My shoes were the cheap tennis shoes I'd bought with Owen and my toes started to protest. The promise of water and a flat surface was the only thing that kept me going.

That and the desire to be able to take care of myself.

When we turned back on to Mavis's street my lungs were screaming and my legs felt wobbly. I used to love to run. It was the perfect time to think, but I'd passed that time mark an hour ago.

"Want to do the circuit again?" Mavis looked over her shoulder at me.

I didn't respond. The only words I was capable of at this point were of the four-letter variety and I honestly didn't want to waste any oxygen on them. Which was a new thing for me. Instead I went around to the back of her house intent on a giant glass of water.

Owen was wearing sweatpants and a white t-shirt that stretched over his muscles as he walked Kenny through some sort of exercise. I had to remind myself I was irritat-ed with him as I walked past to go in the kitchen. An older man was busy at the counter and I froze. Slowly I walked backward until I was again on the patio.

"Um, Owen?" I checked behind me to make sure I was at the right house. Yep. I had walked into the right kitchen.

"Yes?"

"There's an old man in the kitchen."

"That's Mr. Felding. He's the butler," Kenny explained. "He'll get you anything you need. And he makes great sandwiches."

"Uh huh." I frowned. I hadn't noticed any household staff last night. Then again, we had arrived very late.

I walked back into the kitchen and the old man turned to smile at me.

"Good morning, ma'am." He bobbed his head. "Are you hungry?"

"No." Just the thought of trying to process food after that run made my stomach queasy. "I'd really love some cold water, though."

"Still or sparkling?" He moved toward the large refrigerator.

"Still." I managed to sit at the island instead of falling flat on my face. My throat was raw from sucking in cool air during the run.

"Here you are, ma'am." He set the glass down in front of me. "Can I help you with anything else?"

"No thank you." I picked up the glass and chugged half of the water. "Call me Ava, please."

"Thank you, ma'am." He wasn't one for chit-chat which was more than okay with me. I had no idea how much he knew about his boss.

Mavis sauntered in a few minutes later and went

straight to the refrigerator for a drink. She poured herself a glass of green juice and I grimaced. It would figure that Mavis was a health nut.

"Good morning, ma'am." Mr. Felding gave her a little head bob.

"You kept up." Mavis slid onto the stool next to me.

"I'm not sure if you noticed, but I was about ten yards behind you for most of the run." I grimaced. "I was the one sweating and groaning. You might have mistaken me for a zombie."

"Oh, I know you were there. The point is that you kept pace, even if you were ten yards behind me." She tapped her glass of stinky green juice against my cup of water.

I took another drink of my water. It certainly hadn't felt like I'd kept pace with her. She had blown past me without even trying. My eyes cut in her direction and I frowned. Looking at her, you would never know she had gone for a run.

"Okay, we've had a long enough break. Let's go work on forms." Mavis drained the rest of her drink and hopped off the stool.

I leaned over and placed one of my hot cheeks against the cool marble counter top. I didn't want to do forms. I just wanted to die here against the cold stone.

"Get up. You've got a lot to learn." She put her hands on her hips and for a brief moment I had a vision of Jazz-ercise Barbie.

"How much is this going to hurt?" I narrowed my eyes.

"Just remember, you asked for this." She smiled sweetly before turning and going out the back door.

Groaning, I stood up and followed her out, knowing that she was right. I had no one to blame but myself. I wanted to learn and Mavis was the one that had agreed to help me. Or course, I didn't delude myself into thinking she wasn't going to enjoy herself. She was going to love every minute that she got to beat me up.

The forms weren't the bad part. Learning how to take a punch was the hard part. Or rather, trying to learn to avoid being punched was the hard part. I had no idea how to block, so being fast and moving out of the way were my best options.

"That's it. You are not human!" I pointed at the tiny ninja in front of me. "You're an evil elf sent to torture me."

"Stop whining and put your hands up!" Mavis moved forward at the speed of light and I back peddled. "Stop doing that."

"You're a spider monkey on steroids. What else a I going to do? Oof!" One of her tiny fists slammed into my stomach.

"You're bigger than I am. Use your size." She twirled and her foot shot toward my head.

I ducked and dove for her leg which seemed to catch her off guard. We tumbled together to the ground and I fumbled to keep my hold on her. She wiggled and fought, slamming her knee into my chin.

"That wasn't bad." She twisted out of my grip and rolled into a standing position. "You had me for a second."

"I almost bit my tongue off." I stuck my tongue out and touched it gingerly.

"Get up. There is no crying in sparring."

I stood up and brushed my backside off. Maybe I

would be better once I'd practiced the katas more. Those would teach me how to move and weave around my opponent.

The loud sound of flesh meeting flesh made me wince and I looked over at Kenny and Owen. Kenny was bent over and cursing under his breath. Owen was patting his shoulder with a pained expression. It looked like I wasn't the only one suffering.

That afternoon as I sat on the grass next to Kenny, I tried to give myself reassurance. I'd picked up the katas pretty quickly which had made me feel better after the long run. It was a soothing exercise. Owen approved of my stances, but otherwise didn't say much to me.

Katas were where my self-praise ended. Mavis had thrown me around like a ragdoll and despite that, I'd still found it hard to actually try to hurt her. My punches were weak. I needed to punch through the foam paddles she held up, but pulled back each time my knuckles met one. My kicks were pathetic because I wasn't limber enough to touch her nose with my toes. When it came to escaping choke holds and flipping Mavis over my shoulder, I'd been a complete failure.

At least I wasn't bleeding, which was more than I could say about Kenny.

"Here, you need more tissue." I unrolled some of the toilet paper sitting between us and handed it to him for his nose.

"Phanks." He discarded the bloody paper he'd been using and replaced it with the new stuff, careful to keep his head tilted backward. "Phis bows."

I snorted. Yep, it really did blow.

"Maybe we aren't as bad as we think. Maybe we're

doing okay for our first day." I stared up at the sky and prayed that was the truth.

"Phight." The young guy sighed, his frustration matching mine. "Veast ooo ahn't bweeding."

"Not from a lack of effort on your aunt's part." I plucked a piece of grass and held it up between my fingers. Yep, grass was pretty much the same no matter where you visited.

Owen and Mavis had gone on a cool-down jog, leaving me and Kenny to bleed to death in her backyard. I didn't even have the energy to be jealous over the time Owen was spending with Mavis. Not that I thought he wanted Mavis, but because she was getting time with him, period. But nope, I was content to lay here on the ground and pass tissues to the bleeding teenager.

"Maybe we could feign comas and get out of whatever torture they have planned for us when they get back." The sounds of the city were muted, but I closed my eyes and tried to pick them out. Cars, people, music from a store floated past my ears.

Regular people doing regular things.

"Have you two eaten yet?" Owen walked through the house, using a towel to scrub the sweat out of his hair.

Kenny and I looked at each other. The thought of food made me want to curl into a ball, and blood was dripping past the tissue in his nose. I pulled off more paper and handed it to him.

"No." I managed to prop myself up from the ground. "I'm not sure Kenny can swallow anything right now."

"Noth wifth outh bunch o' bwood." Kenny sighed.

"Mr. Felding is making dinner." Owen leaned against the door frame and looked at Kenny. "I can ask him to cut your steak into tiny little pieces."

"I'd fwip ooo off if my fwinger didn'f hurf."

"Here, let me." I raised my middle finger.

"Later, love." Owen's laugh rolled through the back yard and despite how tired I was it still made my heart jump.

"Too sore." I laid back on the grass and closed my eyes, hoping Kenny didn't notice my blush.

"Your nose wouldn't be hurt if you had done what I told you." Owen walked over and made Kenny look up at him. "You let your anger get the best of you."

Kenny just grunted.

"Right, well, I'm ready to shower." I pushed myself up and started to stand. He held his hand out to me and I let him help me the rest of the way to my feet. "Thanks."

His eyes ran over my and he pressed a soft kiss to my temple.

I knew he wasn't happy about watching Mavis throw me around, but he hadn't tried to stop it. Which I appreciated. I wasn't going to be worth anything by the time we got to Paris, but at least it was a start.

Somewhere in the back of my mind I knew that if I was going to keep Owen in my life, I'd need to learn how to take care of myself. If I could take care of myself then he wouldn't do stupid things like jumping in front of bullets to save me.

Hot water helped work the knots out of my back and neck, but nothing was going to help the deep ache from muscles that hadn't been used for too long. By the time I got out, there wasn't much warm water left, but I didn't care. I hobbled back to the bedroom I had shared with Owen the night before and collapsed face-down on the bed. Putting clothes on seemed like too much work, so I just lay there to finish air drying.

I was a wimp.

I heard the door open, but I didn't look up. I didn't care that I was naked in a strange house full of staff and assassins. And wanna-be assassins if you included Kenny. I was comfortable and that was worth more than my modesty at the moment.

The bed dipped and a hand ran down my leg, working the muscles with strong fingers.

"I really hope you're Owen. Otherwise, he might be pissed."

"Not might, love." I could hear the smile in his voice.

"Good. It's you." I sighed as he worked down the other leg. "That feels great."

"Mavis pushed you hard today."

I attempted a shrug and winced. "I've got a lot to learn."

"I understand wanting to be able to take care of yourself." His voice was low. "I just don't like that you feel you need to."

"Is that your pesky male ego talking?" I turned my head so I could see his profile.

"No." He frowned but continued working on my legs. "I don't like you being involved in all of this."

"Sorry to point out the obvious, but I am involved in all of this and I don't want to just sit around and cower behind everyone."

"We have two days. You won't be ready to take on the bad guys, Ava." He switched legs.

"I know that." I closed my eyes.

"Then why are you torturing yourself right now?" He

stopped and met my gaze.

How to answer? We hadn't even defined our relation-ship. Blurt out that I wanted to keep him in my life? That I needed to be able to protect myself so that I wouldn't slow him down?

"Ava?" He shifted so he could pull me onto his lap.

"A girl should know how to take care of herself." I didn't meet his eyes. "Life has really highlighted that point for me lately."

"After this, you can go back to your life. Find a job and not worry about people trying to kill you." He used his fingers to make me look at him. "You can get a security system and a big dog."

"How can you be so sure?" I frowned. "After this I'll still have to deal with the police and God knows who else. I've got to find Tessa, too."

"I'll help you find Tessa." Calm, clear eyes watched me.

"What about after?" I hated that my voice shook on the last word.

"After that." His eyes clouded. "I'll make sure you're okay, Ava."

"I...I want more than okay. I want to be happy." I want you, you stupid, hot, perfect man.

"Ava." He leaned forward and pressed his head to mine. "I don't know how to keep someone happy long term. I'm not cut out for happy."

"Have you ever tried?" My tone was sharp. "I thought you liked being with me."

"I more than like being with you. I love it—" he curs-ed under his breath. "Damn it. Ava, love. I want to wake up with you every morning. I want to see what kind of jewelry you make and how you look cooking breakfast naked. I want all of that and things I can't even let myself think about, because I don't deserve that. I'm not that person. I don't live in that world and I can't give you what you want, what you deserve."

"How do you know what I want?" I captured his face in my hands. "I don't even know what I want. Shouldn't I get to have a say in that? To decide?"

"I've never wanted anything as much as I want you." He took a deep breath. "You're so innocent and kind. You're everything I'm not. I kill people, Ava. You can't have a future with someone that works for death."

"You kill bad people." I narrowed my eyes. "And I'm not as sweet and innocent as you think. I did kill and then run over the dead body of a pimp. I've stolen a car, used fake identification, and carried an illegal weapon."

"All of that happened after you met me." He frowned.

"The point is…I don't feel bad about any of it. Not even Mr. Song." I shook my head when he started to say something. "I did at first, because I was the one that did it, but then I realized that I wouldn't have been upset if someone else had done it. I mean I can't be upset if the world lost one more bad guy."

He opened his mouth but I gave him a stern look.

"It's like those people that are okay with eating beef and Thanksgiving turkey as long as they don't actually have to kill, skin, de-feather, or whatever the hell you do to prepare an animal to cook. You've been getting rid of all these horrible people so everyone else could eat their turkey. You deserve to have some turkey, too."

His lips trembled and I realized he was fighting a laugh.

"I'm not explaining this very well." Heat filled my cheeks. "Damn it. I'm trying to convince you to be happy, but I can't make you. You have to decide to be happy. I read that in a book, but it's true. You're a fucking assassin, Owen! You don't follow the rules and that works for you. You take what you want, what you need."

I clamped my mouth shut. Any minute I was going to be using one liners from rom-com movies and ask him to love me—just a girl sitting naked on his lap.

His face turned serious and I felt my stomach drop.

"We don't celebrate Thanksgiving in England, love." He trailed a finger down the side of my cheek.

"You know what I meant." I narrowed my eyes.

"And you compared yourself to a turkey." A glimmer appeared in his eyes.

"Okay, I wasn't making much sense—"

"You were rambling." He leaned forward and kissed my chin, then the tip of my nose. "But you did say something that made sense."

"I did?" My voice was breathless as he kissed one cheek and then the other.

"Yes, my American turkey, you did." His chuckle lifted the weight that had settled in my stomach.

"You reminded me that I'm an assassin." He wrapped his arms around my waist. "And I'm a really good fucking assassin. I've always had my own code of ethics. I do what I think is necessary. Even when that means stealing something important." He kissed my neck. "Something valuable." He kissed my shoulder. "Something I needed."

I took a deep breath, trying to focus on what he was saying.

"I've been fighting what I wanted, what I needed. I

wasn't strong enough though. That wasn't working for me." In a quick move he rolled me onto my back and propped himself above me. "So I'm not going to fight it anymore. I'm keeping you, Ava. You're mine and no one is taking you from me."

I looked up into his eyes and felt my eyes sting. "That's good, because you didn't really have a choice."

"I'm not much for words, Ava, but I want you to know something."

"What's that?" I brushed his hair out of his eyes.

"I love you." The amount of sincerity in those three words brought tears to my eyes.

If I wasn't looking up at him I would swear that I was floating. My body felt alive and my soul felt full. Full in a way that I hadn't experienced in a long time.

"I love you too, Owen."

CHAPTER TWENTY-FOUR

Owen

EVERYTHING WAS BATHED in a dark shade of red. I would kill them all. Staring at the floor was the only way I could keep from meeting other people's eyes and sending them scattering. The monster I kept carefully caged was prowling behind the bars, thirsty for blood and the need to cause agony.

Every single man that turned and stared at Ava's ass as we walked through the airport was on my shit list and that wasn't a list people wanted to make.

Her skirt hung well past her knees and yet that only seemed to enhance the sexiness of her curves. The teal of her low-cut sweater made her eyes almost glow. She'd added a little extra sway to her walk with the mile-high heels.

I couldn't really blame the men; she was a knock-out.

But she was my knock-out and watching other men enjoy what I'd just claimed made me want to rage. Jealousy was a nasty emotion. No wonder some people paid to kill off their rivals.

"Ms. Gardner, can you hand me the information for the flight?" Mavis held her hand out without looking.

"Of course." Ava reached into her bag and pulled out a sheet with flight information and placed it in Mavis's hand.

"As you can see, we have all the appropriate information." Mavis cocked her head at the woman manning the private terminal.

"Of course, Mrs. Thomasino."

"Miss Thomasino," Mavis corrected her curtly.

"Yes, ma'am." The woman smiled and it almost looked genuine. "And I'll need the documentation for the people flying with you."

"It's in with the rest of the papers." Mavis looked away from the woman, boredom radiating from every pore.

"Ah, yes. I see it here." She punched some information into the computer before stepping around the corner and lifting a rope. "This way, please."

Private planes came in different makes, sizes, and opulence. From the grandeur of the terminal we were being led down, I felt it safe to assume the company wasted no money on their planes. Flying wasn't something that I minded, but doing so on an expensive private jet certainly made it more enjoyable.

The woman from the gate handed us off to a different attendant that placed our bags on a cart and led us onto the tarmac. White paint so bright it almost blinded us was broken up by a thin silver pin-stripe that ran from nose to tail. A tall bloke ducked out of the door and quick-stepped down the stairs.

He pulled his idiotic captain's hat off his head and

watched us as we approached, a giant smile splitting his face. His eyes tracked Mavis as she swayed toward him before darting past her to check out the other possible conquest and stopped dead.

The wind ruffled Ava's hair around her face and Captain Horny's smile grew to unbelievable proportions. Mavis held out her hand and said something I didn't catch, but it brought the dickhead's attention back to her. I'd seen Mavis using her full charm before and it wasn't something most men were able to escape, but the captain's eyes kept darting toward Ava.

My Ava.

He took Mavis's hand and brought it to his lips to kiss and I used the time to move closer to Ava. I shouldn't have moved closer because it made his next words all the more clear.

"Sexy little Ava." He grabbed her hand and lifted it to his lips for a lingering kiss. "I didn't think I'd ever have the pleasure of seeing you again when I found out you had left the States, but today is my lucky day."

"I didn't realize you worked for this charter company." Ava smiled at him and I tried to not be annoyed. She was merely playing a role.

"Come now, Ava." His voice lowered and I had to strain to hear it without looking interested. "How many times have I begged you to run away with me? And now, here you are."

"But I'm not running away with you, Captain." She tossed her hair over one shoulder, almost hitting me in the face. "I'm here on business."

"Business and pleasure often mix." He winked at her.

Winked. At. Her.

"You two know each other?" Mavis stepped closer with a seductive smile. "Ava, darling, you didn't tell me you knew the captain."

"I didn't realize I did." Ava cleared her throat and pulled her hand away from the pilot's. "Captain, this is my employer, Miss Thomasino. I work for her now."

"Moving up in the world, then." The captain replaced his hat and motioned for our group to move onto the plane. He held Mavis's hand as she stepped onto the stairs and did the same for Ava. With a short nod to me and Kenny, he followed Ava so closely he needed to place his hand on her waist to keep from tripping on her. When they reached the top step, his hand dipped low enough to cup her ass. Ava stiffened when he touched her before willing herself to relax. A soft giggle floated back from her when he leaned down to whisper in her ear.

The other men in the airport had just received a reprieve. I would unleash all my hatred on the pilot.

Captain Horny must die.

A slight tug on my sleeve had me jerking around to wrap my hand around a thin wrist. I looked into Kenny's annoyed face.

"Dude, you're growling." The teenager's voice was low as he pulled free.

I clenched my jaw and stared into his eyes, trying to reign in my temper. The boy was right. I needed to get it together. If that bloody cocksucker was going to hone in on Ava, it wasn't her fault. The fact that she hadn't told him off was just her sticking to her part. We needed the fucking idiot.

"I don't like him." My teeth clenched shut after the words escaped. Emotions were a double-edged sword.

297

"Yeah. I get that." Kenny straightened the suit jacket he was wearing. "There is a schedule to keep, though."

He was trying to remind me that we needed to stick to the plan, as if I'd forgotten. I hadn't forgotten our agenda; I was just debating if I still wanted to follow it.

Leaning forward, I lowered my voice. "If you play your cards right, I'll let you use him as a practice dummy."

"We need him to fly the plane." Kenny grinned. I wasn't sure if he believed me or not. "And other stuff, you know?"

"After, then." I narrowed my eyes.

"Sounds good to me." His smile grew even more. "Would be nice to not be the punching bag for once."

A bruise still showed along his left cheek and his nose was a bit swollen. I slapped him on the shoulder and steered him in front of me. He hadn't bitched once during the last couple of sessions, even if his face had warranted a good curse. He'd thrown himself into the work with vigor.

"You're a good kid, Kenny." I walked up the stairs slowly. "But you really need to learn to duck."

"I duck just fine. I need to learn to be faster, is what I need to learn." Kenny shook his head as he dipped into the plane. He hesitated for half a second before clearing the doorway. I knew by the way his eyes darted briefly in my direction that I wasn't going to like whatever he had seen.

Ava was sitting in a chair across from Mavis and the pilot was crouched down next to her blocking the aisle, his hand on her knee as he asked her if she had been to Paris before. Not sure what to do, Kenny turned and grabbed the seat at the front, which left me with nothing to do but push past the prick hitting on Ava.

"Pardon me." I let the bag I was carrying swing into

the back of his head. "These bloody planes are so small inside."

The pilot looked up at me with a careful smile. "Not used to flying in a private jet?"

"Not this small." I threw my bag into a seat. "The last one had a gold toilet seat and a stripper pole."

"That sounds like some plane." Captain Horny stood up and looked around the plane. "What do you say, Ava? Think your old employer would throw in a stripper pole and gold toilet seat for a loyal customer?"

Ava dragged her eyes away from me with a grimace. I wasn't sure what I'd said that had upset her. It wasn't like I'd alleged anyone had been using the stripper pole.

"I'm sure they'll put in whatever you want." She smiled up at the pilot and I had to busy myself with the contents of my bag to keep from decking him while he stared down her cleavage.

"I'll have to give that some careful thought."

"Which arrondissement is your flat in?" Mavis crossed her legs and leaned back in her seat.

"Oberkampf," he said.

"Oh, that's a great area." Mavis smiled. "I keep a place in Avenue Montaigne."

"Rubbing elbows with the stars, eh?" He looked from Mavis to Ava. "If you want to see the real Paris, I could show you two around. It would be my pleasure."

"You could really show us around?" Ava sat forward, a slight blush to her cheeks. She was a horrible flirt, which made her even more adorable. Bloody hell. "I'm so excited. I've always wanted to travel and Paris is at the top of my list, but I don't want the tourist version. I want the nitty-gritty version of Paris. The real Paris. Exciting and

299

edgy. Not just museums or tombs, you know?"

"Is that why you decided to work with Miss Thomasino?" The prick sat down on the arm of her chair like they were long lost friends. "She offered to show you the world?"

"I basically dangled it in front of her like a carrot," Mavis laughed. "I couldn't let someone like Ava slip through my fingers. She's so efficient. Isn't she, dear?" She looked over at me with a gentle smile and I tried not to sigh.

Looked like I'd landed the role of arm candy for this trip.

"Mmhmm." I leaned the chair back and closed my eyes. "She's got an eye for numbers."

"How did you two meet?" I heard him shift but I didn't dare open my eyes. Pretending indifference was the best I could offer at this point. It was that or the blade strapped to my left leg.

"I'm friends with the owners of Heartland Entertainment. I went with Penelope to see her plane and Ava assisted us with a few things." I could hear the smile in Mavis's voice. "I snapped her up. You can only be as profitable as your employees are diligent."

"Well I'd be happy to show you both and your friend around. Not sure the boy is old enough to go everywhere and get the full experience, though."

"That's fine. Kenneth is my newest investment. Brilliant with numbers, horrible with people. He'll be much happier staying in."

I assumed the pilot had turned to look at Kenny. I could hear the boy's fingers dancing across the keys of one of his newest toys.

"Right then, it's settled."

"Thank you, Patrick. I'm so excited. I used to dream about visiting Paris. Even took French classes in high school." The wistfulness in her voice made me grimace. I could just imagine her big eyes shimmering like something out of an anime film.

I needed a stiff drink.

"What drew you to Paris? Why not Italy or Greece?" Mavis asked.

I cracked open an eye and watched as Ava shook her head and sighed.

"It just seems so romantic. I watched Les Misérables and became obsessed."

"Well, it's my pleasure to show you around." Captain Dick-Head stood up. "And if you need a refresher on your French, let me know."

I snapped my eye shut and imagined strangling him. Slowly.

Was I being reasonable? Hell no.

"Would you care for anything to drink, sir?" The flight attendant leaned down to ask in a quiet voice.

"Scotch." I opened my eyes. "Thank you."

Silence rang through the cabin by the time the plane had leveled out. Ava had taken a book out of her bag and was thoroughly engrossed in the contents. I bit my cheek to keep from laughing at the kilt-wearing hero on the cover. As if she could sense my amusement she looked up at me and wiggled her eyebrows before diving back into the story.

I flipped through the New York Times, The Telegraph, and a few Parisian papers. Eventually I pulled out an old deck of cards to busy my hands.

I let my mind wander as I shuffled and flipped cards. While it was important to stay loose and roll with whatever happened, it never hurt to have back up plans and open options. I'd make contact with some of the people I could trust. And by trust, I meant 'not need to kill on sight.'

The door to the cockpit opened and Captain Dick-Head strolled out. He stopped at the coffee pot and refilled his mug. Leaning against the bulkhead he took a sip from his cup and watched us with a smug smile.

Ava looked over her shoulder, her eyes going round. "Shouldn't you be flying the plane?"

"Auto-pilot. I'm mainly here for take-offs, landings, and emergencies." He lifted his mug in salute. "Need to be able to use the bathroom from time to time."

"And refill your caffeine tank." She smiled at his cup.

"Would you like some?" He pulled another cup from the cabinet.

"That would be great." She tucked her hair behind her ears and leaned forward.

"So, you're a card man." He looked at me over the rim of his cup.

"I've been known to play a hand or two." I looked over at him and forced a smile. "You want like cards?"

"Indeed. It's a hobby of mine." He took another sip.

"Care to play?" I raised an eyebrow.

"Oh, sweetheart, don't steal the poor pilot's money." Mavis looked over at me with a sly smile. "I'm sure you can find someone to challenge in Paris."

I shrugged. "Let the man decide."

Captain Bellend looked irritated, but hid it behind a cool expression. "Now, I'm not exactly a novice. I've held my own before and walked out with more money than I had going in."

"You know a table that would let me in?" I flipped the cards overs quickly before folding them back into the stack. "I've got the paper."

"I might know a place." His eyes studied me over the coffee cup. "I can make some calls."

"Ugh. I don't want to sit around in a dingy place filled with smoke while you take everyone's money again." Mavis leaned back and closed her eyes. "I'll just stay in tonight and work. Ava, we'll make calls to the Americans. We should get ahead while we can, I suppose."

"Yes, ma'am." Ava closed the book in her lap and did a horribly perfect job of hiding her disappointment. "Excuse me, I need to use the ladies' room."

"Ah, of course." The pilot stood up and motioned toward the head.

"Thanks." She skirted past him, keeping her face down, but letting her body brush his.

It was surprisingly well executed. A damsel in distress. Which was hilarious when you considered how she had cussed and hollered at me when she really was running for her life.

"I feel bad, going back on my promise to show you Paris." The captain sat down in Ava's seat.

"I'm well used to Owen's need to gamble." Mavis waved a hand. "We're here for business anyway. I'll give my assistant tickets for the holidays."

"Still, I might know a good place to visit that would appeal to all of you." His smile was back in place. "It's a real big deal in town, but I have to warn you, it's not exactly government sanctioned."

"That sounds like it's exactly up our alley," I said.

CHAPTER
TWENTY-FIVE

Ava

LEANING AGAINST THE railing of the Juliet balcony, I sighed. The Eiffel Tower glowed in the dimming light and I couldn't stop looking around in awe. I was finally in Paris. I hadn't been lying on the plane. I'd dreamed of visiting France from the time I was twelve.

Jasmine wrapped around the wrought iron railing and I took a deep breath. Tonight was a trip into the lion's den, but I'd be damned if I could help enjoying this brief moment.

"Gold straps or pearl heels?" Mavis walked into the room from the spacious adjoining bathroom. She held up two pairs of shoes.

I pursed my lips. "Gold straps."

"They're definitely more eye catching." She tossed them on the bed and put the other shoes back in the closet. "And on the plus side, blood washes off these with no problem."

"I guess that's something to consider." I hoped my face didn't show how I really felt about that tidbit of information. Instead I held up the slinky dress Mavis had suggested for tonight. "Are you sure this is the right one?"

"Trust me. You could be packing a bazooka in that thing and Captain Horny would never notice. He'll be too busy checking out your ass and cleavage." Mavis finished strapping on her last shoe. "He's really not that bad. I've had to deal with much worse. One guy stuck his tongue in my ear while his wife watched. I would have killed him for free."

She squirmed and rubbed at her ears while I tried to not laugh. "So you'd already been contracted to kill him?"

"Yes. The bastard had cheated on and beat his wife. After years of trying to have a baby, she got pregnant. She finally saw the light and tried to leave him, but he wasn't having any of it. He pushed her down the stairs and she lost the baby. It was ugly and she almost died. He forgave her." Mavis snorted before standing up and brushing the wrinkles out of the gold cocktail dress she was wearing. "Someone gave her my contact information. I accepted."

"What a fuck-head." I shook my head.

"Yeah, so at least Captain Randy hasn't done any-thing so heinous."

"No, he's just busy chasing skirts and running from venereal diseases." I frowned. "He's like a used car sales-man trying to park something dirty in my garage."

Mavis's deep laugh filled the room before she man-aged to get a grip. It was followed by a snort. She wiped her fingers under her eyes, careful to not smudge her makeup once she finished laughing.

"I thought Owen was going to encourage him to go sky diving without a chute," I mused. He hadn't said much to me since we'd arrived at Mavis's place. The original plan had been to lay low at his place, but it made more sense to look like big wigs. He'd left pretty quickly with some explanation of trying to find backup.

"Don't worry, dear. He's not used to feeling jealous. It got to him." She stood in front of the mirror and refreshed her makeup. "You've got to think about the world he lives in. He does what he thinks appropriate, even when that means killing someone. Watching someone grope the person you love isn't easy. It would hit him harder than most people. Honestly I was coming up with a plan on how I'd explain the blood stain on the interior when you hugged Captain Horny. I thought for sure he was going to break the pilot's neck."

"I know." I'd have been chewing on one of the plastic and wood tables to keep from killing a woman that rubbed all over Owen. The fire glowing in Owen's eyes had been intense.

"You've got just over an hour before your used car salesman shows up," Mavis said. "Go get changed and primp. You're a bit ruffled."

"Why thank you, Mother. You know exactly how to warm my heart." I fluttered my eyelashes at her before picking up the dress I was supposed to wear. The shoes were something I wouldn't wear for a runway job, much less somewhere I might need to fight.

There was a smaller room next to Mavis's that I had procured for my stay. I slipped out of the outfit I'd worn on the plane and changed into my new dress.

I pulled my hair up in a sophisticated ponytail, leaving my bangs to shield my eyes, and amped up my look for a night time date. Normally I didn't wear this much makeup. It made me feel fake and I'd swear I could feel my pores getting clogged, but this was a special occasion. I needed Captain Horny to think he stood a chance. Wanted him to think I'd dressed up for him, not so I could sneak in a pistol tucked into a band around my waist nor the knives I'd strapped to my inner thighs and between my shoulder blades. I might not be able to do much with the deadly blades or new pistol, but I could at least act like a pack horse for Mavis and Owen.

Kenny had gone with Owen, which had made my heart bump a little harder. Despite his initial disregard for the teenager, he seemed to have really taken him under his wing. It was sweet. He was teaching him how to break bones, shake someone down for information, and stay out of sight. Yep, very assassin-sweet.

"How do I look?" I turned to look at Mavis. The dress felt more like lingerie than attire appropriate to walk the streets. Scratch that. It was appropriate when combined with street walking.

She turned to look at me, her critical eyes running over the ensemble. She twirled her finger in the air and I performed on cue. The shoes were much more comfortable after breaking them in over the last two days. I'd even gotten used to the extra height.

"Perfect." Mavis nodded her head. "Seriously sexy with a touch of innocence. Which seems to be the captain's weakness."

The sound of someone moving downstairs announced the arrival of Owen and Kenny. I could hear the two different sound of footsteps as they moved around. Suddenly the reality of what we were attempting that night hit me like a ton a bricks. We were going to sneak into an underground casino in an attempt to catch a woman that had put a hit out on my best friend, but had mistakenly targeted me instead.

My gut clenched and I knew we weren't going to make it out unscathed. We might die. If Mavis died tonight, she would be leaving behind a nephew that needed her. If Owen died tonight...I couldn't even think of it.

Tears filled my eyes and I turned my attention to the ceiling. How fitting would it be that I finally came to Paris just to die?

"We're going to be okay." Mavis touched my shoulder. I opened my eyes and looked down into her concerned face. "You have to focus on one step at a time. Don't try to anticipate the outcome. Just know we'll all be fine and we're going to get what we needed."

"You should stay here with Kenny. We'll say you got sick." My stomach rolled and I couldn't shake the feeling that something was very wrong.

"I have to find Laura." Her eyes narrowed. "I owe it to her sister."

"What happened?"

"I had a job go wrong. I was so intent on keeping Kenny out of the sights of someone wanting revenge that I accidently led them to Laura. Kenny was tutoring her in maths one day. I was observing, he didn't even know I was back in town." Her eyes swirled with regret and guilt. "Laura is petite with blonde hair. They must've thought she was the one I was protecting."

"Oh God." I tried to keep from gasping.

"So, I'm going tonight. Kenny knows what to do if things go bad, but I have to try and right this wrong." Mavis frowned at me. "I shouldn't have told you, but there is something about you that makes people...comfortable.

You're already at your edge. Just forget what I said and focus on distracting Captain Horny."

I took a deep breath and looked back at my reflection. I could do this. I could pretend I was on a blind double date with a grabby guy. While the man I loved pretended to be on a date with another woman.

This was completely do-able. It was practically normal. Someone had probably written a scene just like it in a book. A romance novel set in France.

Okay, it sounded like a bad romance novel. Or some kind of spy flick. Only we were bad guys against very bad guys.

Stop thinking about it, I commanded myself.

"Better?" I tried to smile at Mavis. Footsteps sounded on the stairs and I looked toward the door.

"Let's find out." With more strength than someone of her stature should possess, she pushed me into the tiny hallway.

I practically fell into Owen's arms and fought to keep my footing in the stupid heels.

"Sorry." I untangled myself and stood up. "Mavis is like the Hulk stuck in Barbie's body."

Her snort came from behind me and I shot her an angry look. I turned back to look at Owen. He hadn't said anything yet but his eyes were a little wider than normal.

"Owen? Are you okay? Did something happen?" I placed my hand on his chest, surprised by how fast his heart was beating.

"You're wearing that tonight?" His eyebrows drew together.

"Yep. It's perfect," Mavis announced before stepping back and closing her bedroom door.

"Does it look bad?" I dropped my eyes to the dress and frowned. It wasn't something I would normally pick out, but I hadn't thought I looked gross. Was my butt hanging out? I looked over my shoulder but couldn't really tell. I didn't feel a draft so I hoped that was a good sign.

"No. It doesn't look bad." Owen placed his hand on my hip and pulled me closer. "It looks entirely too good."

"Oh." I smiled. "Thank you."

"But I think it's missing something." His eyes turned serious.

"A coat would be nice. I feel like I'm wearing nothing but underwear."

"That's not what I was thinking." Stepping back, he led me to another bedroom.

As soon as the door was closed behind us, his mouth was pressed to mine. His teeth tugged on my lips, forcing them open so his tongue could explore inside. My breathing hitched and I kissed him back with just as much force.

The horrible feeling in my stomach came back in full force and I needed his hands to push it away.

His fingers slid along the soft material of my dress, tracing the guns strapped to the small of my back and the knife that ran between my shoulder blades. He broke our kiss and rested his forehead against mine.

"You look scared, love." His soft breath washed over my face.

"I am." A shudder ran over my body.

"That's normal." His fingers traced my jaw. "It's okay to be scared."

"Are we going to die tonight?" My fingers tightened on his shirt.

He didn't answer, his breathing slow and even, but he

closed his eyes. "No, love. None of us will die tonight. We're going to be fine."

"You promised to not lie to me," I reminded him.

Wrapping our fingers together, he lifted our hands and pressed his lips to where our skin met. "I'm telling you the truth, Ava. We're going to be fine. I did some scouting today and found the location of the casino. One of my contacts has guaranteed to have transportation waiting for us when we need it and to provide a distraction for a getaway. If we're lucky we'll negotiate a truce and walk out of there free and clear. If not, we've got an exit planned."

I took a deep breath. "We're going to be okay."

"Yes. Trust me, love. Everything is accounted for." He lifted my chin so I could look into his eyes. "Now, you need to relax and not look so worried. You have to look excited."

"I'm not sure I can relax. I can't turn off my worry." I shook my head. "It's just there, gnawing at my stomach."

"You need a distraction." He pressed his body closer to mine. "I can help with that."

"Owen—"

"Shh, love. Let me distract you." He lifted me from the floor and set me on a table.

He kissed me, slowly, with tender fingers cupping my face. When he pulled back to breathe I was surprised to hear him whisper. "I need you to distract me, too."

His hands moved along my legs and slipped my skirt up my hips. He traced the lacy edge of the knife sheath wrapped around my thigh as if surprised to find it there. When he knelt in front of the table, I leaned back and threaded my fingers through his hair. I focused on his hands, his warm mouth, the way he made me feel.

When he stood up and slid inside of me, our movements were slow and tender. There was nothing hurried or urgent, just a need to love and be loved. When the climax came it hit us both at the same time. A shocking wave of pleasure that made him groan my name.

Later, once he'd changed and I'd fixed my makeup, we joined the others downstairs.

A somber tone filled the apartment as everyone took care of last minute details. Mavis decided to change her jewelry to something that had a GPS Kenny could track and a microphone so he would be able to hear what was happening. Owen had hidden several knives along his person, including a simple pocketknife in a front pocket.

"If you hand them what they're searching for, they usually don't look much further," he explained.

Mavis went to the kitchen and came back with two glasses of champagne. She handed me one and sipped from the other.

"We're supposed to be living it up." She clinked glasses with mine before turning on an mp3 player. Music filled the room and she started dancing around as if she didn't have a care in the world.

Kenny glared at his aunt before pulling a pair of noise cancelling headphones out of a bag. They apparently didn't have the same taste in music. He had spent most of his time sneaking through back doors of the casino's security system. This way he would be able to remotely help us if we needed anything.

"C'mon, Ava. Move your ass! Show me what you've got." She did a little shimmy and I laughed.

I took a gulp of champagne and decided dancing

wouldn't hurt anything. It would be easier to look stupid here than try to be sexy at the casino.

When a Taylor Swift song came on, I didn't find it too hard to start dancing and shaking my butt. I was more than happy to try and shake off my bad mood.

Mavis finished her glass of champagne and pranced around the living room, gyrating and wiggling. For someone so poised and posh she was a truly terrible dancer. Laughter exploded from me when she wiggled her butt all the way to the floor and almost didn't make it back up.

I went over to help her up, not noticing when someone knocked on the door. It wasn't until I'd gotten Mavis off the ground, giggling, that I realized someone else had joined us in the room.

"Looks like the party started without me." Patrick was wearing a tux, though not nearly as well as Owen. He was holding two bouquets of flowers and wearing a smile.

"Sweetheart, our guest has arrived." Owen took Mavis's hand and pulled her toward Patrick.

"There's our lovely pilot!" Mavis leaned forward with a smile that was a little too large. "Would you like some champagne? I think we still have some!"

Without waiting for a response, she wandered off to the kitchen, her steps a little uneven. When she came back out she was holding a bottle that was almost dry. There couldn't be more than a couple of tablespoons left inside.

"I'm sorry, Captain, but apparently Ava and I drank most of it." She giggled.

Considering that I'd not finished my first glass, I knew there was no way we'd gone through an entire bottle. Mavis was putting on a good show though.

"Not to worry, Miss Thomasino." He handed her a

bunch of flowers. "Your company is more than enough. And please call me Patrick."

"Flowers! Oh, look at this, Ava." She turned and gave me a sly smile. "He brought me flowers."

"I've also brought some for the lovely Ava." He handed me a bunch of red roses wrapped in newspaper.

Giving him a large smile, I leaned forward and kissed his cheek. "Thank you, Patrick. That's so sweet."

"Most definitely my pleasure." He smiled down at me and his fingers chucked my chin while his eyes ran over my tiny dress. I ignored the nasty smirk and let him throw his arm over my shoulder. "Are you ready to go eat? I'm starving."

His thumb rubbed a little circle on my arm and I suppressed a shudder. He hadn't stuck his tongue in my ear yet. If Mavis could get through that, then I could definitely get through his leering and innuendos.

I had to. If we didn't figure out what was going on, I was going to end up dead eventually and they might find Tessa.

If they hadn't already.

CHAPTER
TWENTY-SIX

Ava

DINNER WAS TORTURE. Pretending to find Patrick interesting was exhausting. I still didn't understand why he had latched onto me instead of Mavis. Things would have been much simpler. Owen had slipped into his comfort zone, despite his occasional glare in Patrick's direction. The drive around Paris would have been wonderful if Patrick hadn't been so intent on running his hand up my leg. I tried to pretend I didn't care, but when he came dangerously close to my thigh sheath I tapped his hand playfully and made a tsking sound. His eyes glinted with amusement and his soft chuckle tickled my ear.

That was the key to stringing the idiot along. He liked the chase and enjoyed the final conquering. If I kept playing hard to get and giving him little rewards from time to time, he would keep following me.

No lights announced the illegal casino. No intricate signs declared the location. Cars were staggered in a way that you couldn't see anyone as they exited their vehicles and went inside.

Two men were visible just outside of the door, but I knew from the research Owen had done that there were a dozen more within a few feet of that entrance. Would they search me for weapons? Did I look suspicious?

I shivered and Patrick looked down at me.

"Are you cold?"

"I should have realized that it would be chilly tonight," I sighed dramatically. "But I really wanted to wear this dress."

"Well, I'm glad you did." He winked at me before pulled out of his tuxedo jacket.

Owen was watching him with a carefully guarded expression.

"Oh, no. I couldn't take your coat. I'm sure it'll be warmer inside." I shook my head with a sad smile.

"I'll be fine." He wrapped the coat around my shoulders and for the first time I thought maybe he wasn't as bad as I had thought. "I like seeing you wear my clothes."

And that thought didn't last very long.

I looked out of the limo window and barely made out the profile of a man melting out of the shadows. I pulled the jacket tight around me and allowed the young guy to help me out of the car. Patrick placed his hand on the small of my back and I pulled away. Had he noticed the guns strapped under my clothes?

"This way." He nodded at a large man standing to the left of the door. "Good evening, Vitz."

"Nice to see you, Patrick." The man stepped forward and I tried not to wince at the scar running down the left side of his face. His voice had a slight accent. If I had to guess I would say he was originally from Russia, but had lived elsewhere for a long time. "Have you cleared your guests?"

"Of course. She's aware that I added them to the guest list." He rattled off our fake names and passed Vitz a business-card sized piece of cardboard that he pocketed.

"Go on." Vitz looked us all over with an expression of disinterest...until he got to Owen. "Hold on. What's your name?"

"Owen Vander." He kept his hands calmly at his side. Patrick turned to watch, but didn't offer any help.

"Vander." Vitz said the name slowly, as if he was waiting for something. "Where are you based?"

"I'm sorry?" Owen leaned his head toward Vitz with a confused expression.

"You freelance, or do you work for a firm?" Vitz leaned his head back, taking in Owen's appearance.

"I'm an investment manager." Owen shrugged. "I do contract work from time to time, but right now I'm working with Miss Thomasino full time."

"I think he believes you're my bodyguard." Mavis wrapped her arm around Owen's waist and smiled up at him. "It's a compliment. He thinks you look tough and scary."

"Me? Of course I'm tough and scary." Owen jabbed a thumb into his chest and stood up a little taller.

"You don't guard?" Vitz frowned and in that one show of emotion I could see the wheels turning quickly in his head.

"Um, no. Not really the type to throw myself in front of a bullet, you know." Owen flashed a cheeky smile.

Oh, no, he wouldn't jump in front of a bullet. It wasn't like he'd been shot just days ago when trying to save my life. But if I hadn't known that fact, I would have been convinced by his charade. Vitz, however, didn't seem inclined to jump on the I'm-just-a-playboy-scoundrel train.

"He is the type to play in a high stakes poker game, though." Mavis's lips curled into a sensual smile and she looked up at the scarred bouncer. "I have a thing for bad boys. I think I want to reform them, but in reality I just want to enjoy them being naughty."

"A little thing like you should be careful. Most bad boys turn into bad men." Vitz looked down at Mavis. Nothing in his expression changed, but his eyes took on a softer light.

"A woman needs a good challenge from time to time. Keeps me on my toes." Mavis's smile looked genuine.

"Are we good?" Patrick spoke up from next to me. "We ran the records like usual. Nothing popped. And you're holding up the drivers."

There was a line of cars behind our empty one with agitated drivers glaring in our direction.

"We're good." Vitz stepped back and waved his hand. Several men stepped out of the shadows and lowered their weapons. "I believe I must recall you from a card game. Your face is familiar."

"I probably took your boss's money." Owen's laugh was higher than normal. He slapped Vitz on the shoulder and the bouncer stared at his hand as if it was a leech. "Uh, sorry."

Owen took his hand back and frowned before pulling Mavis against his side.

Patrick wrapped his arm around my shoulders and steered us inside of the rundown building. Light filled the cavernous space, not from holes in the roof as I had expected but from hundreds of chandeliers dangling from the beams that ran across the room. People mingled underneath all the crystal and gold, long skirts twirling, short skirts fanning out, and tuxedos that would make Valentino proud. Music pumped from unseen speakers, filling the air with an upbeat tempo and lyrics about being the best.

I forgot for half a second that I was stuck next to Captain Horny and gaped at the splendor. Slot machines pinged, people cheered, and the sound of shuffling cards bombarded my ears.

"Wow." I bit my lip. "I never would have guessed it would be like this inside."

Patrick leaned forward, his lips ticking the delicate hairs along my neck. "It's never the same. Every time they move it's something new, something mind boggling."

"They aren't always in Paris?" I let my eyes get big and turned to look at the man next to me. "How can they move all of this stuff? It would be impossible."

"It might seem that way, but they manage." He led me toward a group of men standing near a metal detector.

"Are those metal detectors?" Mavis asked. "Are they going to make me walk around without my shoes like an airport?"

I shot a glance back at Mavis and Owen. Hopefully Kenny hadn't fallen asleep. I wasn't sure if there was a way to disable metal detectors but hopefully the computer whiz did.

"This is just a precaution. We want to make sure everyone is safe." Patrick stepped to the side as if he was going to leave us. "I'm going to sign into the building. The owner allows certain people to worry about their own protection." He tapped his side to indicate something in his pocket. "You have a gun?" Owen's eyebrows rose. "Those are terrible things."

"I'd rather do terrible things than have terrible things done to me." He frowned at Owen. "These settings are always safe, but you can't be too careful."

"Are you sure we're safe here?" I cringed away from him a little. "I don't like guns."

"You're the American!" He laughed. "Don't worry. I won't let anything happen to you."

Stepping away from him, I took off his jacket and handed it back to him. It gave me an excuse to put a little more space between us again. Without a care he turned and walked through a door marked personnel.

Mavis tapped her earring, which was probably a signal for Kenny. Owen smiled and threw an arm around each of our shoulders before guiding us toward the burly men next to the scanning machine.

"Do I have to take my shoes off?" Mavis scrunched her nose.

"No, ma'am. Please put your purses on the conveyor belt and step through the metal detector." He motioned to move past him. "If you have any weapons you can check them here and we'll make sure you will get them when you leave."

Owen let his arms drop from our shoulders and pulled the pocket knife out and held it up for all to see.

The guard took it and handed it another man. "Tell him your name and he'll put it away for you."

Owen stepped to the side while Mavis and I sat our purses on the conveyor belt. As I turned to walk away I noticed the rolling belt hiccupped.

Mavis went through the metal detector first, her amused smirk in place. No alarms or flashing lights announced her weapon cache. Smiling I followed her lead and stepped through the machine. When I stepped through, I was quickly followed by Owen.

Once we were through and into the main weapons check, Patrick joined us and really seemed to light up. People said hello, waved at him from across the room, and offered him seats. He ate up the attention, especially when it came from someone of obvious wealth.

Disgust twisted my face and Mavis frowned at me. I tried to school my features into something happier, but it was like trying to rearrange a mountain. Some of the people were friendly, witty even. I would have enjoyed talking to a few if I had been anywhere else. Instead, I just felt nauseous.

"Well, how do I cash in?" Owen rubbed his hands together, spinning in a small circle.

"Let me introduce you to a friend first." Patrick smiled and wrapped his hand around my upper arm to guide me in a different direction.

"You're holding me a little too tight, Patrick." I pulled at my arm, but he didn't let me go.

"I'd hate to lose you, dear." When he leaned closer to me his hand dipped down to my ass. "I'd hoped to get between your legs before we came here tonight, but you ignored all of my attempts to get you away from your bodyguards. If you get out of this alive I'm going to take what you've been teasing me with."

"What?" My eyes widened and I pulled a little harder on my arm.

"Don't make a scene. You won't get away from this alive if you don't do what I say." Yanking at my side he pressed me to him and looked over my head. "Don't do it, asshole. They're all watching you."

From the corner of my eye I saw Owen's blank face. His eyes darted from side to side and I realized that the guards around the room were all turned in our direction.

"Hello, Ava." A cultured voice caught my attention.

I spun around to see that I was face to face with a tall brunette woman. I knew immediately that this was Maria. Not her assistant, but the woman herself, and she was just as cool as she had seemed on the videos. There was another woman standing behind her, but she didn't have quite the same frosty veneer.

"Maria." I swallowed, trying to wet my throat. "It's nice to finally meet you."

"Manners. I'm surprised." She raised an eyebrow. "I thought you might curse at me."

"I don't think that would get us anywhere." I relaxed and stood up straight.

Maria held her wine glass out and her assistant stepped forward to take it from her. "What do you think of the casino?"

"Honestly? I'm not much of a gambler." I looked around, not wanting to look scared. "I guess it's nice if you're into illegal gambling. I expected something danker."

"Danker?" She laughed, drawing the attention of a few people nearby. "No, I cater to a different clientele."

"The kind you can blackmail." I narrowed my eyes.

"Yes. I'm a firm believer of being prepared." She looked at Owen and Mavis. "I've found that if you can control people without violence, it makes life much easier."

"Or you could try not bullying people and being honest." If we weren't standing in the middle of an underground casino with millionaires floating about and armed guards staring us down, you'd think we were having a discussion in an office break room.

"I'm always honest, Ava. That's how I got to where I am." She lifted her chin a little. "The truth is the sharpest weapon."

"Then why are you trying to kill me?" I yanked hard on my arm and Patrick let go.

"I wasn't trying to kill you." Her calm voice was starting to grate on my nerves.

"Let me rephrase this. Why did you send people after me? Why did those people shoot at me?" I leaned forward, the words falling out of my mouth in a rush. "What brilliant reason do you have for that?"

"That was simply a mistake." She turned and started walking through the room. "It had nothing to do with you."

I looked at Mavis and Owen, but they were both wearing the same expression, which was more like no expression.

A guard fell in behind us and Patrick and I had no option but to follow the two tall women in front of me.

"Is that an apology?" I ignored Patrick as he stepped closer to me.

"I don't apologize. It's not my fault that you were targeted. It was an unfortunate twist of events." She patted one of the gamblers on the shoulder as she walked by, leaning down to whisper in something in the old man's ear that made him chuckle.

"If you weren't trying to hurt me, what's going on? And why all the guards?"

"You came to my casino with two heavily armed assassins. Of course I'm going to have guards." She turned and smiled at me. "As for what's going on, I believe I owe you a check."

"Check what?" I stopped walking and Patrick bumped into my back. He slid his hands around my waist. I shoved him with all my strength. "Get off me, jackass."

"Watch it." He grabbed my arm and squeezed.

"Patrick, let our guest go. We don't want a show." Maria kept walking.

Captain Horny pushed my shoulder to get me moving again. If I could have hurt him I would have done it. My disgust for him had reached new levels and had quickly turned into loathing.

"Keep your hands to yourself." Owen's voice was a deep guttural growl that made Patrick stand up a little straighter.

As if nothing had happened, Maria continued walking and I had to speed up to hear her.

"You completed an assignment for me. Granted, it wasn't accomplished in a manner quite as extraordinary as I had hoped, but the end result was the same and I always pay for services rendered." She glanced back at me. "Though if you prefer, I have cash."

A man joined us as we were walking, a black bag in one hand.

"She's talking about Song." Owen's voice was smooth and cool.

"But—"

"You removed a very big problem for me and I appreciate it." Her assistant opened a door into a dark hallway and we had no option but to follow her. "Forgive me, but you'll need to leave your weapons here."

Several guards ran their hands over the two assassins, searching for and removing the weapons they had tucked away. When no one made a move in my direction, I didn't offer up any of the items I'd hidden away on my person.

"You still haven't explained why you were trying to kill me." There were steps leading down into another hallway. The further we went from the crowd in the casino, the more nervous I became.

"Well, it would seem that you were the wrong American in the wrong place at the wrong time." She stopped in front of a door and pulled a key out of her pocket. "We were looking for someone else and you happened to fit her description."

"Tessa." I watched as she pulled a key from her pocket and opened the door.

"Yes, your friend." Maria walked into the office and I realized it was the first door I'd seen her open.

"Why do you want to kill Tessa?" The office was mostly bare. A desk, a couple of chairs, and one computer. As we crowded in, Patrick took a spot by Maria's desk and several of the guards covered the door. The nameless assistant stayed outside.

"Her husband has something of mine."

"Your issue is with him. Leave Ava out of it." Owen stepped forward, his arm brushing mine.

"She's free to go." Maria flicked her fingers at the door.

"No. I won't just let you hurt Tessa." I leaned forward. "I don't know what Danny has that is yours, but keep the money and we'll call it even."

"Ava." The aggravation in Owen's tone was clear.

"It's not about the money." Maria sat down behind her desk. "I want the piece. That's why I commissioned him to get it for me."

"You mean it's the principle," Owen said.

"There is that, too." Maria smiled. "I can't let people think it's okay to back out of deals."

"You can't hurt Tessa." I glared at Maria. "This isn't her fault."

"How do you know?" Maria folded her hands on her desk. "Have you spoken to her? She chose to marry the cat-burglar after all. This very well might be her fault. Perhaps when she left you at her apartment, she knew you'd be in trouble."

No. Tessa and I had been friends for too long. She never would have willingly put me in danger.

And Danny is a cat-burglar. My best friend, the art history buff, had married a thief. Go figure.

"I haven't seen her. I've been a little busy," I explained. "Running for my life and all."

"You're free to go now. No one will bother you." Maria cocked her head to the side as if waiting for something.

What was she thinking? I was free to go. Oh. Just me.

"Owen and Mavis?" I looked at her in fear.

"Owen is a favor for a business partner." She smiled sadly and looked at Owen. "It's a pity. You're truly an artist when it comes to your craft. Unfortunately, business comes first. I have spent many years cultivating that particular branch of my company and find it in my best interest to keep them happy for now."

From the corner of my eye I saw Owen stiffen at the mention of his brother. My heart broke even more for the man I loved. If I got out of this alive I was going to kill

Marcus. He'd asked his boss to murder his brother. That's low even for a criminal.

"And me?" Mavis stepped forward.

"You are a problem." Maria turned to look at my friend with cold eyes. "And I believe it's better to trim those types of things early on."

"I'm not going to just walk out of here while you kill all of my friends!" I stepped forward.

"I thought I was being generous." She shrugged and stood up.

"You're not being generous. You're a criminal that does what's best for yourself. I'm sure that if I left now you'd find some use for me later and blackmail me in to being a drug mule or something." I put my hands on the desk and leaned forward. "So you can take your money and shove it up your—"

A knock on the door made everyone in the room jump. Well, I jumped. Maria, Owen, and Mavis merely looked at the door.

"Enter." Maria's cool voice echoed in the tiny room.

Vitz walked in with a package, followed by a man. No, not just a man. Danny.

"You instructed that Mr. Myers be brought to you if he showed up on the premises." His boredom with the task was clear. "He had this with him."

"Well, apparently all of the interesting people are in Paris." Maria smiled. "How nice to see you, Mr. Myers. I'm assuming that's my painting?"

For the first time emotion shined in her eyes. Anticipation.

"Hello, Maria." He glanced at me quickly. "Ava, sorry about all this."

"Sorry?" My anger had hit all new levels. I marched up to him and smacked him as hard as I could. "Sorry? You bloody Englishman! You didn't spill wine on my dress. I've been shot at! This woman is planning on killing my friends. I killed a man with your car! And you're sorry?"

"Er, yes." He rubbed his cheek." I thought the matter had been settled or I would have never let Tessa invite you to London."

"Did she know what you were when you got married? Have you hurt her?"

"Yes and no. She caught me trying to steal something. That's how we met and she's safe, though likely going to try and kill me when I see her next. I locked her up."

Owen grunted and I realized he was thinking Danny had the right idea.

"Enough. Let me see the painting." Maria held her hands out and Vitz passed the package to her.

She tore through the paper like a child at Christmas. With a look of awe she held up a small canvas. "You really did it."

"Of course." Danny cleared his throat. "I thought we were even when I returned your money."

"It was never about the money. It was about this," Maria explained. She cradled the canvas with gentle hands. "It's a Van Gogh. The only artist I hadn't managed to collect."

"Well, then, we're even. You have your money, and the painting, and we'll get out of your hair. Shall we?" Danny reached for the door but Vitz stepped to block the way.

"Why did you back out of the deal?" Maria set the painting down carefully. "What made you squirrel?"

"I saw one of your employees with a drugged woman when I came to deliver. He was talking about stables and orders." He put his hands in his pockets. "I'm a thief, but I don't deal with people in the sex slave trade. I spooked and sent your money back. I thought that would be the end of it."

"No. It was certainly not the end of it." Maria shrugged. "But everything is fine now. I'll call off my people looking for your wife."

"And the rest of us?" Danny rocked back on his heels.

"Loose ends." Maria handed the painting to one of the guards. "Take care of that."

He nodded his head before leaving the room.

"I see." Danny frowned.

"Ava hasn't done anything wrong. Let her go." Owen raised his voice. "You don't need to kill her."

"As I said, she's free to go."

Owen nodded thoughtfully before he spoke. "I would ask a favor, if you don't mind. A courtesy before I'm executed." Maria motioned for him to go on and my stomach dropped. How could he talk about his death so easily? "Have someone remove Ava. Put her outside and let her go."

"You'd have me go against her wishes?" Maria looked over at me, her cold eyes calculating. "What if she fights?"

"Owen." I took a deep breath.

"Restrain her. Just get her out of here unharmed." He didn't look at me and my entire body began to shake. "None of this is her fault."

"Vitz." Maria looked at the scarred guard behind me. "I'll honor his request. Take the bag as well. She earned it."

"No! You said we'd all leave together." I fought as Vitz wrapped a giant arm around my waist. "Owen! Don't do this."

He didn't look in my direction as Vitz pulled me through the door.

"You promised, Owen. You promised and you lied!" I grabbed at the door frame, but it was like fighting a bull. Vitz was headed away and there was nothing I could do to stop him. "Please, Owen."

I saw him look in my direction with sad eyes just before I couldn't see them anymore.

"Put me down, you damn ogre!" I kicked and pulled, trying to get away.

Maria walked out of the makeshift office, her heels clicking on the cement. Her assistant seemed to appear from the shadows, falling into step with the taller woman.

"Stop fighting, girl." Vitz looked down at me, his bored expression fueling my fury. "I'm not going to hurt you."

"Try to keep her quiet." Maria shook her head as she passed us. "I don't want to upset our clients upstairs."

"Yes, ma'am." Vitz tightened his hold on me and I bit down on the thick corded muscle. He cursed in a language I didn't know and switched arms, moving the bag of money to his bleeding arm and me to the uninjured. He gave me a little shake. "Behave. I'm trying to get you out of this alive, got it?"

Why the hell would he care if I got out of this alive? One of my shoes fell off when we reached a grated walkway. He reached down to pick it up and threw it in a trash can.

I didn't care. He could throw away my shoes. He could throw me away.

He might as well. With Owen dead I had nothing else in life. I was alone. Like when my parents had died. Just me and a giant hole in my chest. I wouldn't even have Tessa to help me through it this time. I had no idea where she was.

I looked where we were headed. Maria and her assistant were talking quietly, the assistant carrying the painting in a special case.

All of this for a painting.

Everyone I loved gone, because a horrible woman wanted a special painting.

No. I fought against Vitz, trying my hardest to get free. I stepped on his foot with my remaining high heel, but he didn't even flinch. Tears of frustration ran down my face. I balled up my fist and swung it backward at his groin, but he merely shifted my weight. Making me look at the women in front of us.

They dealt in the sex slave trade.

They killed to keep money.

They blackmailed influential people every day.

They were going to kill my best friend's husband.

Murder my new friend.

Murder the man that I love.

Shatter my entire world.

When the first shot echoed down the corridor, every muscle in my body went still. Someone I cared for was dead. More shots followed and Maria never stopped moving. She didn't care who she fucked over, as long as it benefited her.

My sudden lack of movement seemed to startle Vitz. His hold on me loosened and he turned to look behind us and muttered something that sounded like a prayer.

Maria's high heels met cement with a sharp click, her bun bouncing jauntily as she walked.

I wouldn't be the last person whose life would be ruined by her.

She was evil.

And I was faster than most people expected.

"Maria."

She slowed and turned in my direction, but her assistant never stopped. Reaching behind me, I pulled one of the small pistols from the holster hidden in my dress. It took seconds, maybe less.

Sometimes bad people just needed to die.

When I pulled the trigger I felt no remorse. In fact, I felt hollow. Empty. I watched as her head flew backwards, blood spraying the wall beside the assistant, who never slowed.

And that was how my body count doubled.

CHAPTER TWENTY-SEVEN

Owen

"BLOODY HELL." I held a bunch of fabric from Mavis's dress to my shoulder. Danny shifted me on his shoulder and I winced. I stared down at Captain Horny's blank eyes and was surprised I didn't feel satisfied. He didn't really matter. The only thing that mattered was finding Ava.

"You were supposed to move left." Mavis glared at me.

"Right. It's always right. Why the hell would we move left? We're right handed!" I tried to bat her away, but it was ineffective. "We don't have time for this. We need to get to Ava."

"Then stop getting shot!" Mavis threw her hands in the air before kneeling to pick up one of her discarded knives. "Every time I turn around, you're running into bullets! Do you have aspirations of becoming Swiss cheese?"

"Mavis, we have to find Ava." I took a deep breath and tried to make sense of the spinning room. "I don't trust Maria. She's not safe."

"I'll go. This is my fault." Danny moved to sit me

down on the desk.

"No need." A deep voice with a Russian accent filled the room.

I tried to stand, ready for an attack, but the room spun. Staggering backward, I sat on the desk. I needed to find Ava and get out of there. I was in no shape to fight.

"Oh, God." Small, cold hands touched my face and I looked up at an angel. "Owen? Can you hear me?"

"'Course I can. Wasn't shot in my ears." I watched as Ava looked down at the bloody mess of my shoulder.

"What did he say?" The Russian bouncer leaned over me and I slammed my fist into his jaw.

"Owen, he's on our side. Stop. Be still." Her hands were back on my face, and tear tracks ran down her cheeks. My gut froze.

"Are you hurt?"

"I'm fine." She shook her head. "I thought you were dead."

"Nope."

"The bullet is still in there. I've got to get it out and patch him up before he bleeds out." Mavis moved into my sight line. "Don't do anything else stupid."

"Ava?" I looked back at her. "You're sure you're not hurt?"

"I'm not hurt." Her smile was blinding. "But if you ever pull that shit on me again I swear to every god there is, that I will be the one to put a bullet in you. Do you hear me?"

"Yes, ma'am." I leaned forward and pressed my forehead to hers. "I love you."

"I love you, too, you giant idiot."

"Not to break up the reunion, but where is Maria?"

Danny asked. He was peering out of the office door.

"Dead," Vitz rumbled.

Ava stiffened and I looked over to where the burly Russian was standing.

"You killed her?" Mavis cocked her head to the side as she wiped her knife off on her dress. Her even tone was much scarier than when she raised her voice at Kenny. "I needed her. She has something of mine."

"No." He shook his head and looked at Ava.

He was looking at my sweet, angelic Ava.

The Ava that punched people for kissing the guy she liked.

My Ava that would kill to protect those she loved.

Mavis cursed under her breath, but didn't say anything to Ava. Danny was looking at Ava in surprise and Vitz had his arms crossed as if everything was completely normal.

Red filled Ava's cheeks and she frowned before a fierce look filled her eyes.

"I thought she had killed you," she whispered.

She had killed for me. This beautiful, brilliant, kind woman had killed for me.

"I love you." I didn't know what else to say. I'm not sure there was anything to say for that. It wasn't like the card companies made cards for occasions where your lover kills a villain.

"Of course you do." Her bright smile did wonders for the pain I was feeling.

"Ava killed Maria." Mavis shook her head, a smile forming on her face. She looked a bit like a proud mother. "I didn't see that coming."

"She killed *a* Maria." Vitz grunted. "It was a good

336

shot, though."

"I got lucky." Ava's blush deepened.

"What do you mean *a* Maria?" Mavis demanded.

"It's an organization." Vitz rubbed at his jaw where I'd hit him. That's right. Even with a bullet in me, I packed a punch. "I've spent the last five years infiltrating these damn businesses, trying to find out how it was managed. Every branch is controlled by a woman named Maria. The CIA has been trying to unravel the threads for years."

"Then it was a different Maria that hired me. She looked like this one, but it wasn't her." I frowned. "Are they a cult?"

Vitz grunted. Either he didn't know or they weren't sure.

"You can explain later. We've got to go." Danny leaned back into the room. "I hear people coming this way."

"Wait, where is Tess? Is she really safe?" Ava looked at the thief.

"Yes, she's monitoring me with a GPS from the basement of a building near-by. I locked her in so she wouldn't follow me." Danny grimaced. "She's probably going to divorce me."

"How did you know to come tonigt?" I asked. "You showed up at just the right time."

"We've been following the casino since Tess got Ava's email. I figured that if she was with someone that could help her, you would eventually end up at one of them." Danny rubbed the back of neck. "I couldn't find Ava. We searched all of London. I thought of just sending the painting to Maria but I worried she'd kill Ava either way. I'd hoped presenting it in person would up our odds

337

of surviving."

"That was a big gamble." Vitz frowned. "You should stick to stealing and leave the strategy to someone else."

"Right." Danny frowned. "I'm really sorry, Ava. Tessa is going to be so relieved you're okay."

"Those people are getting closer, we need to split." Mavis nodded at Vitz.

"I have help waiting outside." I managed to haul my sorry ass off the desk and stand. Ava slipped under my arm. I was determined to keep her tucked against me for a very long time.

"Can you tell us a way out?" Danny looked at Vitz.

"Yes. My cover is shot." Frustration laced his words. Without another look he took off in the opposite direction of the way we had come.

"I guess we're moving." Mavis looked at me with assessing eyes. "You can make it out. Don't run into any other bullets, got it, cheese boy?"

"Got it."

"What kind of cheese?" Ava glanced up at me.

"Swiss." I sighed and leaned over to kiss her head. We were alive.

"So you're Swiss Cheese? It works." There was that smile I loved so much.

"Yes and you're my American turkey."

"I can handle that." Her laugh helped distract me as we made our way down the dark hallways.

We ran into very little resistance. Mavis and Vitz took care of it quickly and quietly each time.

Outside there was a boy in black clothes leaning against a wall. He pressed something on a phone and said a few short words in French before a van turned the corner. He walked over and opened the door for us.

"Owen?" Mavis called.

"We're good." I let Ava help me into the van. I could have managed without her, but it was nice to have the help. The man in the front passenger seat turned to look at me. "Where's John?"

"He's getting a physician. Derek said you were bleeding."

"Thank you."

Ava was looking at my shoulder, her face worried. "Are you going to be okay? Mavis, is he going to be okay?"

"Yes, he has more blood than brains." The slender woman leaned over the seat and lifted the material from my shoulder. "He got lucky again."

"Did you want a matching bullet scar on the other shoulder?" Ava's smile wobbled.

"It's manly to have matching scars." I pulled her closer to me.

"Don't get any more, okay?"

"I'll try."

She sighed. "And don't lie to me again."

I lifted my hand and extended my pinky finger.

Her eyes filled with love, she wrapped her finger around mine.

"You're stuck with me, now." I leaned forward the best I could and she met me, her lips pressing to mine.

"Like you could get rid of me."

I wondered if she would ever be the same. Or maybe she hadn't changed at all. Maybe she'd had a little assassin to her the whole time.

"You wanted to shake things up." I pulled back and

339

looked in her eyes.

Her smile was wide. "I think I've officially figured out how to do that. It just took a few lessons from an assassin."

"The world is your oyster. What do you want to do now?"

"After you're patched up and I've yelled at Tessa and Danny? I think we should explore Paris. Visit a bakery." She shrugged. "Maybe I'll design jewelry for Kenny to put little transmitters in. Designer watches with hidden tools."

"Very James Bond." I shifted in the seat, unable to find a position that didn't hurt.

"Hm." She frowned. "I've never wanted to be a Bond girl."

"So true." Mavis said. "We really needed better spy role models."

Danny leaned forward. "Can you drop me off at the next street? Tell me where to meet you and I'll bring Tessa. She's going to want to see Ava right away."

I looked at Ava. "What do you think?"

"I think if he doesn't show up with Tessa we'll go looking for him next." She turned and narrowed her eyes at Danny.

"That's more than fair." Danny frowned. "I really am sorry, Ava. I'll find a way to make this up to you."

"Take this." Mavis pulled her GPS earring off and handed it to Danny before telling him an address. "Give us two hours."

"That wasn't where we were earlier."

"Kenny packed up and headed for the other place as soon as he realized we'd been figured out."

Danny hopped out of the van and saluted quickly before jogging off down a dark alley.

When the van started to move again, Vitz passed something over the seat and Ava looked at it with a frown. It took a second for foggy brain to realize that it was the bag of money Maria had given her.

"It's official now." Mavis announced as Ava took the bag.

"What is?" Ava raised her eyebrows.

"You've been paid for killing someone." I could just see a glimpse of Mavis's white teeth as she smiled at Ava. "You're one of us now."

Her eyes locked on mine. "Yes. I am." She leaned forward again, this time her kiss was stronger, more sure. "And I wouldn't have it any other way."

THE
END

342

ACKNOWLEDGMENTS

I COULD WRITE an entire book filled with the people that I need to thank. Seriously. And I do mean that seriously literally. Okay, maybe a novella. A long novella. But really, it would be nothing but me heaping thanks on the people that have listened to me stress out/ freak out/ panic, cry, have been ignored, put up with my absent-mindedness, and didn't mind eating take-out food one more time because I had a deadline. To save you all from that boredom, I'll keep it quick here and lavish those other people with love in person. How about paragraph form?

KP Simmon, Rebecca Friedman, Becki, Jessie, Nia, Jonathan, Anne, Danielle LeFave, Erika Leonard, Mandy Anderson, Laurie Thornton, Angie Stanton, Tina Hoffman, Heather Darenberg, Nicole Benisch, Brandie, Celia Ottoway (again, thanks for answering my British vs. American questions!), Sarah Ross Abernathy, Laura Bradley Rede, Elizabeth Hunter, The Facebook Accidental Assassins group, and a big thanks to everyone that has read one of my books and helped spread the word—You guys are my heroes.

One last thing. I can't write without music. It inspires me, moves me, helps shape my books. So, let me say a quick thanks to the musicians that helped inspire *The Accidental Assassin*:

Ed Sheeran
Imagine Dragons (I swear, Demons was written for Owen.)
Taylor Swift
Sia
Macklemore & Ryan Lewis
OneRepublic
Ed Sheeran
Adele
Rihanna
Skillet
Imagine Dragons
Katy Tiz (Listen to The Big Bang and tell me that's not Ava. I dare you.)
Muse
Ed Sheeran
Journey (Showing my age here. *cough, cough*)
And did I mention Ed Sheeran and Imagine Dragons? I did? Oh, okay. Good.

Check out www.nicholechase.com for more information about upcoming books and appearances.

NICHOLE CHASE IS the *New York Times* and *USA Today* bestselling author of *Suddenly Royal, Flukes, The Dark Betrayal Trilogy*, and several short stories. She is also the instructor of *Say What?* a dialogue class at the Romance Academy.

Nichole lives in Georgia with her husband, energetic daughter, superhero dog, Sulcata tortoise, and two cats. When not writing, you may find her reading, painting, crafting, or chasing her daughter around the house while making monster noises.

Nichole is represented by Literary Agent, Rebecca Friedman of the RF Literary Agency. If you would like to ask about review copies of her books, public appearances, or Skype chats for a book club, please contact her publicist KP Simmon of InkSlingerPR.

If you would like to learn more about Nichole and her projects, check out her website.

www.NicholeChase.com

Books by Nichole Chase

Suddenly Royal (Royal Series, Book One)
Recklessly Royal (Royal Series, Book Two)
Reluctantly Royal (Royal Series, Book Three)

Mortal Obligation (Dark Betrayal Trilogy, Book One)
Mortal Defiance (Dark Betrayal Trilogy, Book Two)
Immortal Grave (Dark Betrayal Trilogy, Book Three)

Flukes (The Flukes Series, Book One)
A Mermaid for Christmas (A Flukes Novella)

On Christmas Hill (A Christmas Hill Short Story)